The Way Back Home

A Wildflower Novel

ALECIA WHITAKER

POPPY

Little, Brown and Company

NEW YORK   BOSTON

Poppy

Hachette Book Group
1290 Avenue of the Americas, New York, NY 10104
Visit us at lb-teens.com

Poppy is an imprint of Little, Brown and Company.
The Poppy name and logo are trademarks of Hachette Book Group, Inc.

The publisher is not responsible for websites (or their content)
that are not owned by the publisher.

First Edition: July 2016

Library of Congress Cataloging-in-Publication Data
Names: Whitaker, Alecia, author.
Title: The way back home : a Wildflower novel / Alecia Whitaker.
Description: First edition. | New York ; Boston : Little, Brown and Company, 2016. | Series: Wildflower ; 3 | "Poppy." | Summary: "Rising country music star Bird Barrett is out on tour, with her brother and best friend along for the ride. But when the fear of being left behind by those she loves collides with the pressures of being a headlining act, Bird begins pushing everyone away—including her longtime crush, who has joined the tour." —Provided by publisher.
Identifiers: LCCN 2015036992| ISBN 9780316251440 (hardback) | ISBN 9780316251457 (ebook)
Subjects: | CYAC: Musicians—Fiction. | Country music—Fiction. | Dating (Social customs)—Fiction. | Fame—Fiction. | Brothers and sisters—Fiction. | BISAC: JUVENILE FICTION / Family / General (see also headings under Social Issues). | JUVENILE FICTION / Girls & Women. | JUVENILE FICTION / Performing Arts / Music. | JUVENILE FICTION / Social Issues / New Experience.
Classification: LCC PZ7.W57684 Way 2016 | DDC [Fic]—dc23
LC record available at http://lccn.loc.gov/2015036992

10 9 8 7 6 5 4 3 2 1

RRD-C

Printed in the United States of America

This one's for Matt, for reading all three.
And for Bobbie Jo, for making sure I wrote them.

1

"Bird," Dylan whispers in awe, his eyes going wide as we board the tour bus. It's his first glimpse of our living arrangements for the next nine months, and it's obvious that he's as shocked as I was the first time I saw it. After the brutal writer's block I had while trying to create a worthy follow-up album to *Wildflower*, watching *The Road to You* skyrocket to the top of the charts made all the stress and long days worth it. Thanks to the best fans in the world, I'm now headlining for the first time ever, bringing the Shine Our Light Tour to forty-nine cities across North America. We opened tonight and it was the highlight of my life, playing to a full arena and hearing the Memphis crowd sing my songs along with me. Having my big brother in tow was just the cherry on top.

Now, as we step up into the lounge area, he lets out a low whistle. "It's...it's..."

"Pretty awesome, right?" I finish for him, setting my fiddle case down on the plush gray carpet.

"Awesome?" he echoes as we take in the white leather furniture, stainless-steel appliances, and flat-screen TV. "This is insane."

"When Dan Silver promises the best..." I say, trailing off as I allow myself once again to be blown away by the luxury. My label president wasn't lying when he said he'd make my time on the road as comfortable as possible. It feels like I'm in an upscale condo, not a motor home.

I follow Dylan past the spacious bathroom and the three bunk beds with curtains for privacy, and into the master bedroom, where he just stops and stares. This is a level of opulence neither of us could have imagined.

"I'm assuming this is mine?" Dylan asks as he tosses his duffel bag onto the queen-sized bed. He lies down and folds his arms behind his head. "Not bad."

"Very funny," I say, flopping down beside him. We hear the other musicians outside boarding the band bus next to ours, but we don't move. Instead, we lie in silence for a minute and relive the night's performance. This was the first time we had performed live together in a while, but the way we connected onstage felt natural and easy, just like our days growing up in the Barrett Family Band. I know exactly what he's doing right now—going over every song we played tonight and thinking of times he messed up or ways he can improve as the tour continues. And he knows what I'm doing—coming down from the postshow high of my first official tour date.

For months I labored tirelessly with the whole Open Highway team to put together a show that brings my songs to life. I was given unlimited creative input on everything from set to wardrobe, lighting to schedule, and seeing it all come together tonight was indescribably rewarding. When I popped out of the trapdoor in the floor, I could feel the excitement in the arena. They loved the pyrotechnics and video feeds. And the eleven costume changes? Totally worth it.

My manager, Troy Becker, had a brilliant idea. At the beginning of the concert, fans are shown hashtags on the big screen that they can use to tag me and their seat number so I can find them in the crowd. They send me questions through Twitter, and I answer live, right from the stage.

"That guy you posed with in the crowd is going to be the most popular kid in school when he goes back," Dylan says with a grin.

"Like I always was," I reply.

"Bird, we were homeschooled."

I look over at him. "Yeah, but Mom and Jacob clearly liked me best."

Dylan rolls his eyes and screws up his face, with his features so much like my own, and I chuckle. Then I nudge him affectionately. "Kind of feels like the old days again, huh?"

He nods. "Yeah, when we used to tour the country with a massive mural of your big old face on the side of the RV. Like déjà vu, really."

I punch him in the arm.

Okay, so it's not at all like the old days. We aren't scraping by, living payout-to-payout, playing dives and bars hoping to sell a few CDs. Over a hundred and fifty people have jobs because of this tour. It's massive, and if I let myself think about the risk involved, it causes me major anxiety. A lot of people are counting on me. Leave it to Dylan to remind me of all that.

"I wish Jacob could've come," I say with a sigh. "He's the brother I like."

Dylan laughs. "Yeah, he's the brother *everyone* likes. Get this: Adam told me that before Jacob started dating Ashlynn, he was a total player at UCLA."

"That's disgusting."

"No, what's disgusting is"—he stops and bats his eyelashes—"infinity."

I groan. "Oh man, if I'd heard him say 'infinity' on the phone to that girl one more time this summer, I swear I was going to murder him."

"How much do you love me?" Dylan asks in a high-pitched voice.

"Oh, Ashy-poo, to infinity!"

"Infinity?" Dylan continues. "Is that long enough?"

"No, double infinity," I say. "Triple infinity!"

We both crack up.

"I'm just mad she stole my bass player!"

"Aw, take heart," Dylan says. "You've got me. And because you've got me, you *don't* have Mom and Dad."

"And because you've got me—" Stella says from out of nowhere. She flops onto the bed on my other side. "You *don't* have to be alone with him."

"Thank God," I say, and we all laugh.

But it's true. With Dylan taking off a year from college and me turning eighteen in a few weeks, my folks decided to take a break from the road, after a stern conversation about responsibility, of course. They'll check in from time to time and meet me somewhere every other week or so, but my granddad broke his hip a few days ago and they want to stay in Tennessee while he recovers. I personally think it's killing them—at least my dad—not to be along for the ride, but my granddad's on his own and he needs the help.

"Remind me again why you hired her?" Dylan asks me, while looking pointedly over at Stella.

"Because I am a gifted designer with a natural eye

for fashion and Bird's stylist needed an assistant," Stella answers for me. "The *talent* wanted everybody from her dancers to her band members flinging their clothes off backstage."

"Ha-ha," I say dryly, although the show *is* quite a spectacle.

"I thought it was because your grades tanked," Dylan goes on, trying to get under her skin.

Stella shrugs. "That too. I suck at math...and English... and apparently Design Fundamentals." She gives me a big grin. "Aren't ya glad you hired me?"

"Oh, please," I say.

"But enough about my fabulous college crash 'n' burn. Why'd she hire *you*?" she asks Dylan.

"Because she's a platinum-selling recording artist who needed someone up to her level to play guitar in her band," Dylan answers.

"Oh, not because you're her brother?"

Dylan scoffs. These two have been volleying jabs back and forth like this ever since the first dress rehearsal. "No, Bird wisely plucked me from the many talented Nashville up-and-comers before another megastar caught wind of my potential."

"Huh," Stella says. "I thought maybe it was because of all the jailbait."

"Jailbait?"

"Yeah, Anita has been going on and on about what a draw you are for Bird's young fans. You have that bewitching…boy-band look," she says with a gleam in her eye.

Dylan sits up, clearly offended. " 'Boy band'?"

"Yeah, that look," she goes on. "You, Harry Styles, Nick Jonas, the Biebs. If we put you in skinny jeans and got you a signature 'do, you'd all be the same person basically."

Dylan is utterly and completely speechless as the back of his neck gets red. His mouth hangs open in shock, and Stella cracks up next to me. I just stare at the ceiling and grin, still flying on the high of tonight's show and so happy to be back on the road.

2

"How much longer 'til he gets here?" I ask Stella at a stop in Sacramento.

We've been on tour for a week, and Stella started a practical-joke war on the very first day. She mismatched every sock in my drawer, so I retaliated by short-sheeting her bunk. Then Dylan hid just one earring from every pair Stella had brought with her. Today I'm helping her get back at him, and she's going to record the whole thing for my YouTube channel. We were meticulous in the planning of this prank, but I've been squatting inside this huge—and thankfully very clean—garbage can for at least fifteen minutes, and I'm getting hot...and cramped...and bored.

"Any minute now," Stella assures me, shoving me back down into the garbage can. "He's almost here."

"You've said that a million times," I groan, just barely peeking out.

"I know, I know. But I just texted him again, and he said two seconds so *shhh*!"

"Stella?" Dylan calls from down the hall. Hidden by the vending machines next to me, I close the lid all the way, and my pulse picks up as Stella leans against the can, pretending to text but secretly recording.

"I'm here with Dylan Barrett," she says quietly in a fake broadcaster voice, "heartthrob older brother of your favorite country music star, Bird Barrett, and my personal knight in shining armor."

She stops talking abruptly, and I hear Dylan's footsteps echo on the concrete floor. I can tell from the sound that he's finally getting close.

"SOS?" he asks skeptically. "What's the emergency?"

"I think I accidentally threw away a piece of wardrobe jewelry," she says, affecting a very anxious voice. "Amanda will murder me if I lose something like that, and I don't want to tell Bird or she'll regret hiring me."

"What is it?"

"A bracelet," she says. "It's so pretty, and I just wanted to wear it for a few minutes, and now..." She sniffles. I have to cover my mouth not to laugh out loud. "It's only been a week, and I've already made a huge mistake!"

"Hey," I hear Dylan say, softly and a little closer. "Don't cry. Seriously."

"I tried looking for it, but this trash can's so deep, and I'm so—"

"Short," he cuts in with a little laugh. "I know. Listen, calm down. I'll help you. It's in here?" he asks, his voice right above the trash can. My legs tingle. I'm ready to pounce.

"Uh-huh."

When the slightest sliver of light slips into the garbage can, I flip the giant lid all the way back as I shoot up to my feet and roar, "Ahhhhhhhhh!"

Dylan screams. Literally, he screams like a little girl, totally spazzing out and slamming into a vending machine. Stella is trying to hold the camera steady, but she can hardly stand, she's cracking up so bad. And I lose it. I absolutely lose it. I am laughing so hard that I lean back to catch my breath, not realizing that the garbage can has wheels. Suddenly, I feel the whole thing start to slide, and I topple backward with a loud *thud*.

"Bird!" Stella calls. The camera is on me now, and I feel tears streaming down my face.

"I can't breathe," I whisper.

"Me neither," she manages.

"You guys are idiots," Dylan grumbles.

Stella swings the phone his way again. "Dylan, you should've seen your face!"

Ungracefully, I crawl out of the empty garbage can and try to get ahold of myself. I can tell that my brother wants to kill us both, but with the camera rolling, he fakes a laugh and says, "Y'all need a life."

Announcer Stella turns the camera back toward herself and says, "And that's what you don't see on the Shine Our Light Tour. Even from the good seats. Bye-bye, Birdies!"

The second she cuts the video, Dylan lunges for her, pinning her arms and swinging her around in a circle like she weighs nothing. "Bird did it!" she shrieks, selling me out. "I'm innocent! Get Bird!"

"What?" I call, feigning naïveté.

"Oh, I know this was your idea, Crossley," Dylan says. "I just don't know how I'm going to get you back."

"No matter what you plan," she says, "I guarantee I won't scream as high as you did."

"Agh!" Dylan growls, swinging her around again.

I wish I could watch the video and laugh at Dylan and myself, but I look at my phone and realize that I was supposed to be in my dressing room two minutes ago.

"Hey, guys, hate to prank and run," I say, "but I'm late."

"Shoot, you're right, Bird," Stella says, looking at her own phone.

Dylan sets her back down on her feet, but he doesn't let go right away. She twists in his arms, smiling up at him, and he grins, definitely not mad anymore. Stella pushes against Dylan's chest to free herself and grabs my hand. "We have to go be serious professionals now," she says as we walk past him. Then she calls over her shoulder, "Remind me never to go through a haunted house with you!" He lunges for her again, and we race down the passageway, laughing like hyenas.

"Paybacks are hell!" he calls.

When we burst through the doors to my dressing room, my styling team looks at us like we're crazy. Amanda especially makes a big show of examining the time on her watch, but we don't even attempt to explain.

"Had to be there," I simply say as I sit in my chair and reach for a tissue to dab at my eyes. "You really just had to be there."

"Bird, you were fantastic!" my manager exclaims backstage at *Conan*. The tour headed to Phoenix after Sacramento while Troy and I drove south to LA for a quick appearance.

"Thanks," I say as I pull my earpieces out and let them dangle around my neck. "His audience was fantastic."

"Oh, they ate it up," he agrees.

Producers and guests mill around us, and we step out of

the way as they prepare for the next segment. A production assistant is leading us down the back hallway toward my dressing room when a door opens up ahead and I hear a loud and very unhappy person shout, "What is *she* doing here?" I glance over and nearly choke, stopping dead in my tracks as I come face-to-face with none other than Kayelee Ford, another country music singer my age who has hated me since before we ever met.

"Kayelee!" I manage as I wither beneath her look of death. My legs stop working, my feet suddenly like concrete blocks. The PA leading me down the hall exchanges a look with the other PA, who was leading Kayelee out of her room, and I can tell that they had purposefully tried to avoid this very encounter.

Ever since I turned down Great American Music for a record deal and they signed Kayelee right after, we've been pitted against each other in the media. Everyone's constantly comparing our sound, our image, and our success. Last year we both got caught up in the drama, but I've tried to rise above it all since then. Clearly she has no intention of doing the same.

"God, this *would* happen," she complains as she pulls down on the shortest miniskirt ever made. She focuses her angry eyes on the group of people filing out of the dressing room behind her and gripes, "I knew I heard that stupid 'Shine' song. Who said it was just the radio?"

"That would be me." A very handsome, very British guy steps around Kayelee and gives me a wide, warm smile. "Miss Barrett, I don't believe we've had the pleasure. Colton Holley."

But of course Colton Holley doesn't need an introduction. The filthy rich (thanks to his family's hotel empire) twenty-three-year-old is the current "it" boy of the young Hollywood crowd. He looks like a Calvin Klein underwear model. In fact, he's on this month's cover of *GQ*. And I know this is totally lame, but I get butterflies when he takes my hand, kisses it, and says, "You're even more beautiful in person."

I just gawk at him, speechless.

"God, Colton, keep it in your pants," Kayelee fumes. She throws her long fake hair over her fake-bronzed shoulder and brushes past me, snapping at Colton like he's a pet. "The producers are waiting. Let's go."

His amber eyes don't leave mine, his smile mesmerizing. "My new nightclub opens tomorrow, so..." he says with a shrug, "promotion."

"Cool," I manage.

"If you're ever in Vegas, you should come by."

"Oh," I say. "My tour goes through there in a couple of weeks actually. My birthday."

"Then we have to celebrate!" he says, eyes gleaming.

"Colton!" Kayelee calls. "Stop wasting your time with 'Wanna Be Me' and let's go."

My jaw drops, and I gape at Troy, who just shakes his head.

"Mr. Holley, we really do need to get to the stage," the visibly nervous production assistant says quietly.

"I'll be in touch," he says softly before following Kayelee and the rest of the *Conan* production team down the hall. I make a beeline for my own dressing room, totally unnerved by the whole encounter.

"Ready to go eat?" my mom asks in a cheery voice as I walk in. She immediately sees the scowl on my face and jumps up off the couch. "What's wrong?"

"Colton Holley happens to be taping here today as well," Troy explains. "And he brought along our friend Kayelee Ford."

A look of understanding crosses my mother's face. "He's that British playboy all over the tabloids, right? Are they dating?"

"Who cares?" I cut in. "Let's just go." I grab my purse and a piece of chocolate from a basket on the end table. "I can't even with her. She is the rudest, snobbiest, brattiest, most selfish, ignorant, ridiculous, phony—"

"Okay, okay, okay," Mom interrupts. She throws her arm around my shoulders. "Let's not let her ruin our night."

I sigh heavily and try to shake it off as we make our way out of the studio, but my heart is pumping fast and my whole body feels hot. That girl infuriates me more than any other person on the planet.

"Nobu, West Hollywood," my mom reminds our driver as he holds the door open for us outside. "You know," she says as we get settled, "I think Kayelee's just threatened, Bird."

I crack my window and take a deep breath. I want to push the run-in out of my mind. This is my first night out since the tour started, and all I want to do is eat sushi and enjoy time with my mom. I do not want to think about poor little rich, successful Kayelee Ford.

3

"THAT IS SO disgusting," I hear Stella say from outside my door on the tour bus a couple of days later.

"Why?" Dylan asks.

"You licked my ice cream cone!" she cries. "Your tongue touched my food."

I yawn and look over at the time on my phone, nap officially over.

"So? It's no worse than kissing."

"Exactly," she says. "Disgusting."

"As if you don't dream about it every night."

"I dream about ways to strangle you, not kiss you."

I smile.

"Denial is the first sign," Dylan goes on.

"No, 'da Nile' is a river in Egypt."

He groans. "Oh, you are even cornier than Bird."

At that I laugh out loud.

"Bird, are you awake?" Stella calls. "Your brother is an idiot."

"Your best friend wants me!" Dylan calls in response.

I giggle and stretch as I throw my covers back and get up. We've played seven cities in the last two weeks, and on top of that, Troy booked me a big-time sponsorship meeting yesterday back in LA that I couldn't miss. It was nice to stop by the California condo and sleep in my own bed, but getting up at five this morning to fly back and meet up with the tour for tonight's performance in Boise was torture. When the Open Highway team and I originally worked through the tour schedule, we agreed that I'd push it and do eleven to fourteen shows a month. My dad worried that was too extreme, but I really wanted to go hard. That's been my motto since the early planning stages: Go hard. My show is a little longer than ninety minutes, and I want it to be full of surprises and excitement the whole time. I don't want my fans to think, *Now is the perfect song to go grab a hot dog.* No. There is no perfect time to eat, to pee, to do anything other than watch the show, because every minute of the Shine Our Light Tour is packed with drama.

In those planning stages, I figured a schedule like ours meant I'd only be working half of each month, which would still give me plenty of time off to rest; what I didn't count on was how fatiguing the travel would be and how often I'd be spending many of those "free" days working. Troy has all kinds of things in the works, constantly reminding me how important it is to "capitalize on tour momentum." Who am I to argue? Thanks to yesterday's meeting, I get to be the face of the new Sephora campaign!

"What time are we walking over there?" I hear Dylan ask Stella.

"My call time's not for an hour."

Ugh. I've only got an hour to shower and eat before sound check.

The tour itself is going more smoothly than any of us could've dreamed. We started rehearsals in June and worked out all the kinks, both onstage and backstage, going over each song meticulously. I'm working with Jordan again. She was the stage manager on Jolene Taylor's Sweet Home Tour, which I opened for last year, so I feel confident that she can handle making the show actually happen each night. Meanwhile my tour manager, Marco, is a friend of Dan's, and he deals with the business end of life on the road. Yeah, I've got three managers now. *Who knew I was so high maintenance?*

I grab my shower caddy and a towel and make my way to the bathroom.

"Bird, look at this," Stella says when I slide the divider open.

I look up at her bed but am surprised to see her sharing the middle bunk with Dylan instead.

"Sit with us," she says, patting the spot next to her. Dylan has his laptop open, and they're looking at something on his computer. "It's the photos from the World's Largest Ball of Paint." I throw my stuff onto the vacant bottom bunk and hop up beside her, smiling as she scrolls through pictures the three of us have taken in the very little amount of time we've had to sightsee so far.

"That was really fun," I say.

"Yeah, and all the pics are linked to this map, see?" Stella clicks on a pic of us at Disney, and it minimizes to Orlando.

"So each of these pins is a tour stop?" I ask.

"Yeah, he's pinned the pics to each place," she gushes. "It's so cool."

Dylan clears his throat. "I just made it to document our trip," he says, a little embarrassed. "I found a template when the tour started just to, you know, remember all of this or whatever."

Stella leans her head on his shoulder. "This ol' softy is a sensitive guy after all," she says mockingly. He shrugs her off.

"Can I see?" I ask.

He passes me the computer, and I expand the pin on Alexandria, Indiana. A couple of pictures pop up, and I laugh at one where Stella is pretending to lick the paint ball.

I click on Seymour, Wisconsin, the Original Home of the Hamburger, and a few more funny images of us maximize. "This is awesome!" I say as I continue clicking across the map. There we are stuffing our faces at the chocolate factory in Birmingham and laughing our butts off as Dylan model-poses on a race car at the Nascar Hall of Fame in Charlotte.

"Oh man," I say, giggling. "I'm glad I was able to find the two biggest dorks on the planet to come with me on tour."

"Takes one to know one," Stella fires back.

"This would be so cool on my website," I say, looking over at Dylan. "Can I steal it?"

"I don't know," he says, shrugging. "It's not that fancy."

"Who cares? Anita will love it." I look back down at the screen. "My fans will eat it up."

"Yeah, but, I mean, I wasn't really doing it for that," Dylan says uncomfortably.

As I keep clicking through the map, I realize why he's not so eager. I expand the photos from Denver and see some of just the two of them, making faces by the gorillas and roaring by the tiger exhibit. "You guys went to the zoo?" I ask.

Stella squirms.

"You had a ton of radio interviews, so we went out on our own," Dylan explains.

"Okay, but why didn't y'all mention it?" I ask. "I mean, I wouldn't be mad or anything. It's not like it's your fault I have to go promote my own tour."

Stella shrugs. "I don't know. FOMO?"

"Ha," I say, faking a smile. "Yeah right."

FOMO. It's not fair—I know it's not fair—but I do feel like I'm missing out, especially when I click through another few cities and see more of the same: the two of them having fun without me. And since they didn't tell me about any of these adventures, it all feels a little intentional, a little personal. I realize they can't be expected to sit on the bus all day while I'm working, but as I take in their silly selfies, it looks like my brother is spending more time with my best friend than I am.

"Why are you pretending to fall in this pic?" I ask Stella.

Her eyes twinkle. "Because Dylan had just tripped that lady in the background."

"I didn't trip her!"

"Oh, I'm sorry," she amends. "Dylan just happened to be walking when his feet interrupted the feet of that lady."

"So that's why you wrote, 'Having a nice trip in Rapid City'?" I ask.

They both laugh way harder than seems appropriate. *I guess ya had to be there . . . and I wasn't.*

"Seriously, I didn't trip her," Dylan says with tears in his eyes. He looks down at Stella. "But it *was* pretty funny."

Obviously I see Stella every night in my dressing room and in the quick changes during my show, but I thought there'd be more BFF time on the road than there has been. The first few nights, she shared my bed and we talked and laughed until really late, but the shows started to take their toll and lately, I've been so beat that I've just crashed afterward. Plus, I leave the tour a lot. Now it's like Dylan is my stand-in.

I stop at a shot of Stella goofing off in front of an enormous true-to-life dinosaur screaming as if it's chasing her. "This one's funny," I say with a big smile, determined not to make them feel bad. I'm the boss, it's my tour, so it makes sense that I have less free time than they do. But when I look up, I nearly do a double take. Dylan's eyes are closed, and Stella is wiping away an eyelash on his cheek.

"Make a wish," she says, placing it on the back of his closed fist as if they've done this before. He grins at her and pounds his hands together, then she squeals and claps her hands when it jumps to the back of his other fist. "It's going to come true!"

He blows it away and grins down at her. "Hope so."

Suddenly I feel like I'm interrupting an intimate moment. But that's dumb because Stella and Dylan are as good as brother and sister, and Stella has personally told me she doesn't see Dylan in *that* way. Still, I close the laptop and hop down from the bunk feeling a little off-center.

"This is awesome, Dylan," I say, passing him his computer. "But I really have to get ready or I'll be late. Can't afford to miss anything these days."

He nods, and Stella opens his computer again. They are immediately lost in their photo map. I open the bathroom door feeling a little lost, too, but I'm not giggling the way they are.

4

"Okay, so right after this appearance at the Venetian, I'll meet y'all and we can walk the Strip or whatever until our dinner reservation," I say as we hustle through a back entryway of the luxury Vegas hotel.

"This Emeril guy better be a good cook," Dylan grumbles. He tugs at his collar, still pouting about wearing a sport coat and button-down on his day off.

"Um, he's on *Good Morning America* all the time," Stella says. "And besides, you look really nice tonight."

He smiles down at her and, again, I feel a niggling thought at the back of my mind that maybe they're into each other...which would be so weird.

"Are you sure you don't want us to come with you, Bird?" Stella asks.

"No, seriously," I say. "It's stupid promo stuff for this weekend's shows." I lower my voice. "And the Hicks from Thirty-Six are going to be there. Do you really want to hear those guys play on your day off?"

Stella and Dylan exchange a look, all of us having agreed that my opening act is not our cup of tea, onstage or off. "We'll just walk around, then," Dylan says. "Text when you're done, and we'll meet back up and kill some time before dinner."

"Sounds good."

One of the Venetian resort staff members leads them to a hidden exit, and they duck out into the throng of tourists. They blend in easily, in a way I no longer can. The door closes, and I follow my bodyguard and my hotel security team down the passageway, but then I remember that I wanted to give Stella my VIP pass. I hustle back over to the door to try to catch them, but when I peek out, I am stunned to see my brother buying Stella a rose from an "Italian street vendor." The moment is so picturesque. Dylan really does look dapper tonight, and Stella is a vision in ruffles and ribbons that only she could pull off. The look on her face is so blissful that I figure she already feels like a Very Important Person, and it hits me like a ton of bricks that they do like each other. It's so obvious. Stella and Dylan are more than friends, even if they don't realize it yet.

I close the door and catch up to my team, back to the

grind, trying with all my might to ignore the terrible ache of envy that is settling in my chest. To be looked at like that, and outside of a spotlight, is something I'd kill for.

"Have you been to Vegas before, Ms. Barrett?" a private concierge asks me now.

"Oh, um, yeah, but somehow I keep missing all the sights," I say.

"Well, if there's anything I can arrange to make your stay more enjoyable—a spa visit, a VIP booth at Tao, dinner reservations—please don't hesitate to ask."

"Thank you," I say on autopilot. But when she mentions the nightclub, I remember my run-in with Colton Holley and how he mentioned his new club on the Strip. "You know, I have been wanting to check out COLT," I say. "Do you think it's too short notice to get in tonight? It's my birthday."

She pulls out her cell phone with a big smile and opens the door to a very posh greenroom. "You get to work, Ms. Barrett, and I will, too. How many?"

"Three," I say, walking into the suite with a satisfied smile. "Thanks so much."

* * *

"Okay, that's it," the producer calls from off set. "Thanks, Bird. You were great."

"No problem," I say as an assistant takes my mic pack.

I make a little small talk with the Hicks from Thirty-Six, then allow my handler to lead me back to the greenroom, where I can grab my two most important accessories: my purse and my bodyguard. Once I've checked my hair and reapplied lip gloss, I grab my phone to text Dylan and Stella. But before I can send a message, I hear a knock at the door and am frozen in place when I look up to see none other than Colton Holley standing in the doorway.

"Ms. Barrett, I hope I'm not intruding," he says with a confident smile.

"Colton, hi," I manage.

He strides into the room, full of poise—and full of himself—and grabs my shoulders. He leans in for what I now think of as the Hollywood Hello: an air kiss beside both cheeks. Then he steps back and puts his hands in the pockets of his slacks, smiling at me as if he's won the lottery. "I heard you're stopping by COLT tonight?"

"The concierge arranged it for me, but I didn't expect you to track me down."

He grins devilishly. "Ah, you underestimate me."

That accent.

"Are you in town long?" he asks.

"Nope, just a show here tomorrow and we're moving on," I say, flashing him a smile that I hope will exude even half the self-assuredness of his own. "But I remembered your invitation at our *Conan* run-in and thought I'd check it out."

He cringes. "Yes, the *Conan* run-in. That was uncomfortable to say the very least."

" 'Uncomfortable,' " I repeat as I head toward the door. "That's one way to put it."

He touches my bare upper arm and I shiver. "For what it's worth, I'm sorry about that."

"You don't have to be sorry," I say as we walk through the dim hallway and across the set, where a few crew members are still cleaning up. "You were charming and sweet. Kayelee just knows how to push my buttons."

He grins. "Join the club."

I stop at the back door. "She's not in town, is she? I do *not* want to spend my birthday with your girlfriend, no offense."

"No worries," he says. "She's not in town and she's not my girlfriend. No matter what you've read in the rags, I'm not seeing anyone at the moment."

"Oh," I say, surprised by the delight I feel at this news.

"So it's your birthday, is it?"

"It is. I'm celebrating tonight with my brother and my best friend."

"A Vegas birthday celebration," he says with a roguish grin. I feel myself weaken a little at the knees when he looks at me as if I were a present for *his* birthday. "It would be an honor to play tour guide for you. We can walk around, have dinner, hit up the casinos. Anything you want."

I just stare at him, at his amber-flecked Robert Pattinson eyes and his Tom Brady jawline, and feel utterly flattered. I swore off dating after Kai, but it's been nearly eight months and I'm tired of protecting my heart. Plus, I've been working like a dog all summer to get this tour ready. Everybody else gets a break every now and then. Why not me?

I bite my bottom lip and consider my options: (a) Find Dylan and Stella and be the third wheel on a possibly romantic gondola ride through the Venetian resort before having dinner with them, or (b) Ask super-sexy male celebutante Colton Holley to join us and spend the rest of the day as his arm candy.

"You know what, Colton?" I say with a grin. "I think I'll take you up on that." He offers his elbow, and I loop my arm through his. "But only if you let me get you backstage passes to tomorrow's show."

"Confession," he says, leaning his head close to mine once more. "I already have tickets. Front row."

I look at him in shock. "Really?"

"It's the hottest show in town," he says. "And that's high praise in a city with as much going on as Vegas."

"Then I'll make sure not to disappoint," I say, flirting.

"Oh, Miss Barrett," he says, his voice low, his eyes twinkling. "I doubt you could ever do that."

"That was delicious," Stella says, staring down at the rest of her banana cream pie mournfully. "I wish I had room for every last bite."

"Yeah, for the first time in my life, I can't even do cleanup," Dylan says, pushing away from the table.

Dinner was everything we had hoped. Colton, our Vegas pro, ordered for the table. To start, a seafood tower with everything from oysters to lobster tail. That was followed by the juiciest filet mignon I have ever eaten and buttered asparagus that would make my momma cry. We assured Colton that we were all too full for dessert, but he insisted that we try Emeril's famous banana cream pie and strawberry shortcake. And now, I could die and go to heaven.

"Should we go?" Colton asks, looking at his Rolex. "I should probably get to the club."

"I can't believe we're VIP at Club COLT," Stella gushes. "Didn't Zooey Deschanel just throw a party there?"

"Indeed," Colton says as he stands and buttons his jacket. "Has anyone ever told you that you favor her?"

Stella beams at him. "Thank you, Colton. I adore her style."

Colton pulls out my chair as we all stand to go. "If Zooey saw you tonight, I'm sure she'd say the same of you."

"Give me a break," Dylan mutters, but luckily Colton gets a call and turns his attention to a situation at his club.

I glare at my brother, who glares back until Stella cuts the tension by asking him if she's got anything in her teeth.

I knew Dylan wouldn't be happy about going on a double date with his little sister, but I didn't realize he'd be this obnoxious. Ever since I introduced them, Dylan has been the most caveman version of himself, grunting his responses to anything Colton asks and snorting in disgust at Colton's jokes. My brother has always been overprotective, but Colton's playboy image has put him on high alert. I guess I worried about that a little, too, at first. The tabloids paint Colton as a party boy, but he's been a total gentleman so far. As someone who has been on the ugly end of tabloid rumors, I'm going to give Colton the benefit of the doubt.

"Thank you," he says into his phone now. "We'll be there within the hour."

I look around for our server.

"If you're waiting for the bill, it's been taken care of," he tells me softly.

"Oh," I say, surprised. "Oh no, you shouldn't have."

"I wanted to," he says, squeezing my hand. "I was looking at a very boring evening until I ran into you."

Dylan rolls his eyes yet again, but Stella and I exchange an excited look. As Colton offers me his arm, I almost can't believe the way my birthday is turning out. While celebrity has made it hard to have a private life, perks like these make it all worthwhile.

5

"TWENTY-ONE!" EVERYBODY AT the blackjack table hollers.

"Bird, you're on fire!" Stella says next to me.

After dinner, we hit up Colton's gorgeous nightclub. He escorted us right to the VIP area, where we had an overhead view of the entire club and unlimited bottle service. We danced hard, took lots of pics with random people, and I let loose in a way that I don't think I ever have.

Now it is way past midnight, and we are hitting up the casinos, making our rounds through the games. With Colton by my side, it's like the whole resort is our playground: Nobody has carded us and nobody has asked me for an autograph. He has consistently led me to the calmest tables with the fewest tourists, and we've played roulette, been on the slot machines, and even shot craps. It's been so unbelievably nice to have a real night out, especially since I get to spend it with a hot guy who can relate to the insanity of living life in the public eye.

"Bird, after this, Hold'em?" Dylan asks, his eyes twinkling.

"Oh, good idea! We'll clean house." We high-five, reminiscing about the many hours we spent playing poker growing up on the RV.

Dylan has really loosened up since dinner, partly because he's been a lucky gambler tonight and partly because the free beer keeps coming. As for Stella and me, we've discovered that while we don't care for beer or champagne, strawberry daiquiris are delicious. I can't even taste the alcohol. And they just keep coming, like magic.

I like that I've been able to impress Colton Holley. He has been right at my side, or like now, standing behind me with his hands on my shoulders, at every table. He whispers encouragement and continues to tell me what a "shrewd" gambler I am. He's five years older than me, but I feel like I'm holding my own, like the age difference doesn't matter.

"You are a timeless beauty, Miss Barrett," Colton mumbles into the nape of my neck. Involuntarily, I lean into him. My body feels loose and alive all at once.

"You have to hit that," I hear Dylan tell Stella.

"No, mate, *you* have to hit *that*," a tipsy Colton jokes, nudging Dylan's upper arm. He laughs heartily at his own joke, but I cringe. Dylan shoots him a death stare.

"Colton, what time is it?" I ask, trying to diffuse the tension. The round continues as he pulls out his cell phone.

"Three."

"Three in the morning?" I ask. That feels impossible, but as I look around the casino, I realize that there aren't any windows and that the vitality of this place, the constant high of winning—or determination to win back what's been lost—keeps people going.

"We should probably go upstairs," I say. I stand up and stumble into him.

Colton wraps his arms around me and murmurs in my ear, "That sounds like a marvelous idea."

I giggle. I meant my room, but he thinks I meant his room. That's funny. Why is that so funny?

"Bird, Hold'em?" Dylan asks. He and Stella have gathered their chips and are standing next to us now.

"I don't have to hold him," I say slowly. I am fully in Colton's arms now and don't feel capable of standing on my own. "He's holding me!" I giggle again. Stella laughs, too. "Why is that so funny?" I ask her.

"I don't know," she says, tears in her eyes. "But it's really funny."

"Oh-kay," Dylan says. "It's late. Let's get you girls back up to the suite." Stella reaches over to the table for our drinks, but Dylan intercepts her, putting them on the tray of a passing waiter. "I think y'all have had enough tonight," he says. He wraps his arm firmly around her waist and motions for us to follow him toward the elevators.

"This is why you should never party with your big brother," I tell Colton.

"And why you definitely shouldn't after-party with him," he says softly. His hand is rubbing circles on the bare skin at my neck. I feel tingly all over. "Plus, your best friend is going to want some alone time with her boyfriend."

"They are *not* together," I say.

He raises one eyebrow. "Yet."

"Ugh, don't," I say, worried that he's right. I've been watching them tonight, how effortless they are together and how strong and obvious the chemistry is.

"Which is why," Colton continues, pulling me behind a slot machine, "you should come sober up with me." He runs a hand over my shoulder and up my neck, then locks his fingers in the hair at the base of my head. And before I realize what's happening, Colton Holley is kissing me. He kisses me hard, pinning me against the slots so that I have to reach out to steady myself.

I have never been kissed like this, with this much urgency. With his body pressed up against mine, I feel like maybe my thoughts about romance have all been wrong. Colton Holley isn't a sweet boy from a country song, but he is sexy as hell, and rather than back off, I hold on tight, all in.

"Bird, let's go," I hear Dylan say firmly. I open my eyes, but Colton doesn't stop kissing me. "Bird, now!"

"Listen, mate," Colton sneers, pulling away with a stormy look on his face. "The girl is eighteen years old. She doesn't need her big brother telling her what to do."

"Oh yeah, *mate*?" Dylan says, stepping up to him toe-to-toe. "She doesn't need a slimy player pawing all over her, either."

Colton doesn't step down, but he does look amused when he faces me. "Bird, who's running this show? You or your roadies?"

"That's it," Dylan says, pushing Colton with both hands so that his back slams against a slot machine.

"Dylan, stop!" I shout, stumbling in between them. "I'm going to date, okay? Get over it."

He clenches his jaw, madder than I've ever seen him. "You're drunk," he says quietly.

"I'm not drunk," I reply thickly. My mouth feels so dry. "I mean, I'm not wasted or anything. I know what I'm doing. And it's my birthday, and I'll make out if I want to."

Dylan turns around and runs his hands through his hair, on the verge of exploding.

A very smug Colton puts his arm around my waist and kisses me on the forehead. "Let's get out of here," he mumbles.

I look at his handsome face and nod.

"Bird," Stella interrupts softly. "I don't want to tell you what to do or anything, but some of these people could have cameras and..."

She trails off, gesturing to a couple eyeing us from the Wheel of Fortune Slots, and as tipsy as I am, I get her meaning: I am in public, therefore I am still on the clock. It's my night off, but in public I will always be Bird Barrett: Role Model. Everybody else on the planet can have a little fun once in a while, but not me. Oh no. And I don't know why, but suddenly I get mad. Really mad. At everybody. At everything.

"Fine!" I say, pushing Colton away. I wag my finger between my brother and my best friend. "You guys go ahead and be really happy and enjoy the vacation, oh, I mean, *tour*, and I'll just be alone for the rest of my life."

I walk away fast, feel myself veering, feel the instability in my steps, and wonder if I actually am drunk. Drunk, like, bombed. I bump into a few people and finally make it to the elevators, but when I look through my purse for the VIP card, I'm so angry that I can't see straight. This place is spinning. When the others catch up, Dylan uses his own card to magically open up the portal to the upper floors and I march in, pulling off my high heels.

Ooooh, the cold floor feels good. I grin. Why is that funny?

Colton stands next to me in the back, quiet but still

determined. His hand slides up the underside of my arm and then down my spine, grazing the top of my butt.

"It's not gonna happen, Colton," I say, annoyed.

I hear Stella laugh, but it sounds like she's in a tunnel.

The door opens and I lurch out, leaning against the wall until Dylan takes my hand and leads me toward the right room. Colton follows us down the hall, but I'm pretty sure my brother slams the door in his face. Once inside, I throw my arm around Stella and glare at Dylan. "She's sleeping in my bedroom, got it? If I can't make out with somebody tonight, then you can't, either."

He opens his mouth but shuts it again, at a complete loss for words. We all just stand there, glaring back and forth at one another like some kind of stare down, until Dylan finally busts out laughing. Stella joins in, falling to the floor as she hoots, and then I flop back onto the sitting room sofa, laughing so hard I feel like I could throw up.

Uh-oh.

And then, I throw up.

"I'm dying," I croak the next morning. "Or no, I'm dead, I think. My skull was crushed, and the pieces are piercing my brain. I'm definitely dead. And I didn't go to heaven. Which sucks."

"Oh, terrific. Not only are you an angry drunk but you also have dramatic hangovers," Dylan says from somewhere. He must've died, too. Our parents will be so sad. "Bird, take this."

I open my eyes and everything looks blurry. A person who resembles my brother is sitting in front of me on the coffee table with a glass of water and two aspirin. "This helps," he assures me. He places his hand under my head and lifts me a little so I can take the pill and wash it down. Water never tasted so good. "And for some reason, McDonald's does, too."

I feel my stomach lurch and clap my hand over my mouth, slamming my eyes shut again and lying back on the couch. *Did I sleep on the couch?*

"Don't you dare throw up again," Dylan commands.

Again?

"I'm dying," I hear Stella moan.

I turn my head and barely open my eyes as my best friend stumbles into the room. She folds herself into a giant armchair, looking worse than I've ever seen her, which is saying something since I've seen that girl with the flu. "Stella, your hair," I manage. Her thick bangs are sticking out everywhere, like a sign giving conflicting directions, and it looks like there are pieces of something matted in her shoulder-length tresses.

"Oh my gross!" she shouts when she notices it. "Bird, I'm going to kill you!"

She stumbles out of the room, and I hear a door slam. Then I hear water running from the bathroom and assume she's in the shower.

"What'd I do?" I ask.

"Stella helped you last night," he explains. "When you got sick. We cleaned it up, but she was pretty hammered, too, and I guess she missed some spots."

Mortified, I realize my puke is in her hair. "I'm a terrible friend," I whisper, closing my eyes again. For some reason, I feel my eyes well up with tears.

"We've all been there," he says, which is weird because I'm waiting for the Dylan Barrett holier-than-thou speech about being responsible and making good decisions. "Consider this your first semester in college. Just...pace yourself next time, okay?"

I nod. He pats me on the shoulder, and I wince. I ache all over.

"I am never drinking again," I say from the backseat of Dylan's rental car as I chow down on a Quarter Pounder with Cheese on our way back to the resort for rehearsal.

"I am never *ever* drinking again," Stella says. "But this Big Mac really is making me feel better."

"Told ya," Dylan says. "The first time I got drunk was at a kegger off campus, and I felt like y'all did this morning. But a buddy swore to me that greasy food and a sugary soda would turn things around, and he was right."

"Well, I wouldn't say it's turned things around," I respond. "I still feel like tiny elves are chiseling my eyeballs and worms are eating my innards—"

"Bird!" Stella protests. "Weak stomach up here."

"Right, sorry," I say, my mouth full of fries. "But I'm seriously never ever *ever* drinking again."

I roll the back windows down and let the cool desert air whip through my hair. Cool desert air, except deserts are hot. That's funny.

"Uh-oh," I say, leaning forward between the front two seats. "Can you be drunk the day *after* you were drunk?"

Rehearsal is actually a blast. If you'd have asked me this morning, I'd have told you there was no way in the world I'd be able to perform tonight, let alone rehearse. But I guess I caught a second wind because I feel okay, even if I have missed a few cues.

"I drag the sleep from my bed, I shake myself in my head," I sing, then start laughing when I realize I goofed the lyrics to "Sing Anyway." "Oh my gosh, y'all, sorry, sorry," I say as the band stops playing. "Let's go back. Sorry. I'm a little tired. Sorry."

I see my fiddle player and drummer exchange an exasperated look when the music starts up again, which is so lame. I messed up a few lyrics in *rehearsal*, big deal. Ignoring them, I start the number again, dancing with a few of the guys in the band and even walking through the crew in the wings, giving this sound check a fun vibe for once as I sing through this song for the bazillionth time.

"Bird, are you going to mark the quick change?" Monty asks a few minutes later. I turn around and realize that the band is offstage, mocking their costume changes, and I'm still standing at the front of the T, zoning out at a spot in the upper decks.

"My bad," I say, running back to the main stage and then to the wings, where Stella waits.

"Rip off," she says, pantomiming pulling off my dress from the previous number.

I gasp and cover myself as if I'm really naked. "Excuse me, miss, but you have to at least buy me dinner first."

Stella laughs and rocks back on her heels. Then she grabs the imaginary shirt I'm wearing next and tosses it at my face. I swat my hands around and say, "I can't see! I can't see anything!"

My flailing is making her laugh so hard that she's shaking and people are starting to stare. I can barely control myself, either. "Step in," she commands. I mime one foot stepping into the leg hole. "Other leg," she says. "And up!" She jerks the imaginary shorts up, and I grab my crotch and bend over, crossing my eyes. At this point, she falls back against what she thinks is a wall but is actually a curtain, and she lands flat on her butt.

"Stella!"

She is laughing so hard now that she's not even making any sounds. "I can't get up, Bird," she barely ekes out. "Can't. Get. Up."

"Bird!" Dylan shouts. Everyone near me backstage looks up as he storms toward us. "Are y'all done goofing off over here? Some of us actually want to practice before playing in front of a sold-out venue, if you don't mind."

I look at him like he's crazy and say, "Sor-ry," with as much sarcasm as I can muster.

"Oh yeah, you sound real sorry," he says, shaking his head. "You think you're so grown-up, but if you want to be treated like an adult, you have to act like one."

I roll my eyes. "Good point, *Dad*. I'll take that to heart, I truly will, just as soon as this young lady down here zips me up."

I reach my arm out to a giggling Stella and pull her up, but Dylan explodes. "Zips you up?! It's not a real costume change! Just fake it like the rest of us and let's play some music already!"

Now all eyes are on us. Everybody, from the catering team to the grips, is staring holes through us, and I feel my face flame. "Listen, Dylan. This is *my* tour, and if I want to have a little fun once in a while, I don't need one of my *band members* coming down on me. Got it?"

He looks like I slapped him in the face, and then I see his nostrils flare. But before he can respond, Monty steps between us and suggests we all take five. Dylan storms off, and I turn toward the onlookers and say, "Sorry you had to see that, folks. Just a little sibling spat. Let's all take five."

And true to my word, I turn to my best friend and say, "Zip me up?"

Which she does. "Ow." She pouts playfully. "My pinkie got caught in the zipper."

Grinning, I kiss it. Then we throw our arms around each other and head for Craft Services, where we each pound a Gatorade before getting on with the show.

"Tammy, can you please stop jerking at my hair?" I complain in my dressing room later. My hairstylist looks at me with surprise and nods crisply. "And Sam, seriously, my eyes are really sensitive, and you're practically gouging them out with that shadow brush."

"Mm, mm, mmm," he murmurs. "Somebody's in a bad mood today."

"Sorry," I say, reaching for the aspirin bottle Marco just brought me. My tour manager is cool. I think my parents were hoping he'd step in as a sort of chaperone, but he rides with the band and lets me be. He didn't even ask questions about last night—just brought me the pills and got back to his job. "My head is pounding."

I take two aspirin, drink some more Gatorade, and check my cell phone again. Anita is trying to squash a story about me "partying hard with playboy Colton Holley," and her constant judgmental texts aren't helping my headache. Luckily, he was spotted with a tall, redheaded model in a skimpy bikini this morning at the pool, and the images they do have from last night are too grainy to confirm anything. Anita is threatening libel if the rag mag links him to me. I think I dodged a bullet, both with the story and a fling with Colton.

But I still feel stupid.

There is a knock at the door, and I look up. "Come in!" I shout, but then I wince from the effort.

"Hey, it's me," Dylan says, stepping inside. "When you have time, can we talk a minute? In private?"

"Sure," I say, rolling my eyes. "Can y'all give us a minute?"

My styling team exits the dressing room, and I swivel around in my chair to face my brother. He doesn't look as angry as he did before, but he doesn't look apologetic, either.

"Bird, I know you're eighteen, and you can make your own decisions," he starts. "And I know that this is your tour. Believe me, I'm aware. It's awfully hard to forget when your face is plastered on billboards across the country." He points at me. "But *you* have to remember that, too. This is *your* tour. *You're* the boss." He steps back and opens the door, and the sounds of equipment rolling by and crew conversations fill the dressing room. "Look around. All those people out there? They depend on *you* for a job. For some, like Stella and me, who are just starting out, our *careers* could be based on the success of this tour. Don't you feel some responsibility for us? For everybody?"

"Yes, Dylan, gah!" I swivel back around and lay my head down on the vanity. "I had a bad night. I made poor decisions. But I swore off drinking, and you can trust that I'm paying for it enough without you coming down on me, okay?"

"Okay," he says simply. And leaves.

My styling team files back in quietly, but it's pretty apparent that they heard everything we said after Dylan opened the door. Stella is the last back in, and when I see her, I say, "Can you believe him?"

She surprises me when she picks up a handheld steamer and shrugs noncommittally. "Well, you *are* the boss now."

I gape at her, but she doesn't meet my gaze. She sided with Dylan. They've been hanging out for, like, three or four weeks, and she sided with Dylan. I thought they were just friends—I was *hoping* they were just becoming better friends—but she has always had my back until now. She likes my brother, and she sold me out.

"Unbelievable," I mutter. I pull out my earbuds and iPhone and blast my Now Is Not a Good Time playlist, determined to block out everybody else.

Okay, yeah, I am the boss. Except I'm not. I still have to answer to my parents, my label, and my fans. Oh, and *I'm* the bad guy, but they were both there *partying with their boss* last night. Unbe-freaking-lievable.

I close my eyes and quietly fume. Dylan and Stella may be right, but they don't have any idea what it's like to be me.

6

"BIRD?" STELLA CALLS outside my door. The bus is making its way over to Salt Lake City, and I'm trying to hold tree pose without toppling.

"Come in," I call.

She slides open the divider and holds up a DVD. "Want to watch *Pitch Perfect*?" she asks. I can see from her expression that she's trying to smooth things over.

I give in to the rhythm of the bus and let my foot fall to the floor. "You sure you want to mix business with pleasure?" I ask a little snidely. "Hanging out with the boss can get pretty tricky."

"Don't be like that, Bird," Dylan says, squeezing past Stella to sit on my bed. "Listen, we were all hungover and we all acted dumb. Can we just agree to that and move on?"

I chew my lip and consider.

"Bird?"

"Yeah, fine," I finally say. "But Dylan, we can't fight like that in front of everybody."

"I know. I should've kept my cool."

I sigh heavily. "And I shouldn't have been acting so ridiculous. I do take this seriously, and now everybody probably thinks I'm losing it."

"Nah," he says. "You just have to have boundaries."

"Oh, like you?" I retort. "One minute you want me to be the boss of the tour and keep it all together, and then the next minute you want to be my overprotective big brother who doesn't let me make out with hot, rich guys."

Stella laughs and sits by Dylan. "That's true."

He just shrugs.

"Hey, Colton was there last night in the front row," Stella says to me now. "Did you see him?"

"Yes, I saw him and his *two* dates."

"See?" Dylan says. "It's sleazebags like that dude that make me act all 'overprotective' or whatever. And I'm not sorry for playing the big brother card at the casino the other night." He stands up and holds out his hand. "But I do promise to dial it back otherwise, okay?"

"And I'll do better at treating you like a respected member of my band instead of the annoying nerd that you are," I say, shaking on it. "Deal?"

"Deal."

Dylan leads us out to the living room area and crashes on the couch as Stella loads the movie. I grab some snacks from the kitchenette, relieved that we're putting the stupid spat behind us. With three of us cramped on the same bus all the time and working together, too, we are bound to have a few tiffs, but I'm glad we could work it out and get back to normal. When I head toward the couch, Stella slips down next to Dylan before I can sit, her expression that of attempted nonchalance although she clearly cut me off. Then Dylan oh-so-casually drapes his arm around the sofa, not necessarily across her shoulders, but the two of them look quite cozy as they stare past me at the television, apparently super absorbed in the opening scene, as if we haven't seen it a million times before.

I turn around slowly and drop into the recliner with the unsettling feeling that it may be too late for normal.

It was a madhouse in my dressing room tonight. Troy was prepping me on a few talk show appearances he wants me to make, and Stella was frantically trying to get a lipstick stain out of my opening costume. Sam and Tammy were talking nonstop about a *Real Housewives* scandal, and Amanda was in a mood about us being five minutes late.

All that to say that by the time I took the stage, there still hadn't been a private moment to talk to Stella about what is going on between her and Dylan, because clearly something is happening there and clearly she wants me in the dark.

And it hurts my feelings. Yeah, okay, the likelihood of a "Stylan" relationship is a little, um, *yuck*, but I'm her *best friend*. During the last couple of costume changes, I've just wanted to shout, *Hello! I'm not an idiot. Talk to me.*

"Let's bring it down, one time," I say near the end of "Notice Me." The band softens and the instrumentals play as I talk, totally off script. "Is there somebody out there you've been friends with for a long time? Maybe you're thinking about being more than friends. Maybe you want to take things to the next level, but you have absolutely no idea if that person feels the same way." I glance back at Dylan and raise my eyebrows. He looks away. I knew it. "In fact," I go on, stronger now, "maybe you think they like you back, but there's another factor, another person maybe, that's in your way. Or that you assume might be in your way. Anybody out there want somebody to see you as more than what you've always been?"

The crowd cheers.

"Salt Lake City, let 'em know!" I shout out. I cue the band, and they play louder at my lead, nearly fifteen thousand voices filling the arena as we sing: *"Is it real? Do you see? Say you notice me.* Come on! *Notice me. Oh, say you notice...me."*

As the crowd goes wild, we cut the song and I race backstage. A short video plays on the giant screens onstage, a roadie hands me a bottle of water, and Stella rips off my fire-engine-red sequined dress. We're going fifties-mod for the next song, the one I wrote with Adam last year called "Worth Being in Love." I know now is not the right time to bring this up, but I can't stop myself, blurting out, "Do you like my brother?"

Stella has a vintage black-and-white polka-dot dress halfway up my body, and she stops cold. "What?"

I tug at the dress. "Keep going. I've only got another minute until this video is over, but it seems like you guys have been flirting lately and, I don't know, maybe I'm crazy, but do you like Dylan? Like *that*?"

She looks away, pulls the dress all the way up, and steps behind me to zip me in and tie the halter. "Yeah," she says quietly. "I do."

I shake my head.

"See, I knew you'd be mad," she says, walking around and fluffing the full skirt with its tulle peeking from the hemline. "That's why I didn't say anything. Well, that and I don't think he likes me back."

"Are you serious?" I ask. "First of all, I'm not mad that you like him, although I do question your taste in men. But why didn't you tell me? I asked you about him before, and you said he wasn't your type."

"That was, what, almost two years ago?" she asks, pulling my boots off. "I didn't even really know him then. And this just sort of happened over the past couple of weeks, where I realized, 'Oh, for real, I think I like this guy. And he's my best friend's brother, and it's weird.' I've wanted to tell you, but I've been like, 'Ah! What do I do?'"

I slip my feet into a pair of retro-style pumps and sigh. "Honestly? I can sort of see it," I admit.

She clutches my forearms as I balance. "Seriously?"

I look down at her face, at the excitement there and the childlike hope that I've never seen in her before. Suddenly it feels like there's some sort of distance between us even though she's right in front of me. I shake it off. "But Stel, it sucks that you didn't tell me, 'cause you're the only person in my whole life that I can be one hundred percent totally real with twenty-four-seven. And I want you to feel the same way with me."

She nods. "I do!"

"Then why—"

Jordan hands me my microphone. "You need to get out there," she says, looking at her wristwatch. The video onstage ends and the audience cheers, meaning that even though Stella and I should probably have a real talk, we can't. Not right now.

"Okay, we'll talk later," I say as I back toward the stage. "But I'm pretty sure he likes you, too."

"Really?" she squeals from the wings. "How do you know? Bird Barrett, don't you dare leave me hanging like that!" she calls. "I want details! Come back!"

I smile as she pantomimes fishing for me, but I feel anxious inside as I rush to my mark. If Dylan and Stella get together, I'll definitely be a third wheel. And then if it doesn't work out, life on my bus will be miserable. Will I have to fire one of them?

I stand between two male dancers behind a door in the big screen, and as the music starts, they lift me onto their shoulders. When the spotlight hits and the crowd swells, I plaster on a big smile and focus on the show, on the moment, on being a professional musician instead of a worried teenager. This is who I need to be now, so I sing with all I've got, even as I chew on the quickie backstage convo.

I obviously want them both to be happy, but as I belt out the chorus of "Worth Being in Love," I can't help but think that, in this case, it may not be worth it at all.

"So, basically, after the Salt Lake show, when you jetted off for LA again, it was just me and Dylan on the bus," Stella says a few days later. Troy had a town car waiting for me at the back door of the arena the other night, but I had called Stella on my way to the airport and we talked about every single nuance of her crush on Dylan. I felt thoroughly filled in on Stella's feelings for him, but now that I'm back on the bus and she's sitting across from me on my bed with a ginormous smile, I have the feeling that something happened—with my brother—and I'm not sure I want to hear every juicy detail.

"So you know how the other night in the wings you were saying that you think Dylan might like me back?" she asks. I nod. "Well, I *think* I found out while you were gone that he does!"

"Oh, wow."

Stella throws herself back against the pillows beside me and rushes into the whole story. "Okay, so that night it was just Dylan and me—alone on the bus—and I was charged from telling you I like him and admitting it out loud and everything. Like, that made it real, you know?"

She rolls her head toward mine, and I face her and nod. "Totally."

"And every time he squeezed past me on the bus, I swear I thought he could hear my pulse, it was beating so loud. Or he could read my mind or something. But he acted totally normal. Just regular ol' Dylan zoning out after the show on his Beats, staring up at the bottom of my bunk, so I just got ready for bed like usual except, with you not here, I was, like, 'Um, what do I do now?'"

"What did you do?"

"I climbed up into my bed and started watching *10 Things I Hate About You*."

"Oh man."

"I was feeling romantic!"

"Okay, so did something actually happen between you guys, or what?"

"Wait for it!" she says, grabbing my arm. "So I was all into Heath Ledger and his bad-boy charm, but at the same time, I was thinking about being on the bus *alone* with Dylan. So finally I kind of flung my arm off the side of the bed, like, so casual, and I was waiting and hoping he'd just, like, touch it or hold it or something."

"You thought he was going to hold a hand that was just hanging out there in the wide open?" I ask, teasing her.

"I just—I don't know! It was stupid. But I fell asleep with my hand like that. And I guess Dylan had to get up later, and when he did, he closed my computer and set it to the side and tucked my arm back in my bed—obviously I woke up but pretended I was still totally asleep—and his face literally lowered toward mine, and I was like, '*Oh my God, this is a freaking Snow White moment.*' But he didn't kiss me or anything. He just whispered, 'Good night, pretty girl.'" She pauses, looking at me expectantly.

"Whoa," I say, a beat or two later than a best friend probably should in a moment like this.

And then she screams and kicks her feet. "It was amazing!"

Okay, he's not your brother, he's not your brother, he's not your brother. Act like he's not your brother.

"Stella, I would die," I say honestly.

She turns toward me on the pillow and keeps going. "It gets better."

"There's more?" I ask.

"Bird, you were gone for a few days."

"Still."

"This is too big for text!" she squeals. "I wanted to see your face."

I purposefully arrange said face into an expression that mirrors her excitement and try not to be bummed that I missed so much while I was working in LA. "Okay, what else?" I ask.

"So the next day, I was emboldened. I asked him if he wanted to watch a movie and he did, but instead of watching something we already have on the bus, he suggested we go see something in town."

She looks at me again. I can tell this is really big for her, but I can't connect the dots. "Cool," I say vaguely.

"Bird!" she cries. "He clearly wanted to take me on a real, thought-out date."

"Did he call it that?"

She considers, and I see her deflate slightly in front of me. Guilt twists my gut.

"I mean, it probably was," I amend. "Sounds like it was."

"*Anyway*," she goes on. "When Grantuam finally fought for Janelle's freedom—" She stops abruptly and covers her mouth. "Oh, sorry."

"Stella, I promise you that is not a spoiler. There is no way I'm watching an alien black belt save the world, not in a million years."

She grins. "Okay, so he saved her, and it was a semi-romantic part but actually also really funny 'cause, you know, aliens and karate. Well, Dylan and I looked at each other and laughed, and then, like it was the most natural thing in the world, he grabbed my hand. And he held it until the end. And it was just"—she sighs and closes her eyes—"the most perfect day."

"I did *not* realize how much you liked my brother."

She nods. "I've got it bad."

I look up at the ceiling and think about it all. I do want them to be happy. I just don't want to deal with the fallout if things go badly. I've lived on an RV with Dylan after a breakup, and it is not a pretty sight.

I face her. "So, should we make some ground rules?"

"What do you mean?"

"Well, if you guys do start dating, how's that going to work?"

"I don't understand."

I exhale loudly. "Like, I don't want to be in the middle if there's any drama, you know? And I don't want to be the third wheel on all your dates. And I definitely don't want to hear you guys making out at night."

Stella starts laughing. "Bird! It's not like he's my boyfriend. I don't know what we are or if we'll even be anything."

I look over at her. "My brother is a lot of things, but he's not stupid. You're a catch. Any guy would be a fool not to date you."

She beams at me and squeezes my hand. "What if we make a code name?" Stella suggests. "What if I can still have your feedback as my best friend without compromising your situation as his sister? Like, I can still tell you everything, and you can imagine that it's...Channing Tatum, a hot, tall, delicious guy with amazing eyes who makes me melt every time I hear him play the guitar."

"Channing Tatum, huh?"

She giggles and nods.

"Okay," I say. "So has Channing slipped you the tongue?"

"Excuse me!" Stella exclaims. "Mr. Tatum is a gentleman."

We laugh. We laugh and it feels good, and I realize that, as usual, I've been making things more complicated than they have to be. I'll listen when either wants to talk, I'll keep everything they say about the other to myself, and I'll stay Switzerland on all possible conflicts.

"He hasn't kissed me," she says softly now. "I definitely would've called you if things had gotten that far."

"I would hope so," I say.

"We spent our days off together, but he didn't really make another move. It just seems like we touch a little more often now, like he'll lean against me in line for lunch or I'll scratch his back while we watch a show. There's tension like something might happen, but it hasn't."

"Maybe you intimidate him," I say.

"Or maybe he knows when he kisses me it'll make it all real," she says. "Maybe he's not ready for real."

She picks at a loose thread on her shirt, and I can almost hear her thoughts. I wonder if they echo mine: *What does it mean when it all gets real?* I can't help but think about Kai and how perfect our relationship was when we were on the road together last year. And then I remember how impossible it was once we were apart. I wonder if we would still be friends if we'd never taken it to the next level. I used to tell him everything, we shared every part of our day, and now all I get are snippets of his life from his Instagram account.

The same thing happened with Adam. We were always so comfortable together, and I nursed a crush on him well before I let him know about it because I was always worried that he looked at me as nothing more than Jacob's little sister. We finally went on a date, and it was so perfect. I thought we had a chance. But he stopped it before we really got going, and now it's only the occasional text message or tweet that keeps us in contact.

I close my eyes and am inundated by painful memories from two failed relationships. I haven't been on a single date since my breakup after New Year's. There really is a lot at stake on the brink of things getting real.

7

"I'M STANDING HERE with three-time-VMA-nominated Bird Barrett, who looks stunning this evening," Sway Calloway says on the red carpet.

I smile. "Thanks, Sway. It's so good to be here."

"Now, I just spoke with your old pal Devyn Delaney, and she said your performance is the one she's most looking forward to tonight."

I'm surprised to hear that after our falling out last year, but as my publicist looks on from a few feet away, I know I make her proud by not letting it show. I am very familiar with the PR machine that is Devyn Delaney. Before she betrayed me by setting me up for a spat with Kayelee Ford on reality television, I learned a lot about the business from her. So, smiling broadly, I tell the MTV reporter, "Oh, Devyn's just the best."

"She's a cool cat," he agrees. I glance at Anita, who smirks back at me. "Tonight you're nominated for Best Video with a Message for your monster hit 'Shine Our Light.' That's what you'll be performing later, correct?"

"Yes, and that performance is going to be really special," I say.

"The video is also pretty special," Sway says. "Fifteen million views on YouTube in the first week. We've all heard the rumors that it was penned about another singer here tonight," he goes on. "What do you think about when you sing that song?"

I pause to think about my answer as the fans surrounding the red carpet swell in their cheers. I briefly wonder who just arrived, but then I focus on my response. "Well, it does take me back to a hard time in my life," I say, "but a friend helped me see that we all shine brighter when we're casting light instead of shadows—of doubt, or negativity, or whatever else—and I think about that."

"Love the positive message. Good luck tonight, Bird."

I finish the interview and meet up with Troy, Anita, and former country music sensation and personal mentor Bonnie McLain, who are waiting for me off to the side. "The VMAs are madness," I say. "Last year I was just excited to be here, but this year all I see is drama around every corner." I nod toward the carpet as Kayelee herself appears in front of the stands, stunning in a provocative gown that looks like it's made out of purple zip ties.

"Well, all I see is skin," Bonnie says loudly. Of course right at that moment, somebody walks by in a leather tube top and some sort of grass skirt.

"Bird, let's walk," Anita says, business as usual. "I want to get you ahead of Kayelee, and I don't know if you saw, but she brought your good buddy Colton Holley as her date, so let's march while she's waiting for her interview."

I know I shouldn't look, but I immediately whip my head around and lock eyes with Colton on the spot. He smiles broadly and waves, so handsome and polished in his tailored tux. *Is he dating Kayelee or not?* Either way, I am mortified that I got smashed and almost hooked up with him in Vegas, so I just give him a quick smile and follow Anita toward the row of reporters eagerly awaiting a brief conversation. I never thought I'd rather talk to the press than a hot rich guy with a sexy British accent, but my life is stupid sometimes.

Bonnie hangs back with Troy as I get down to business, posing my way down the red carpet for the next half hour, giving the photographers and fans every possible angle of my strappy, sparkly red cocktail dress. I felt dangerous and sexy when I chose it a few days ago, but now that I'm actually at the VMAs, I feel like a Catholic nun. Bonnie was right: Less is more for MTV fashions.

Once I reach the end of the carpet, I manage to drag Bonnie out for a few pictures before we head inside. The photogs love it. She may have retired at the top of her game, but that doesn't mean people don't know who she is. I can only dream that one day my shelves will sparkle with as many awards as hers do. And she may be older than my mom and not one for the spotlight anymore, but when the song she helped me write was nominated for Best Video with a Message, I didn't want to bring anyone else.

When we get to our seats, I see that I'm close to the front of the stage, behind Nick Jonas. Dan is there waiting for me, along with a bunch of other Open Highway execs from LA and their dates. Everybody is dressed to the nines and excited. It's fun celebrating with the whole team.

Throughout the show, we get to see performances by everyone from Justin Bieber to Tori Kelly. And although Bonnie doesn't have a clue as the rest of us sing along with the Weeknd, she sure knows every word when Madonna makes a surprise appearance. She breaks out some eighties dance moves that both amaze and mortify me, and I desperately hope someone gets it on camera.

After Madonna's final bow, when fandom took over Bonnie's body in a way that made me think she might need an exorcism, she crashes down into her chair for a breather.

"Thank you for bringing me, Bird, honey," she says, patting my back when I sit next to her.

"I wouldn't want anyone else by my side," I say truthfully.

"You know, I've always wanted to see this show live," she goes on. "Seems like there's always a few crazies trying to out-crazy each other, and it's a hoot!"

Twenty minutes later, Kayelee Ford, who is not even nominated for an award, proves Bonnie's point. She struts onto the VMA stage in the middle of the Bitter Boyz's live performance, and it's not only a shock, but it's a head-scratcher. *Why is a country music singer featured with rappers?* But as she sashays around the stage wearing next to nothing, it's clear that her solo is secondary.

"Is that a cash register?" Bonnie asks as Kayelee marches past our section. She's wearing a tiny bra made out of hundred-dollar bills and has a cash register strapped around her waist like a belt. Her legs sparkle in shimmery tights, and she keeps whipping her long blond hair around like it's a bug she's trying to shake off.

"Why?" I ask, more to myself than to anyone else.

"I think the lyrics are saying that the lifestyle is the dream because you'll get rich, but then maintaining the lifestyle is impossible because you spend all your money keeping up the image," Bonnie says.

"No, I understand the song," I say. "I just don't get what

Kayelee's doing. Or why she would want to demean herself like this." I scan the crowd for Randall Strong, the president of Great American Music, and wonder why in the world he approved it. Then I lean across Bonnie and ask Anita, "How is this good for her image?"

"I would kill you," Anita says simply. "But this will be the performance they'll all be talking about tomorrow."

"What?" I exclaim, looking at her like she's lost her mind. "This is gross! Look at how she's grinding on them. They're totally objectifying her."

Bonnie nods. "Anita's right though."

And just because I want to prove them wrong, I pull out my phone and open my Twitter app. Immediately I see that Kayelee Ford is trending. "Are you serious?"

At that moment, Kayelee brings the mic to her sparkly pink lips and ends the song with an admittedly impressive vocal run that brings even the most reluctant of the crowd to their feet, but as I stand and applaud, I am only more furious. *The girl can actually sing! So why not just wow the audience with her talent?*

The houselights come up and the cameras move away, everybody standing to stretch and take a break. I overhear snippets of conversation, and it's as if nobody else has performed all night. I certainly didn't feel this energy after my own performance, and not to be conceited or anything, but I brought the house down. I'm just baffled that it's "Kayelee this" and "Kayelee that"—not all of it pleasant but all of it about her.

"Your award's up next," Anita says matter-of-factly. "There's no way you'll lose this one, so forget what you just saw and be gracious."

Bonnie clearly agrees. She grabs my arms and shakes me from side to side, smiling big and trying to pump me up. "You've always wanted a Moonman!"

I throw my phone back into my purse and frown. Yeah, I wanted to win, both for me and for Bonnie, but at this point, it's not like anyone will even care.

8

"Post-VMAs in da limo!" I shout, holding up my iPhone to get a quick video of the whole Open Highway team. Turns out winning really did boost my spirits.

"I can't wait to text this to your mom," Bonnie says as we pull into In-N-Out Burger and she takes a picture of the neon sign. "She always goes on about me eating this garbage. It'll kill her."

"Oh, let's take a selfie then," I say, leaning over. "Really rub it in!"

"And get that Moonman in here!" Bonnie says, holding my award up between us.

Like I imagine most kids do after their prom, we all file out of the limousine dressed to the nines and make our way across the parking lot to the greasiest and yummiest fast food joint on the planet. Once we're inside, my bodyguards stay close as people scream and stand up from their tables, their camera phones already held up high. I feel like a jerk when our group heads straight for the counter and the restaurant manager asks waiting customers to scoot over for my entourage.

"Hi, may I please have a cheeseburger, fries, and a strawberry shake?" I ask the guy taking my order. He looks a little flustered and it's super cute. "And then whatever all these people behind me want, too. I'll cover it."

"So the people, like, in tuxes and whatever?" the cashier asks, confused.

"No," I say, scooting over to gesture to all the people we cut in line. "Well, yes, but also, *all* these people. Anybody behind me right now. I'm buying their dinner."

"Hell, yeah!" some dude shouts, giving his buddy a high five. "That's what I'm talking about!"

Troy takes care of settling the bill, so while we wait for our food, I walk around the restaurant, taking pictures with fans and signing a few napkins. It's nice to have this mini-celebration, especially since I'm missing out on a ton of fun VMA after parties. I have a show in Toronto tomorrow night, and we have to get to the airport.

"Number thirty-nine," the cashier calls. I look over and see greasy bags appearing on the counter and know it's time to roll.

"I'll grab ours," Bonnie says. "You go ahead."

I wave to a few fans as I make my way out of the restaurant with my bodyguards and am a little surprised when I see Dan and Anita in a heated argument near the limo. They completely stop talking when they see me, so I give them space and climb in, not in the mood for drama anyway.

One by one, the rest of our group trickles into the car, and we start chowing down on burgers and fries, the party atmosphere still in full effect. The radio is blasting, and everybody is talking about their favorite acts of the night (conspicuously leaving out the Kayelee Ford spectacle, which I appreciate), but after a while, I start to wonder why we aren't back on the road.

"What's taking so long?" I ask no one in particular.

"I don't know, but I need some air," Bonnie says. I crack my window, and she does the same on her side. That's when we hear the shouting.

"This is ridiculous!" Dan yells.

"Uh-oh," I say. "That doesn't sound good."

Somebody lowers the music in the limo and everybody, including myself, cranes their neck to see. It looks like Dan is arguing with Troy now, while Anita is on her phone nearby. She holds a hand to her other ear to block out the guys and looks as furious as I've ever seen her.

"What in the world's going on?" I ask.

Bonnie shushes me, leaning toward the open window.

"They signed a contract!" Dan booms.

Troy responds quietly, but Dan can't be pacified.

"Throat nodules?" he explodes. His normally pinkish face is as red as a tomato, and he rips off his bow tie, looking like he's going to use it to strangle my manager. "You tell those momma's boys spoiled-rotten little brats that they're finished. They've been completely unprofessional this whole tour, and I'll make sure their label and every other label in Nashville knows it."

Troy nods, looking thoroughly whipped, the epitome of the old saying "Don't shoot the messenger."

"Right, but in the meantime," he replies calmly, "we've got a show in Toronto tomorrow, and we don't have an opening act. We have to find somebody fast."

"This is such bull," Dan mutters, pacing the parking lot.

Everyone exchanges looks, but no one says a word. I feel like I'm in the eye of the storm right now.

"Okay, what about Sugar and Sukey?" Troy finally suggests. "They're talented, and we know they're professional. You can keep it in the label."

"I need them recording," Dan says. "They're not ready to launch."

"Okay, then what about Dust on the Dash?"

"We can't afford them," Anita cuts in as she ends her phone call. "Greedy little punks."

As they go back and forth with names of possible replacement acts, I sit back in my seat, stunned that this is all going down the night before my next show . . . in another country!

"Don't worry, Bird," Bonnie says, patting my knee. "This stuff happens all the time. There's a slew of up-and-comers who'll gladly step in."

"By tomorrow?" I ask dubiously.

"They may not stick, but somebody's going to say yes."

"Bonnie, the show's in less than twenty-four hours."

"Bird, honey, trust me," she says. "Wouldn't you have hopped on a plane?"

I take a sip of my shake and consider her question. Yep. I definitely would've dropped everything to open for Jolene Taylor last year. And actually, that's kind of what I did.

"Who was opening for you, anyway?" Bonnie asks.

"These completely annoying guys called the Hicks from Thirty-Six," I reply. "Their music's not terrible, but their set has run long at least three times and they party nonstop. Dylan hates the lead singer."

"Well, then maybe it's a blessing in disguise."

"Bird," Troy says, opening the door.

"I heard," I say as he gets in.

"We're going to figure something out," he assures me.

Dan and Anita don't say anything as they take their seats. It's a considerably more somber group than the one that arrived half an hour earlier. When the limo starts rolling again, most of us turn to our phones, checking Twitter and Instagram and basically doing anything but talking about the problem at hand.

"Somebody's popular tonight," Bonnie finally says.

"Sorry!" I say, turning my phone on silent. It's been beeping nonstop with notifications and message alerts. "It's just a bunch of congratulations texts and stuff."

Bonnie leans over and reads from my screen. "Your momma, Jacob, Stella, Adam... Hey, why don't you call him?"

"I don't know," I say. "I think it'd be weird to return a text with a phone call."

"No, why don't you call him to *open* for you?"

I gasp. She's right. That's a perfect solution.

"Isn't that his single on the radio right now?"

I hush a few people talking near me and turn up the radio again. Adam's deep voice fills the speakers, and I feel my stomach flip as he belts out his country rock anthem "Make Her Mine."

Troy's date says, "That guy is really cute and his song is, like, kind of sexy. The girl is totally stonewalling him, but he's going to do whatever it takes to make her his girlfriend. So romantic."

"Who's that?" Dan asks, leaning toward us. "Who's that you're talking about?"

"Um, Jacob's best friend," I say. "Adam Dean. He used

to tour on the same circuit we did growing up. Now he's signed with a label and doing really well."

"Adam Dean," Dan says thoughtfully to Anita. "Know him?"

"Of course I know him," Anita says. "This is his first single, but he already has a big fan base. The ladies love him."

I feel myself blush, remembering how crazy I was over Adam, as my team talks about him like a commodity rather than a person. I know it would be an amazing opportunity for him, but if he said yes, it could end up being painfully awkward, considering how we almost sort of dated... and he broke my heart.

"I know this song," Dan says as it fills the car. "It charted."

"In the first week," Anita adds.

"It's a great song," Troy says. "And he's a writer, too."

Yeah, he wrote this in my living room last Christmas.

"You think he'd be a good fit for the tour?" Dan asks.

I roll my eyes, remembering back to that day in the studio when I suggested that Dan use Adam on my album. Dan said he only wanted pros, but here he is considering Adam for my tour when he had the chance back then to sign him to our label. I could speak up now I guess, but he's accused me of using my fame to help my friends make it before. This time, I'm hoping he'll see Adam's talent for himself.

Troy looks up from his phone, where he's been Googling Adam, and says, "I think he'd be great. Same fan demographic, good-lookin' kid, and appears to have some good momentum. It's very short notice for anybody we reach out to, but since he's Bird's friend, maybe his people won't try to gouge us on the price like everyone else who knows we're in a bind."

Everybody in the limousine looks my way.

"What do you think, Bird?" Dan asks.

I smile. "I think . . . I hope he doesn't steal the show."

9

"Guys! I'm home!" I call from the bottom of the bus steps. Troy and I flew into Toronto so late that we just crashed in a hotel by the airport, but now that I'm meeting the tour in the parking lot of the Rogers Centre, I can't wait to dish with Stella.

Dylan's playing Black Ops on our Xbox and doesn't even look up at me when he says, "Oh, hey, congrats on the VMA."

"Yeah, thanks," I say, rolling my eyes as I walk past him to my room. "Your text was so sweet."

"I didn't send a text."

"Oh, that's right."

"Hey!" Stella says when she sees me. She takes off her headphones and swings her legs over the side of her bunk.

"I was wondering what time you'd be back. Your dress for the VMAs was gorgeous."

"Thanks, Stel," I say, throwing my stuff on my bed.

She picks up the Moonman poking out of my purse and says, "Hello, handsome."

I smile and rush behind her, closing the dividing door for some privacy. Then I turn around and quietly say, "If you think he's handsome, wait 'til you see who else I brought back to the tour."

She looks at me quizzically, but I play coy. I grab my makeup bag and scoot closer to her. "Work your magic. I need to look cute, but not on purpose. You aren't going to believe what happened last night."

There is a loud knock on the door of my tour bus. Suddenly my pulse picks up. "Bird?" my tour manager calls.

Stella immediately dives over the couch and looks through the blinds. "He's here," she says in a whisper.

"Coming!" I take one more look at myself in the small mirror by the stairs, smooth a stray hair back, and breathe deep. Adam is here.

"It's just Adam," Dylan says behind me. "Why all the fuss?"

I glance over my shoulder and can tell that he's being

deliberately obtuse. He may not know every gritty detail, but he knows that Adam and I almost dated, he's seen me try on three different outfits this morning, and he had to have heard at least snippets of Stella and me wondering whether the spark will still be there. Dylan knows exactly why the fuss, but he's either messing with me or doesn't want to be involved. As usual, I ignore him.

"Adam!" I say as I open the door and step out into the bright day.

"Hey, stranger," he says with a lopsided grin. He steps toward me, and before I know it, I am in a full-on embrace, almost giggling out loud when I think back to the butterflies I used to get every time I spotted him in the crowd at one of our shows: *Adam is here.*

"Thank you so much for filling in on such short notice," I say as we pull away.

He smiles. "How could I refuse Lady Bird?"

I feel myself blush and then we just stare at each other, nearly the same height, his face sun-kissed and a little fuller than before, his green-brown eyes sparkling, his lips just as full and pink and kissable as ever. The expression on his face must mirror my own; we're one part happy to see each other and the other part in awe that we ended up back on the road together, full circle. I *know* Adam. Even if we haven't spent much time together lately, I know him like I know my own heart. This is like a dream.

"I'm so glad you're here," I say.

"*I'm* so glad I'm here!" he replies.

Marco clears his throat, and I shake my head, snapping out of this semitrance. I remind myself that I already learned the hard way—*twice*—that business doesn't mix well with romance. *Be the boss, Bird. Be the boss.*

"So what's the plan, Marco?" I say, clapping my hands and turning toward my tour manager. "These guys going to be ready to go tonight?"

"Adam's band is getting settled on the bus now," he answers, diving right into the business particulars. "After we load in, the guys can have a few hours to play in the arena and get a feel for our stage. Might push your sound check a little if we need, but we'll play it by ear and see how it goes. That work?"

"Sounds good to me," I say.

"Yeah, thanks, man," Adam says, offering his hand for a shake.

"And give me a call if you need anything at all," Marco adds.

"Come on," I say when I see a curtain move on the bus. "Dylan and Stella are dying to see you."

We board my bus and the reunion is really fun. While Dylan and Adam exchange their standard bro hug, Stella slyly shoots me a look that asks, *Is he even hotter than I remember?* to which I reply with an adamant nod. Adam's brand of handsome is completely effortless. He's in a soft green T-shirt and dark jeans, his boots worn in and well traveled. His brown hair is shaggy as usual, and there's stubble across his jawline. As we all crash around the common space on the bus, he tells us about getting signed to his label and the promotion they've had him doing.

"I don't know why you keep thanking me for helping you out," Adam says, turning to me. "My manager was looking for me to open for a big act next summer. As far as I'm concerned, I'm on the Bird Barrett Fast Track to Success."

"Me too," Stella says.

"Me three," Dylan says. "I probably don't thank you enough for that actually, Bird."

"Oh, please," I say. "None of you would be here if you weren't talented. I just wish I could've helped Jacob out, too."

"Are you kidding?" Adam asks. "Trust me, you've helped Jacob out *a lot*."

"How?"

"Every time I visited him at UCLA last year, whether he took me to a party or we met a girl on the beach, he'd casually bring up that he's Bird Barrett's big brother."

"Ew!" I say. "Did that work?"

Adam shares a knowing grin with Dylan and says, "Let's just say the guy was popular."

Stella guffaws.

I shudder. "That's disgusting."

"He's a changed man now, though," Adam continues. "Ashlynn's got him whipped so hard."

"You mean 'Infinity' girl?" Dylan asks.

" 'Infinity!' " we all quote, laughing.

Adam looks at his phone and stands up. "Well, I'd love to hang out and catch up a little longer, but some big-shot celebrity called me up and changed my life yesterday, so now I have to rehearse." He grins at me, and I'm reminded of how easy it is to fall back into sync with Adam. "First show tonight. I don't want to blow it. I hear the headliner has high expectations."

"Nah, you can relax," I say with a smile. "She only expects perfection."

He laughs. "Oh, is that all?"

"You'll be fine. But you should grab a power nap so you look fresh and rested," I say. "Jacob said Ashlynn and all her friends *love* you."

A deep blush creeps up Adam's neck. "Stop."

"Seriously," I continue, enjoying a chance to tease Adam. "He said they're all like, 'O-M-G, Adam Dean is the hottest guy on the entire freaking planet. I want to make him mine! Me too! I die!' "

Dylan and Stella are rolling as Adam heads for the door, beet red. "I need to get over to my own bus so I can be around people who allow me a little dignity."

We all laugh, and I follow him back outside.

"Hey, how many songs we going to write on this tour?"

Adam asks once we're on the pavement. His lopsided grin is so cute that I feel my heart writing songs as we stand here. "I need you to help me with a few more hit singles."

"Back atcha, mister," I say, holding my hand over my eyes to block out the sun. "'Worth Being in Love' had one foot in the grave before you saved it."

"I guess we make a good team," he says with an easy smile. And before he walks away he adds, "It's good to be back together again, Lady Bird."

I nod and tell myself that the goose bumps I'm getting are due to a light breeze, but as I board my bus all I can think about is the charge I get every time I'm around Adam . . . and how after all this time, it's never gone away.

"I mean, he's so good," I tell Stella as she does some last-minute stitches on a small tear in my opening outfit backstage. "Look at him. The fans are loving it."

"You knew they would," she says through a pin in her mouth. "I can't believe this ripped again."

"Sorry."

"Not your fault," she grumbles. "I told Amanda we need to totally recut this piece, but . . ." She shakes her head.

"I forgot how deep his voice is," I say, my eyes glued to the stage. Adam has only been on tour with us for seven hours, and he looks as comfortable as if this stage were his. "Stella, I think I still like him."

She ties off the thread and pulls the pins out of her mouth, facing me with a knowing grin. "You think?"

"He's just so cute!"

"Yeah, and it doesn't hurt that this song is about you."

I look over at her, trying to feign ignorance.

"Oh, come on!" she says. *"I know a girl who's from every town,"* she sings. "That's you. And then, *I'm right there in her shadow, but always a step behind.* He just got signed, he hit the charts, he's the opener not the headliner, et cetera."

"Yeah, but none of that had happened when he wrote this song," I say as he sings.

She looks at me dubiously. "He still likes you. You still like him. Your fake breakup was just because you were so busy getting famous, but now you are—now you *both* are—so there's nothing keeping you apart."

I chew on my lip and think about that.

"And it'd be so fun to double-date," Stella singsongs as she tucks her sewing materials back into her "styling pouch," or as Dylan and I mercilessly tease, her fanny pack. "All we have to do is convince the boys that they're in love with us. That shouldn't be too hard."

I roll my eyes. "I've found the hard part isn't getting them, it's keeping them." I feel my smile start to fade as I think back to how heartbroken I was when Adam called things off. Yeah, I still like him, but not enough to get hurt again.

"I've got to find Amanda," Stella says. "See you in a few."

I nod absentmindedly as she walks away, but I don't take my eyes off Adam. Any girl would think he's cute. I'm probably just feeling that normal instant attraction. After a week or two on tour, we'll be like old friends, the way we were able to be when I dated Kai…which leads me to wonder now if Adam is dating anybody. Jacob hasn't said anything, but why would he?

"Thanks, everybody! I'm Adam Dean, and I can't wait 'til y'all see the show my good friend Bird Barrett has in store for you," he calls into the mic. "Are you ready?" The crowd cheers. "Oh, come on, Toronto. Are. You. Ready?"

The response is deafening.

"Good night, y'all. Thanks for being so kind."

He waves to the crowd as he walks my way, and the minute he's standing in the wings, he throws his guitar around his back and picks me up, spinning me around so that I squeal. "That was amazing!" he shouts. He sets me back down and puts his hands on my shoulders. We are so close that I can see the sweat beads at his temples and the wet curls at the sides of his ears. "Thank you, Bird. That was a dream come true. Thank you so much."

"You were fantastic," I say honestly.

"Man," he says, draping an arm over my shoulders and leading me backstage. "What a crowd. Your fans are so awesome."

"They know good music when they hear it," I say.

As we walk through the hallway, I feel like I'm watching the Adam Dean *E! True Hollywood Story*. People are giving him pats on the back and fist bumps as we make our way toward the dressing rooms, and I feel like I'm riding his wave. A musician's very first arena performance is the kind of thing that is etched deep in the soul, and I love that I get to watch people discover a talent I've known about for years.

When we get to my door, he stops and leans against the frame. "You're on in twenty?"

I check my phone. "Yep."

"Okay, see you then," he says, but he doesn't move. He just keeps staring at me, and I hold his gaze, having no idea what he's thinking or what to do. Finally, he squeezes my shoulder and says, "Break a leg."

"Thanks, Adam."

He rolls off the wall to walk back to his dressing room, where I hear his band go wild as he enters. It is totally unheard of for a band to join a tour on such short notice, so I know the guys are stoked. As I meet my glam team for final touch-ups, I honestly can't pretend that I'm not, too.

"You are amazing!" Adam says later. He was in the wings for my entire show, and every time I caught a glimpse of him watching me, I felt a new surge of energy. "You had the crowd in the palm of your hand the entire time."

"You were amazing-er," I say, bumping him in the hallway as we head back toward the buses. "It was your first arena performance, and it looked like your fiftieth."

"I don't know about that, but I will concede that it was a good night," he says. "For both of us."

"Yes," I agree. I usually wait for Stella after the show because once I'm out of wardrobe, she and Amanda have to take inventory of all the pieces and get them packed up and secured. But tonight Dylan was crashed on my dressing room couch, and she waved me off.

"You know what would be the perfect way to celebrate?" Adam asks now, stopping dead in his tracks. I look at him blankly. "With a fountain Coke."

My face nearly splits open I smile so wide. "Oh my gosh, yes! There must be some restaurants nearby."

Adam looks at me as if I've sprouted an alien head. "No, no, no, no, no," he says. "The tradition is that we try the Coke at the venue we play."

"Adam," I say in disbelief. "We can't go out there. We'll get mobbed!"

"But that's what you've got him for," he says, gesturing to one of my bodyguards, always good at sticking to the shadows but always nearby. "And oh!" he goes on, digging in his duffel bag. "We can use a disguise."

"A disguise?"

"Here, put this hoodie on. It's probably too big, and it's definitely the opposite of all the skimpy little outfits you wear during your show."

"Skimpy?" I say, mock offended. "You sound like my dad."

"Yeah, except I'm not complaining," he replies with a grin.

I blush and take the sweatshirt, pulling it over my head and breathing in deep. It smells so good, so fresh, so Adam. I am never taking it off. Ever.

"Now put your hair in a bun," he goes on. I do and he takes out a Titans cap, pulling it so low over my eyes that I have to crane my head all the way back to see. He laughs. "Okay, I think that's as good as we can do under the circumstances," he says.

"But what about you?" I say as I adjust the hat. "You were the tour opener."

He shrugs. "At this point, I'd say a lot of the crowd has thinned out anyway. But if it'll make you feel better, give me those shades." He snatches the big sunglasses hooked on the side of my bag and puts them on, never mind that they're bright pink and bedazzled.

"I think that may be the opposite of a disguise," I say, laughing.

Nervously, I let him lead me through the hallways until I'm almost certain we're lost. Finally, we find someone who works here, and she leads us to the upper-level concession stands. They are closing up shop when we get there, but Adam removes the disguises and the vendors immediately fill a couple of Shine Our Light souvenir cups with ice-cold Coca-Cola. I have to take pictures with the workers and sign a couple of T-shirts for lingering fans, but the fuss is worth it to keep our celebratory tradition alive.

"Thanks again, y'all," Adam says, leading me away toward the cheap seats for some privacy.

Once we're settled in the upper decks, watching the crew below break down the stage, I turn to Adam for a toast. But before I say a word, he grabs his wallet and fishes out his old list of the country's best fountain Cokes.

"I can't believe you still have that," I say.

"It's seen better days, but I always hoped we'd play a show together again one day. Consider it my vision board."

I smile, completely flattered. "To Toronto," I say, holding my cup up for a toast.

He meets it with a *clink*, and his eyes lock onto mine. "To us."

10

"OKAY, DYLAN JUST texted that he's with the band, but I don't know how long Monty can keep him occupied," Stella says as she power walks through our hotel lobby, Adam and me on her heels. "So chop-chop, people."

We play a couple of shows in Chicago this weekend and my parents are visiting to celebrate Dylan's birthday, so I sprang for rooms at an adorable little boutique hotel. At Stella's request, I sweet-talked the management into letting us use the kitchen before they open so we can make Dylan a from-scratch birthday cake, but I can't manage to muster up the same enthusiasm about it all that has possessed my best friend. "Why didn't we just send somebody out for boxed cake mix?"

"Or buy one from a bakery?" Adam chimes in. "Or from the restaurant we are currently in?"

"Yeah, why go through all this hassle?" I ask as we enter the kitchen. Stella uses her phone to pull up the recipe she wants to try.

"Because," she says, looking up from her phone with a sly grin, "Channing Tatum finally kissed me."

"Stella!" I shout, attacking her with a big hug. "When?"

"This morning. We watched the sunrise together, and it was perfect."

"You met Channing Tatum?" Adam says, confused.

"Code word for my brother during conversations rife with romantic details," I explain.

"Your brother?" Adam asks, shocked. "And Stella?"

"Yes," I say to him. Then I turn my attention back to her. "Spill."

She beams at me, and it all comes rushing out. "So remember last night when *Channing* was talking about his map and asked if anybody would want to see the sunrise over at the Adler Planetarium?"

" 'TripAdvisor says it's the perfect place to see the whole skyline!' " Adam says in his best Dylan impression. I giggle.

"So while y'all were snoozing away," Stella goes on, "I dragged my butt out of bed and hopped in a cab with Channing Tatum. Yes, I know, I've clearly got it bad. It was hella early, but he met me with a to-go cup of coffee and held my hand the whole way there, and it was just really fun and sweet."

For a second, I think back to my weekend in Chicago with Kai, how romantic it was, what a beautiful place this is to let your heart go. I feel a quiet sadness, a little loss just for a moment, but then I shake my head and focus on Stella. This is *her* story.

"He laid out a sheet from the hotel so we could snuggle up and watch, but this city really is windy, and Channing saw me shivering so he gave me his jacket," she goes on. I think it would be physically impossible for her smile to be any bigger than it is right at this very moment. It's so cute that I actually forget she's talking about my brother. "He helped me put it on and then pulled at the collar and just, like, kept his hands gripped there. And he didn't move. And so then we were just sort of sitting there staring at each other as the sky started to get pink and pretty. And he was nervous, I could tell, and it was like something out of a movie and then finally, *finally*, he asked me if he could kiss me." Her cheeks flame—and I rarely see Stella embarrassed. "And then he did!"

I squeal and squeeze her arm. "Then what?"

"Then we watched the sun come up, and honestly, it really is breathtaking."

"The view or Dylan's kissing?" Adam pipes up.

She giggles. "Both."

"*Channing's* kissing," I say with my hands over my ears. "Those are Channing Tatum's lips."

"Anyway, then we met y'all for breakfast back here." Stella stops and sighs. "And now we're together."

"I cannot believe you made me sit through breakfast without telling me this," I say, slapping the stainless-steel table beside me.

"Bird, your parents were right there!"

"Bathroom break?"

"I tried that, but your mom came with us!"

"Oh, that's right," I remember with a laugh. "Well, anyway, I'm really happy for you," I tell her, and it feels good to mean it. It's definitely going to be complicated, but anybody with two working eyeballs could see it coming. And they do seem to bring out the best in each other.

"So did you DTR?" Adam asks her. I do a double take. I never thought girl talk would include Adam, and I certainly didn't think he'd know the lingo.

"We did," Stella replies.

"Wow!" he goes on. "You're already official? I had a roommate in Texas that went on and on about how guys always take too long to 'define the relationship' and how it drove her crazy."

"I can see her point," Stella says thoughtfully. "But I've known Channing for so long. It's like our friendship laid the foundation first, so now dating just feels natural."

I glance up at Adam at the same time that he looks over at me. We both look back at Stella quickly. While she goes on, I start to wonder about Adam's old "roommate" in Texas.

"So, anyway, that's the first kiss story," Stella says with a happy sigh. "The most romantic moment of my life."

"Who knew my brother had it in him?" I say with wonder. It may be weird that my brother is dating my best friend, but it's a whole lot better than him dating someone I don't like . . . and much more fun.

"And *that* is why Channing Tatum deserves a cake made from scratch," she continues, "so that's what we're doing. Grab an apron."

"Yes, chef," I say, taking a starched white apron from a hook on the wall nearby.

The plan is to hurry, but baking a cake takes a while. The restaurant opens at eleven thirty so every second counts, both to get it done before the staff shows up to prep for their day and to keep Dylan from growing suspicious. Monty called an "emergency meeting" to buy us some time and then my folks will have "computer problems." If all goes as planned, we'll rendezvous back at my room by ten for Dylan's mini-party. Then I've got a full day of promos and interviews before the show. Life on the road means making the time when you don't really have it.

Stella directs us around the kitchen now with all the confidence of Rachael Ray, but finding the ingredients we need is like an impossible Easter egg hunt.

"Baking soda or baking powder?" Adam calls from across the room.

Stella checks the recipe. "Powder!"

"How many eggs?" I call from the fridge.

"Two," she commands.

Stella finds a big mixing bowl and adds the ingredients as we bring them over, stepping around one another as we search. "I need a giant spoon," she mumbles to herself. Unfortunately she bends over to check a drawer at the exact moment that I'm walking by with a big bag of flour.

It's like a scene from a movie that I'm watching in slow motion. I fall forward, holding my arms straight so that I don't spill the flour, but the open paper bag is already out of my control and headed right for Adam, who sees it all happening in time to close his eyes but not in time to get out of the way.

The bag hits him square in the chest and thuds as it hits the floor. We all stand as still as statues, Adam looking like a ghost as he blinks hard once, twice, three times. I wait for him to laugh, but he doesn't.

"Bird," he says quietly. "Am I covered in flour?"

I try not to laugh. "Yes, Adam."

"And Stella, is this all your fault?"

She pauses. "Define 'all.'"

"Well, ladies," he says, opening another fridge. "You leave me no choice."

Before we can react, Adam turns from the fridge with

a can of whipped cream, and we run from him, screaming like banshees. I feel the whipped cream in my hair and then Adam's arms around me. "Let me go!" I wail.

He sprays me at close range, the whipped cream cold on my neck and chin. "Adam!" I scream, laughing like a maniac. Stella squirts my arm with chocolate syrup, and I lunge for a nearby refrigerator. I know I saw ketchup in there somewhere...

"What in the world is going on in here?" Dylan shouts.

"No!" Stella cries. "You're early! You'll ruin the surprise!"

But Dylan's distraction gives Adam the perfect opportunity to cover Stella's hair with whipped cream. "What the hell, man?" Dylan says, and without a moment's hesitation, he picks an egg off the counter and launches it at him.

"Dude!" Adam cries, holding his biceps where Dylan hit him. "That hurt!" He aims the can of whipped cream at Dylan—a direct hit to the cheek.

"Attack!" I holler, coming at everybody with the ketchup.

It is a sugary war zone. Suddenly the lines are drawn, and it's Adam and me against Dylan and Stella. The cake is completely forgotten once the food fight is under way. By the time someone finally calls a truce, we're all tired and so weak from laughing that we can barely stand. We crash on the floor of the kitchen to catch our breath.

"We are going to be in so much trouble," I finally say as I survey the room from my spot on the floor.

And as if on cue, my parents walk in.

"What in the—" my mother begins, but Stella hops up and cuts her off.

"Good!" she says. "You're just in time."

She scoops a bunch of the mess into her hands and lays it in a lump on a baking sheet. She carries it over to a relatively clean spot on the counter near the door, where my mother looks pretty disappointed and my father actually seems amused. Then she pulls a candle out of her jeans pocket and shoves it into the middle, where it leans like the Tower of Pisa. She grabs a book of hotel restaurant matches and lights the pathetic little candle, motioning for us to stand up next to her. We walk over, a motley crew, our hair white from baking powder and flour, our clothes covered in ketchup and chocolate syrup. We are disgusting, cold, and soggy, but we are also happy and here to celebrate Dylan's birthday.

"*Happy birthday to you,*" we start singing.

"The candle's sinking," Stella says, waving her hand in a circle. "Speed it up."

"*Happy birthday to you,*" we speed sing. "*Happy birthday, dear Dylan, happy birthday to you.*"

"Make a wish," Stella says, turning to Dylan with bright eyes.

"Mine has already come true," he says, putting his arm around her shoulders. I would gag, but it's pretty sweet.

98

Even my mom softens, sparing us the lecture and simply saying, "Y'all make sure you clean this up good," before turning to go.

"That took forever," I say, wringing out my wet hair as I join the others in the sitting room of my hotel suite. It took over an hour to clean up the mess we'd made in the kitchen, and I had to swear one early staffer to secrecy by giving him free tickets to tonight's show, but it was nice to have a little fun on tour.

"Okay, everybody," Stella says, sitting close to Dylan on the love seat. "Now presents!"

Adam, who rejoined us after showering in his own room, pulls an envelope out of his back pocket and throws it onto the small pile of gifts on the coffee table.

"I went all out, man," he says.

Dylan grins and leans forward, picking that gift up first. "It's not what's on the inside," he says mock emotionally as he taps the envelope, "it's what's on the *inside*," he finishes, pounding his heart.

Adam fakes wiping away a tear, and I laugh. "Dorks."

"Yes!" Dylan says when he opens it. "An iTunes gift card. I can always use that. Thanks, bro."

Adam nods. "Happy birthday."

Dylan opens the exact same gift from Jacob, something

I'm sure my mom picked up for him. Then he moves on to the big boxes from my parents. "Jeans," he says, Captain Obvious as he pulls out a pair of new blue jeans.

"Since you're touring so much now, I thought you could use some nice clothes," my mom says. She points to the other wrapped gift and says, "And those are shirts."

Dylan looks up at her as if she'd spilled the beans on something really major. "Mom!" he says, clawing his way into the box. "Don't ruin the surprise!"

"Oops!" she says, chuckling.

"These are great," he says when he removes the lid. "Thanks, guys."

"You're welcome, son," my dad says, "but I didn't have anything to do with what's underneath those T-shirts."

Dylan lifts the shirts up and grins. "Thanks, Mom," he says, leaning over for a hug. Then in a loud whisper he says, "But I'll buy my own underwear from here on out, okay?"

I lean forward and pass my brother a small gift bag from the table, knowing he's going to completely flip out. "Here, Dylan, open mine next," I say eagerly.

He pulls the tissue paper out and frowns. "It's empty," he says, turning the bag upside down.

"No, it must've fallen out," I say, looking on the floor for the page I printed in the hotel's business center earlier, a photo of the amp he's been eyeing the whole tour. "Here it is. Happy birthday."

He takes the piece of paper, and his face lights up. "Bird!" he says, gawking at the picture. "This is mine?"

"Yep," I say, beaming. "All yours."

I knew he'd love it.

"I can't believe you did this."

"I had it sent to the Nashville house, so it'll be waiting for you once we're off tour."

"I *cannot* believe you did this," he repeats, standing for a hug. "Thank you. You shouldn't have spent that much."

"Eh, I'll just take it out of your next paycheck," I tease.

"Let me see that," Adam says, and Dylan passes him the picture. Adam lets out a low whistle. "Sick."

"Now mine," Stella says, patting the love seat so that Dylan will sit back down. He opens the last gift, the one that looks like it was wrapped in a fancy boutique but was clearly just wrapped by Stella being Stella. She is looking at Dylan's face with so much anticipation that you'd think it was *her* birthday.

"No way," he says simply, after he lifts the lid. Grinning, he pulls out a vintage red leather guitar strap, flips it over, and then looks down at her face. She smiles up at him and they share a moment, just the two of them, while we all look on. When he looks back down at the gift box in his lap, Stella steals a quick kiss on his cheek. My brother, obviously conscious of all of us in the room, glances up at my mom, whose eyes have gone wide. She looks over at me, astonished, and I nod back like, *Yep. Can you believe it?*

"I love it," he says, looking at Stella again. "Thank you."

"Happy birthday," she replies.

"Looks like a nice strap, son," my dad says. "Something special?"

"Sorry, it's just—I saw this in a vintage shop in Vegas on our first date." He blushes. "Or I don't know, our first hang out or whatever."

"Or whatever," Stella repeats, laughing.

"And it's, well, it just means a lot to me."

Stella can't help but gush as she takes the guitar strap out of his hands and shows us all the back. "He was totally going to buy it, but then he realized the previous owner had written, 'You were right here all along,' on the inside, and he got all cute and embarrassed and changed his mind. I decided to just go for it, and if he never made a move, I'd sell it on eBay."

Dylan laughs. "Oh, really?"

"May I see it?" I ask, eager to eye the guitar strap that upstaged my amp. We all pass it around, everybody heaping praise on Stella for her thoughtfulness, but I realize that once again, I feel like I'm missing out. And it's crazy. Do I not want my brother to be with a great girl who's super thoughtful and makes him happy? Do I not want my best friend to be with a guy who cares about her so much that he's taken things slow? Or do I just not want to be around people who have what I sometimes think is impossible for me?

11

"*I can't do this, go through this, pretend it didn't hurt,*" I sing. We are on our way to Wichita, and I'm writing a song in my room, or trying to, but it's hard because Dylan and Stella are right outside and could probably guess whom it's about. I've tried to play it cool around Adam, even keeping my distance a little, but this week has wreaked havoc on me. The feelings I've always had for him have taken root in my heart again, and it's not professional. I can't date my opener. These nightly Coke meet ups, fangirling in the wings, the nonstop texting, it's all too much. "*When you said good-bye, maybe you didn't cry, but—*"

"Bird?" Stella calls, knocking on my door frame.

"Come in!"

"Hey, we're stopping for gas," she says. I look out the window and see we've exited the interstate and are pulling into a truck stop. "You want to stretch your legs?"

"Nah, I think I'll just chill here," I say.

"Cool. Oh, and Dylan invited Adam to come over and play Black Ops. That's okay, right?"

I sigh. Now I definitely won't be able to work on this song. "Sure."

She winks at me. "I finally did some recon: He's single."

I lay my guitar on the bed and fall back against my pillows. "That just makes it harder!"

"Why? 'Cause of the 'boundaries' and all that?"

"It's unprofessional, yeah, but"—I pause and look out the window, then quietly finish—"honestly, I think I'm more worried about my heart."

"I know," she says. "But I swear to you: Things are different this time."

"Stella! You coming?" Dylan calls from the front of the bus.

"Yeah!" she hollers back. As she backs down the little hallway she points at me and says, "Don't. Worry," and then heads outside. I sit up and watch her through the window, catching up to Dylan and tripping him from behind. He turns around and chases her into the convenience store, and I feel that stab of envy again.

Some people don't know how good they've got it.

" 'Dear Bird,' " Stella reads a few hours later. Marco brought over another box of fan mail that Anita FedExed, and we're going through it as the bus makes its way to our next stop. " 'I saw that you're filming a scene in the new Drew Barrymore movie. Any chance you'll be making a Bird Barrett movie? Like, based on your real life? Even if it goes straight to DVD, I think it would be amazing. I've been trying to break into acting, and I would be a perfect body double for your stunts.' "

"What does this girl think would be happening in your real-life movie?" Dylan asks. "Ziplining through arenas?"

"And why does she assume it'd go right to DVD?" Stella asks. "That's just offensive."

"Listen to this one," Adam interjects. He's holding up a scroll, the back of which is a terrible pencil drawing of my face in profile while a flock of birds fly from my head in what is supposed to represent my hair. I don't have high hopes for this letter. " 'To the one who flew into my heart, I knew you'd be mine from the start. Our stories so similar, our hearts so familiar, only yellow lines keep us apart.' "

But it does make me giggle.

"Please stop," Dylan says, plugging his ears.

"What do you think that guy looks like?" Stella asks. "I bet he's forty and lives in his mom's basement."

"Well, the ones I'm opening are really sweet," I say. "I love little-kid handwriting. This girl writes every *e* backward. It's so cute."

"Okay, here's one you can actually answer," Dylan says. "'I have a major crush on a guy at school, but he's my best friend's cousin and I can't tell if he likes me, too, or if he's just nice to me because our whole group is always going down to the beach together. How did you finally get your guy to notice you, and who is 'Notice Me' actually about?'" He looks up at me and says, "Yeah, Bird. Spill."

But my mouth just hangs open. It's gone totally dry. I can feel heat rising up in my chest, and I know that my neck and face are probably bright red. Adam is sitting right beside me. We were finally having a normal day of hanging out that involved video games and opening innocent fan letters, until my idiotic brother shined a spotlight *directly onto my soul.*

I glance over at Stella, who is shooting Dylan a laser beam death glare that could zap all the hair off a baby bunny. "What?" he asks. The bus is totally silent. And now it's just weird. When Dylan looks at Adam, though, who I notice in a lightning-quick glimpse is also bright red, realization dawns. It's obvious now that Adam knows, too. And I'd say it's pretty obvious that I want to stop the bus, lie down in front of it, and die as the tour goes on without me.

"So this one's pretty good," Adam finally ekes out. His normally low voice is, like, an octave higher at first. He clears his throat as he tries to change the subject. He reads through a long letter about a girl getting bullied at her school because she is overweight, and I have to say that by the end of it, I do realize that there are much worse problems in the world than my crush finding out about my crush... although I am still contemplating ways to murder my brother in his sleep.

"You're bringing your guitar?" I ask Adam. Over the past week, we've wound our way across America to Charleston, South Carolina, where we play tomorrow night. Adam and I had to shoot a few promos this morning, but we have the rest of the day off, so we're going to the beach with Dylan and Stella.

"Hey, my guitar is as important as sunscreen," Adam answers.

"Um, clearly you aren't fair-skinned," I say as I lift the back hatch and throw my stuff into the SUV Dylan rented.

He laughs and loads his stuff, too, then hops into the back, his legs dangling over the bumper. "How much longer? I thought we were leaving soon."

I glance over my shoulder at our bus. Apparently, my brother and Stella are having their first fight—something about her not being able to find her cover-up because my brother is a major slob and his stuff is always everywhere—but

I'm not sure that's something I should share with Adam. I'm trying to stay as far out of it as possible. I am Switzerland.

"Yeah, well, there's no hurry," I say, yawning. "I'm happy for a relaxing day with no schedule."

"Good point," Adam says. "Take the day off today, because you won't be able to relax any when that *Rolling Stone* reporter joins the tour."

Involuntarily, I shudder. "I know. Anita's making it this huge deal. I wish she'd stop talking about it 'cause she's just stressing me out more."

Adam nods. "A *Rolling Stone* feature is a big deal."

"It's huge!" I say. "But why does the reporter have to join the tour? She'll be living on my bus for, like, four days. I'll have to be on my toes twenty-four-seven."

Adam laughs. "Are there many skeletons in your bus's closet?" he teases.

I feel my shoulders relax and I return his grin. "You're right. I'm being ridiculous."

"No, you're being cautious," he says, surprising me by reaching out for my hand and giving it a quick squeeze. "It's hard not knowing what people will write, but just try to have fun with it."

I nod but am only thinking about that hand squeeze. Was it just encouragement from a good friend or something more?

His phone beeps and he frowns. "Hey, a couple of guys in my band want to know which beach. Is it cool if they come?"

"The more the merrier," I say, glancing over my shoulder. "My bodyguard is coming, and I'm hoping he's a Speedo type of guy."

Adam laughs and looks over at Big Dave. "Oh, me too. A Speedo *and* tanning-oil type of guy."

I swat his arm and we both laugh, the thought of my ex–football linebacker bodyguard lounging in a banana hammock too much for either of us to take. I climb up next to Adam in the back, and for the next five minutes we sit in mostly comfortable silence. Every now and then one of us will talk about the tour or a part of the show or Jacob, but mainly we enjoy the time to be still. Our lives are nonstop. There are very few times we can just *be*, and very few people we can just *be* with.

"Hey, so I was going to play this for you on the beach later, but I've been working on something," Adam finally says, reaching back for his guitar.

"Oh yeah?" I ask, lifting up my sunglasses. I shed my big hat, too. With the back hatch open we've got plenty of shade, and at this point, I'm beginning to wonder if we'll even make it to the beach. "Something you just wrote?"

"Kind of," he says, scratching the stubble on his jaw. "More like something that's just now coming together."

"I'm intrigued."

"I think I'm on the right track, but I don't know if it's really my sound," he says with a frown. "My label wants something 'fun'—their word—and I've tried a few things, but they've called it all generic. And I'm like, yeah, generic because it's manufactured. Does that make sense?"

I nod my head emphatically. "Yes. My second album was a nightmare for the same reason. It was like everybody was ordering songs the way you'd order a steak at a restaurant. I wanted to pull my hair out."

"That's it exactly," he says. "So anyway, I've been waiting for inspiration to hit, and I've been thinking back to Dylan's birthday, the whole food fight, and *that* was fun. I scrawled out some images, but I'm having trouble weaving them together into a story."

"I love the premise," I say, crossing my legs. "Sounds 'fun.'"

He grins. "Exactly. It was awesome. But I also feel like there has to be a girl, you know?" He swallows hard, nervous. "'Cause there's not really enough there with just the food fight itself."

I nod slowly, trying to ignore the fact that my pulse just picked up a little.

"So I was thinking, what's the food fight represent?" he goes on. "What are the people in the song fighting over?"

He starts to pick, a fun little quiet melody that surprises me. His usual stuff has a rock edge, but this is almost playful. He doesn't sing, but as he plays, the song fills out and his strumming leads to a chorus that has me bobbing my head. Finally, I comment.

"I love this already," I say.

He nods and smiles widely. "Good. Now sing."

Startled, I ask, "What?"

Adam slaps the strings quiet and laughs out loud. "Bird! I'm stuck! Write me a song. I'm begging you!"

I laugh, too, shaking my head at him. "Oh, Adam, I know we're laughing right now, but this album is killing you, right?"

"Torture."

"You used to just write what you wanted and sing what you loved and go along down the highway from gig to gig—"

"Yes! I just made music, whatever was on my mind."

"—with no pressure."

"Right," he says. Then he considers it and adds, "Well, there was pressure to make money. If I didn't play, I didn't eat."

"Oh." I look out the back of the SUV, remembering once again how different our backgrounds are. We met on the road as teenagers, but I was playing music with my family while Adam was on his own already. We didn't eat at fancy restaurants growing up, or have expensive clothes, but we were always okay, my folks made sure of it. "Did that ever happen?"

"Yeah, occasionally." He picks the strings of his guitar absentmindedly, staring straight ahead. "Not as often as when I was a kid."

"That's crazy," I say at a near whisper. I picture Adam ten years ago. I imagine a skinny kid, lanky limbs, a middle schooler with an empty stomach and big dreams. I know his dad was never in the picture and that his mom wasn't dependable—I think she may have had some problems with alcohol abuse—but I never realized it was to the point that he ever went hungry. "I'm sorry."

He shrugs. "I'm writing a song about this really fun moment, but then it's like I can't believe I was throwing food all around that kitchen when I have literally stolen food from my friends' refrigerators..." He trails off. "Sort of takes the 'fun' out of it."

I glance over. His eyes are faraway and focused not on the horizon but on the past, and it takes everything I've got not to pull him in for a hug. I feel like somebody somewhere needs to hold this boy close and tell him how talented he is and how bighearted and how *worthwhile*. But just then Dylan opens the door of our tour bus carrying an oversized beach bag, and Stella is right behind him with blankets.

"Maybe this song isn't your fun one," I tell Adam as I hop out of the SUV. I face him and say, "Maybe this song is about what really sustains us. Maybe it's a song about how our souls need to be fed, too, or how we need more than food to live—how we need love, too."

Adam slowly lets his hazel eyes drift over to mine.

He locks onto my gaze.

We stay put, staring at each other for what feels like hours but is actually just the fifty paces or so that it takes Stella and Dylan to join us. They throw their stuff in the back, Stella rearranging everything after Adam finally breaks eye contact and gets out of her way.

We stand to the side as they pack the car, and Adam leans over. "You're a special girl, Lady Bird," he says softly.

I turn my head and face him straight on, wanting him to believe me when I say, "You're pretty special, too, you know."

Dylan slams the back door and calls, "Everybody ready?"

Stella walks around to the passenger side and opens the back door instead of taking shotgun, letting everybody know that they haven't quite worked it out yet. I'm sure she'll want to vent later, and then Dylan will give me his side of things in short, explosive snippets, and I'll stay neutral and pretend to sympathize with them both.

But today is my day off. And Adam is here. I just want a peaceful beach day.

"I think I'm going to grab my guitar, too," I say, backtracking quickly toward the bus.

Adam may have writer's block, but after the way he just opened up to me, I am suddenly inspired.

12

"THE *ROLLING STONE* reporter just texted that she is waiting in Atlanta and will board the bus when you roll in," Anita says from my iPad screen. "How long until you're at the arena?"

"Not long," I say, looking out the bus window. "I can see it in the distance, so we have to be close."

"Good." She picks up a pen, looks down at her desk, and without even being there in person, I know that she's got a list of dos and don'ts she wants to go over. "Let's run through a few quick things before you get there."

I grin, glancing up at Dylan, who's sitting in the kitchenette with me. "That woman is relentless," he whispers.

"Who's that?" Anita says, leaning in closer to her screen. "Dylan? Good. Get Stella, too. These are things that you'll all have to remember while she tours with you. Reporters dig, they want dirt, they want their exclusive to stand out from all the other interviews you've given, and no one on the tour is off-limits."

"Then you better tell her about Adam," Dylan says as I move the iPad back so that we're both in the shot.

"What about Adam?" Anita says. "Bird, is that a thing? You know you have to tell me this stuff!"

"It's not a thing!" I defend myself, punching my brother in the arm. "There's no thing. We're just friends."

"The four of us watched a movie on the bus last night, and I'm telling you, you could cut the sexual tension with a knife," Dylan says, all prim and proper. "I was uncomfortable."

"*You* were uncomfortable?" I echo. "Try crying your eyes out to *The Fault in Our Stars* while two other people on the couch are playing tonsil hockey."

"We weren't making out," he says. "We were cuddling."

"And I was gagging."

"Kids," Anita cuts in.

"Like you and Stella aren't constantly talking about what would happen if you and Adam got back together," Dylan goes on.

I feel my jaw nearly hit the table. "Are you kidding me right now?" Then I turn to my supposed best friend as she sits down next to me. "Do you tell him everything we talk about?"

"Bird, the walls aren't soundproof," Dylan says.

"Yeah, neither is the curtain over your bunk, FYI," I fire back, fuming.

"Kids," Anita says again.

"Truce, truce," Stella says, shifting the iPad to fit us all on-screen. "First of all, I would never break your confidence," she says to me. "I feel like you ought to trust me a little more than that by now. And second of all," she says, turning to Dylan, "you don't know how all that went down the first time. I was there, and you're not being cool."

My brother's eyes widen. "Sorry."

"Anita, there's nothing happening there," Stella says to my publicist. "Believe me."

Anita sighs dramatically. "Fine, but this is exactly the kind of thing that cannot—absolutely, positively *cannot*—happen in front of this reporter."

"I was just joking around," Dylan says.

"Joking around right now, but you won't around the reporter, right?" Anita asks. "Certainly not the first day. You'll all be on your best behavior. 'Touring with my best friend is so great,' and 'I love the quality time I'm spending with my little sister.' You think the reporter wants to hear that junk? You think that's newsworthy? No. By day three you'll all be quite chummy, and it's jokes like this that could hijack Bird's whole story."

We all just sit there, thoroughly scolded.

Anita takes a big breath. "Bird," she says, softer. "*Rolling Stone* magazine is major, and they want to do an exclusive feature on you: a day-in-the-life sort of peek into your world. I've seen these go well, and I've seen these go down in flames. Should I fly out tomorrow? Should I see if one of your parents can join the tour for a few days?"

"No, I'll be fine," I say.

"I just want you to be happy with the way the world sees you."

I nod. "Right, but I like the idea that the three of us are touring on my bus and doing just fine without a constant chaperone. I've made it to all my shows, the media coverage has been great, and I've still kept up with all the side stuff Troy books. This reporter's going to be like, 'Wow. This girl's got her act together.'"

Anita frowns. "That's our hope."

"Anita, we'll be fine," an exasperated Dylan says.

"All right, all right," she says, holding up her manicured hands. "So a few things: First, a note to all of you, if you don't want your relationships to be public knowledge, then you have to keep some distance while *Rolling Stone* is on board. Stella and Dylan, I ask you for Bird's sake to keep everything rated G."

"Excuse me, ma'am, but I am a gentleman," Dylan says with a hand over his heart. Stella giggles.

Ignoring him, Anita plows ahead. "And, Bird, I have no

problem with you dating Adam. I want to be clear about that, okay? I think he's a nice boy, and he also fits perfectly with your image."

I roll my eyes. "We're not dating."

"Hey, I was young once, too. If anything *does* happen," she goes on, "a late-night hang out where sparks fly—"

Dylan has to turn his head away to hide his laughter, and I kick him under the table for starting all of this.

"—or a kiss in the back hallways that you think nobody knows about, then you call me. Going public with your first celebrity boyfriend is a big deal. I would much prefer that *we* control the way that information is revealed."

I put my head in my hands and exhale. I'm actually happy when Anita gets to her list, reminding me to let the reporter see me studying so that people will know I'm actively trying to get my GED. She also says that our family history will definitely come up, especially Caleb, and that Dylan and I should figure out what we want to say about that before the grenade is dropped. She reminds me that this woman will be my shadow: She'll be in the wings of the show, in the dressing room, and on the bus, sleeping in the bunk below Dylan's. When someone's constantly in your space, filling up even the moments that are usually private, Anita reminds me, it can be difficult to keep a sunny disposition, so remember my friendly aura.

My publicist goes on and on with tips on how to "control the story," but all I'm thinking about now is the "sexual tension" Dylan supposedly senses between Adam and me. It's messing with my head. Now that Stella spends so much time with Dylan, I've been hanging out a lot with Adam. When he first joined the tour a few weeks ago, I was worried about two things: personally, that my heart would be broken again, and professionally, that I could possibly lose a fantastic tour opener. But now the stakes are even higher. Adam has become one of the closest friends I've ever had. I don't want to lose that.

"We're here, y'all," Dylan announces as the bus slows and we pull into Philips Arena parking lot.

"Okay, good luck, gang," Anita says with a tight-lipped smile. "I know you'll be terrific. Call me if you need absolutely anything at all."

"Thanks, Mom," Dylan says sarcastically. We all wave and I shut down the iPad, feeling like we just went through PR boot camp. "Anita is great at her job, don't get me wrong," Dylan says, rubbing his ear, "but that woman can talk!"

Stella gets up and peers out the window as we roll through the parking lot. "I think that's the reporter. Black skinny jeans and a denim button-down trimmed with plaid." She shrugs. "Total hipster. Cute but cliché." Stella turns toward Dylan and grabs his face. "One final kiss, or are we ready for the world to know about us?"

"I don't know, Stel. The paparazzi will hound us for weeks," he jokes.

"'Stylan spotted at the movies!'" I say, playing along as I run my hand through the air like I'm reading an imaginary headline. Then they kiss and I look away, my standard knee-jerk reaction even though it was just a quick peck. I stand up, stretch, and check my hair and makeup in the bathroom mirror. I'm ready to meet this woman and get on with the interview. A feature in *Rolling Stone* magazine is intimidating, sure, but it's also really exciting. "Let's do this," I say, my adrenaline pumping as I race down the stairs and open the bus door.

I've got my guard up, as Anita instructed, but as Adam's bus pulls in next to mine, I can't help but wonder what would happen if I just let go.

13

"So these are the digs, huh?" the reporter remarks as she follows me back onto the bus a few minutes later.

"Home sweet home," I reply. "This is my brother Dylan. He plays guitar in the band."

"Hi, Dylan," she says, reaching a tattooed arm out for a handshake. "I'm Jase."

"Nice to meet you," he says with a bright smile, and I remember that my brother can be quite charming when he turns it on.

"And this is Stella, my best friend and more important, Master of the Quick Change," I say. "She's working on the tour as a wardrobe assistant."

"Hi," Jase says. "I love your bangs. They never looked good on me."

Stella reaches out her hand for a shake, scrutinizing the reporter intensely. Jase is probably in her late twenties, a petite woman, skinny as a rail, wearing heavy black eyeliner and fresh Converse sneakers. Her jet-black hair is shaved on one side, the rest falling over one eye in an asymmetrical bob, but while her look may be severe, her smile is warm.

"You can put your stuff over here," I say, leading her toward the back of the bus. "The bottom bunk is yours for the next few days."

"Good thing I'm little," she says, tossing her stuff down onto her bed.

"Yeah, try being six foot and squeezing in there," I say. "When my folks are on tour with us, I'm the low man on the totem pole."

Jase grins. "The perks of being a star."

I laugh. "Exactly. So, what do you want to do first? Need a little time to unpack?"

"No, I'm good," she says. "I napped on the plane from New York, and I'm ready to roar. Want to give me the *MTV Cribs* tour?"

"Sure." I turn around in the tight space. "Ought to be a quick tour, but okay ... Actually, this is pretty cool. I never know when I'm going to be inspired, so I keep my instruments on board rather than locked under the bus. So, like, if Dylan or I want to play or write a new song or something, our instruments are right here in this hidden pop-out closet."

"You wrote 'Before Music' together, right?" Jase asks Dylan. "About your brother who passed away?"

"Yes, Caleb," he answers.

"I don't know how you put that much emotion into a record and then replicate it for thousands of people every night."

"Well, I don't think you can let yourself go that deep every time," Dylan answers truthfully. "When we wrote it, the emotion was pretty raw. But now, well, I don't want to speak for you, Bird, but I sing it more as a tribute than as the therapy it was for me at the time."

"Definitely," I concur.

Jase pulls out a small Moleskine notebook and smiles, almost apologetically. "Nerd alert," she says, eyes twinkling. "Hope you don't mind if I take notes." She starts scribbling as I give her a tour of the bus: living room, kitchenette, bathroom, triple bunks.

"Stella up top, Dylan in the middle, and the bottom is our storage-closet-slash-guest-bed-slash-my-bed when my parents are on board," I say.

"Pretty intimate quarters," she comments, and I see Dylan and Stella exchange a look behind her.

"That's life on the road," I say with a shrug. Then I gesture to my room. "And this is the master."

"You do yoga on the road?" Jase asks when she sees a yoga mat that I'd forgotten to roll up earlier. "Impressive. I'm awkward when I'm on solid ground, so you must be good."

"If I lose my balance, I fall on the bed, and if that happens, the session is usually over," I admit. "I'm always tired."

"I bet. What's more exhausting?" she asks earnestly. "The touring or the show itself?"

"Hmmm, I'd say the show itself. It's a workout, and we go hard every night. I want to give my fans the best show I can, so by the time I take my final bow, I'm just spent. The touring part I'm kind of used to." I walk back up to the living room and crash next to Dylan and Stella on the couch. "This is the way Dylan and I grew up, so it's comforting being out on the road. And it's a lot less crowded these days."

"Where are your parents?" she asks. "I was under the impression one of them always toured with you."

I shrug. "They meet us a lot, for a few days at a time, but they also stay busy back home. I'm eighteen now so—"

"So you *got* this," Jase says with spunk, holding out a fist for me to bump.

We pound it out, and I smile. "I got this."

We talk more about the tour and the show, about Dylan and Stella putting school off for a while, and about how well my second album is doing. It doesn't feel like an interview at all, especially since Jase is hardly writing anything down. It's more like a bunch of friends hanging out.

When Stella asks Jase what her story is, the reporter's candor surprises me. She tells us what it was like leaving Iowa for New York, how she never really fit in back home and always had big dreams and big ideas, like dressing according to *Vogue* when everybody else swore by *Seventeen*. Stella nods in solidarity when Jase opens up about dropping out of state university to move to New York for an unpaid editorial internship.

"Nobody's journey is the same," Jase says, "but I feel sorry for the people who always take the straight and narrow and never venture out. I could've stayed in Iowa and married my high school boyfriend, made my parents happy, probably be a mom of three by now. But I never felt like that was my path. I wanted to be a writer, I wanted to hear live music every night, I wanted to follow fashion trends and date a person I connect with regardless of their gender. I wanted something different. Moving away from my family so young was the hardest thing I've ever done, but I feel like I can be me now, without apology. And that's freeing."

We all sit in stillness after that, not really knowing what to say. Jase's words strike a deep chord within all three of us: I can see it in Stella's thoughtful frown and Dylan's unfocused gaze. None of us has taken a traditional path to get where we are or where we're going.

When a production assistant knocks on the door and says catering is set up, we snap out of it and grab our stuff, each of us contemplating the depths of our own bravery as we file off the bus and follow our artistic dreams.

"So, Jase is pretty cool," Stella says backstage. We are in the wings, changing into the "Tennessee Girl" shorts and boots, and this has been the first reporter-free minute we've had for the past six hours. "At first, I thought she was trying too hard—I mean, I still think that blue streak in her hair is a clip-on—but it's cool that she's passionate about her work. That's something everybody on this tour has in common."

"So true," I say. *Who would do this otherwise?*

"For our Tennessee Girl," Adam says from out of nowhere, handing me a handpicked bouquet of purple flowers.

I am stunned as I take the flowers from him, blown away, immediately thinking back to the night I was discovered at the Station Inn. Adam was there, and he left a little bouquet of wildflowers for me, the first time I ever got flowers from a boy. My heart skips a beat.

"Where did you get these?" I say with wonder as Stella ties up the front of my shirt. He looks so cute right now, with his happy lopsided smile and his hair still a little wild from his show.

"I saw them growing in this field over—"

"Thirty seconds, Bird," Jordan interrupts as she holds out my mic.

Stella stands up and examines me, taking the flowers and passing me my microphone.

"Well, thanks," I say, looking at them glumly in another girl's hands.

Adam looks at them, too, a little embarrassed. "Have to work on my timing," he says.

"You made my day," I say honestly. I don't want him to feel bad, so I lean over for a nice, friendly side hug, but he wraps both of his arms around me, tight like always. I get a massive shiver when my cheek presses against his neck, but then I remember that Jase is lurking around and I push away, hard.

Adam stumbles back, stunned. "Hey, what's wrong?"

"The *Rolling Stone* reporter's here," Stella explains, strategically stepping between us as she fixes my collar. "So we all have to cool it for a few days, got it?"

"Cool what?" he asks, sincerely dumbfounded.

I feel the heat rise in my chest. This is so not happening. "Ha-ha, ha-ha!" I fake laugh. "Stella, you're so funny."

As the first notes of my next song start to play, I rush back to the spotlight and beam at my fans, waving at the crowd as my brain tries to process everything that just happened.

Adam got me flowers.

Again!

And then I freaked out over nothing.

Again?

I start to sing this fan favorite, clapping my hands and getting the crowd on their feet, as I think about whether there really is a future for Adam and me and what I'm willing to risk if there is. I glance over at the wings and see a very confused Adam standing beside a very observant Jase. With a Miss America Pageant smile, I face forward and dive into the show. Who'd have ever thought that singing in front of twenty-one thousand people was the one place a girl could hide?

14

JASE HAS BEEN with us for a full forty-eight hours now, and Stella was right; she's pretty cool. She has a dry wit, to the point that we have to double-check sometimes to see if she's kidding. She hasn't actually delved too deeply into my family's past, which has been refreshing, and she's left me alone about the stuff I usually see about myself in the tabloids. Actually, she just seems to be soaking up the tour, watching my interaction with the band and crew, asking about the direction of my third album and when I expect to record it. She's been chill, professional, and somebody we all agree we could hang out with in real life sometime.

But I miss Adam.

I had gotten used to hanging out before the show, eating together, and then walking back to the bus after our

postperformance Cokes. But with Jase here, I've been avoid-
ing him. Anita is right. Even if we were to try dating again,
I'm not sure I want it to be the headline of my first-ever *Rolling Stone* feature. I want that to be about my music.

"Bird, are you in here?" Stella calls from outside my door.

"Yeah," I holler, finishing a quick text to Adam. He
wants me to hear the latest version of his food fight song,
but I've been putting him off:

Slammed today. How about Mon. or Tues.?

Stella slides my door open and walks immediately to my
closet. "Jase wants to take some pictures of the handbag
I made you out of my mom's scratched-up vinyl records.
That cool?"

"Awesome," I say.

My phone beeps again:

I never thought I'd say this, but I hate Rolling Stone.

I laugh and write back:

Aw, you miss us?

Stella plops onto my bed and whispers, "I can tell from
the look on your face who you're texting."

I sit up and look behind her to make sure Jase isn't within earshot. "We're just friends!" I hiss.

"Then why can't he hang out with us?" she asks with a knowing smile. "You afraid Jase is going to pick up on your 'friendship'?"

I know my face gives me away as she starts to laugh.

"Bird! You are killing yourself!" she says. "Just tell him how you feel. Write him a song—*something*. Dylan told me Adam's still totally into you, and I know you feel the same way, so why are you torturing yourself?"

"Because I don't want my feelings for Adam, or whatever, to be the center of my first *Rolling Stone* feature."

She nods. "I get that."

"But it sucks." I groan. "He brought me *flowers*, Stella. We text and hang out all the time and, yeah, it's awesome. And I feel the spark. And I'm ready. But now, because of work stuff, it looks like I'm too busy to hang out with him, which is exactly what drove him away last time."

"Is that what you told him?" she asks. " 'We can't hang out because I like you too much'?"

I blush. "No. I told him that as bad as it sounds, Anita really wanted to make sure the article stayed about me and not my opener so we needed to keep a little distance. He was totally cool about it and said he'd never want to steal my thunder, which made me feel even worse about lying to him."

"Eh, white lie."

Then my phone beeps again and I whip it back out, laughing when I read Adam's message:

You and Stella are ok, but I really miss Dylan. Can't believe I'm grounded from the bus. #RollOnRollingStone

Stella reads over my shoulders and says, "I never knew he was so dramatic." I laugh. "Come on, let's go."

I follow her up to the living room, where Dylan is playing video games and Jase is typing on her Mac. "Ready?" she asks when we sit down with her.

"Yeah," Stella says. "Hey, Dylan, Adam wants you to come over. Or you can stay for girl talk."

Dylan doesn't even reply. He just turns off the TV and bounds down the stairs toward guy time and freedom.

"Okay, so here's the bag," Stella says, passing her my Christmas present from last year.

"Ooooh, this is unreal," Jase says. "I can't believe you made this by hand."

"She has jewelry and hair accessories in her Etsy store, too. I don't know how she has the time," I say.

"Well, I don't now that I'm on tour," Stella says.

"Bird, how do *you* juggle it all?"

"My publicist helps a lot," I say with a shrug. "And I would die without my manager."

Jase shakes her head and says, "That's not exactly what I mean. I'm not talking about juggling a busy schedule." I frown, trying to understand.

"For example, Stella is your best friend and Dylan is your brother, but they're also your employees. And this new opener, Adam Dean, he's an old friend, too, right?"

I nod.

"You can't exactly fire them." She turns to Stella. "Not that she'd want to. I'm just saying it's a serious conflict of interest if any of you flake or overstep or whatever."

"We wouldn't do that," Stella says, a little defensively.

"I'm sure," Jase goes on, "but hypothetically. I'm just asking how you draw boundaries. How do you stay Bird the Boss and Bird the Friend?"

I look out the window and think about her question. "It's not always easy, I guess," I say. "Like the other day when Amanda was mad because Stella takes care of most of my quick changes even though she's not the senior stylist and has no prior experience."

"Exactly!" Jase says. "*That* was uncomfortable."

I glance at Stella, but her smile has vanished.

"I'm sure you don't need the extra drama," Jase plows on, "and you definitely don't want a reputation for unfair treatment or favoritism."

I shift in my seat awkwardly. "Honestly, it just comes down to the fact that I feel more comfortable with Stella.

Knowing each other so well is a big plus. And if you think about it, Amanda actually has a lot more responsibility because she's dressing everyone else in the show."

"Ah, so in reality, you trust Amanda more," Jase says, nodding as if in understanding when I didn't say that at all.

"Speak of the devil," Stella says as she pulls out her phone. "Amanda just texted, and she's willing to give me the opportunity to steam a few of the band members' shirts for tonight, so I better hop to it."

I cringe, wishing I could stop her but knowing she'll kill me if I make a scene. She grabs her headphones and a bottle of water out of the fridge and exits the bus, Jase and I perfectly quiet until she's gone.

"See? Conflict of interest," Jase says.

I sigh. "Sometimes."

"Do you think any of your people have a clue how much pressure you're under? You're running a major tour and balancing a burgeoning career while they're all along for the ride."

I think about it. "Well, I guess there have been a few times with Dylan and Stella where I've been like, 'Um, guys? This is not a real problem. I've got real problems.'"

"Like when your opener quit."

"Exactly." I start to say more but pause to weigh my words carefully. Jase is right: If my guitarist weren't my brother, my stylist weren't my best friend, and my opener weren't my crush, then work stuff like this interview wouldn't be nearly as tricky. "It's like everyone expects me to be what they need. I'm the boss when you need a job. I'm your friend when you need to talk. I think I've blurred the line a few times, but I try to keep business and personal as separate as possible."

"Is that why there's nothing going on with you and Adam Dean?"

I look back at Jase and feel my eyes bulge. "What?"

She laughs and wiggles her eyebrows. "He's a hot piece, and he looks at you all moon-eyed every time he sees you."

"Jase!" I feel my cheeks redden as she laughs. "We're just friends. We tried dating once a couple of years ago, but we're better as friends."

"Maybe he wants another go?" she presses.

"Maybe you've lost your mind," I say, trying to regroup. I can hear Anita's voice in my head: *Everything's on the record.* I probably shouldn't have told her that Adam and I tried dating before, so I think fast and talk about something I've never told another reporter. "But you want to talk boundaries? My first boyfriend was this amazing guy I met on tour last year, but mixing work with dating totally drained us both. It's exactly like you said: conflict of interest. Impossible. You can't be equals in the relationship if you're not equals at work."

She nods thoughtfully. "You were in love with this guy?"

I didn't want my article to be about Adam, and now it's somehow turning into a feature on Kai. I sigh. "It hurt when we broke up."

"Did it have anything to do with your feud with Kayelee Ford?" she asks. "Did he cheat on you?"

Taken aback, I blurt out, "No! Are you kidding me? No and no."

"Okay, okay," she says, holding up her hands. "Just curious."

"Why?" I ask, trying to turn this ship around. "Have you been cheated on?"

Bingo. I see the pain flash across her face before her expression resettles to neutral. "I have. And it sucks."

"Are you dating anybody right now?" I ask, hating that I brought up a bad memory for her but happy to take the spotlight off me. "I bet you get to meet so many interesting people in New York. And there are probably models walking down the sidewalk all the time."

"Yeah, and every one of them asks me out," she says wryly. "It's exhausting."

I laugh. Before she can ask me anything else, Marco knocks on my door, and I have never been so happy to go over a budget issue. He comes aboard and we work a little at the table while Jase types. Then I excuse myself from further one-on-ones with our resident reporter as I shower and prepare to give my Greensboro fans the best show I've got.

15

"I CAN'T BELIEVE I just played Madison Square Garden," Dylan says. We're standing in the wings of New York City's most iconic venue, a landmark performance for any artist.

I glance over at him and smile, on that same high. "We're not done yet!"

"Bird! Bird! Bird! Bird! Bird!" the fans cheer in unison, a chant, a stadium full of happy fans hungry for just one more song. The big song. The one this tour is named after: "Shine Our Light."

Jordan gives the band their cue, and when they take the stage for our encore, the crowd goes wild, the uproar deafening. I rush to the front of the stage and take it all in, arms spread wide. "Thank you, New York City!" I call into the standing microphone.

When the fans settle some, I go on. "This year was really incredible for me. I released an album I'm really proud of, I won a VMA, I'm headlining in the greatest city in the world—" The crowd roars. "And I couldn't have done any of it without you!" I shout. "So thank you! I love you! I have the greatest fans in the world!" They know it's true and they go nuts.

I grab my guitar and pull the strap over my head before stepping back up to the mic. "And on a serious note," I say, bringing it down a little. I start to strum softly. "There were also some bumps along the way. There seem to be bumps on any path worth traveling. I learned the hard way that there are always going to be people who try to diminish the light within us. And it's easy to get caught up in *why* they would want to do that instead of simply not letting it happen. So I wrote this song about that."

The band comes in with me, and I get ready to sing. "If you've got glow sticks or cell phones or anything that lights up or sparkles, hold 'em up in the air for me, okay?"

The music swells around me, and I try to block out anything external to this very moment: *Rolling Stone*, Adam, Stylan, any factor that would keep me from being present right here on this stage. And then I start to sing:

> *"You look at me like it's a natural rivalry,*
> *Like there's just room for one to succeed."*

But this song always reminds me of Kayelee Ford. I wrote it about her. I get so confused every time I think about how much we despise each other, and I always come back to the question, *Why?* Why, really?

I give my audience every last bit of energy I've got as I finish the chorus and start the second verse. I think about the lyrics, how *"Nothing's wrong with being who you really are,"* and how brave Jase was to leave everything behind to move to this very city and cut her own path. When I get to the chorus again, I call out, "Come on, NYC!" and run up a bunch of stairs upstage, stepping onto a hidden platform. As I start the chorus, I am slowly lifted into the air:

"Just rise and fly.
Live your life out loud, yeah, live it outright."

This is Jordan's big cue. As the band, audience, and I sing through the chorus together, my stage manager sends the small platform arcing over the crowd and sets me up front on a tiny stage nestled in the sea of floor seats. As I sing the third verse, our security team allows a few fans to climb onstage with me so that by the time the final chorus comes around, we join voices and sing a cappella:

"Just rise and fly.
Live your life out loud, yeah, live it outright.

Just ride and smile.
On this crazy roller coaster in a whirlwind storm,
We just gotta hold our own, be bold,
And shine our light."

I step away a little and strum, two girls standing beside me with eyes as wide as saucers. I play the rest on my acoustic guitar, going back up to the mic to sing:

"We just gotta hold our own, be bold,
And shine our light."

I smile out at the crowd as they sing along, holding up their glow sticks and cell phones. The tiny lights flicker all around me in the dark arena, lighting up little pockets of people in the floor seats as well as in the upper decks. It's beautiful.

"Shine your light.
Yeah, shine your light."

And I softly strum the last chord as the stage lights fade and at least ten thousand people shine their own light.

"You're going to meet up with us later?" Stella asks the next morning as she wraps a light scarf around her neck.

"Yes, definitely," I say. "This is the last interview with Jase, and then it's adios, *Rolling Stone*."

Stella blows air through her bangs, annoyed. "Thank God."

Dylan arches his eyebrows behind her, but I give my head a slight shake, letting him know not to say anything. Stella is clearly still not happy with Jase after the uncomfortable bus moment the other day, and the last thing I want to do is bring it all up again before our big day on the town. I shot all my promos yesterday, so today is free time with my friends to do all the New York things I've never gotten to do, like see the Statue of Liberty, walk the West Village, and eat my weight in pizza.

There is a knock at the door, and I walk over to answer it. Adam stands in the hallway, looking adorable in his black fleece zip-up. "Another amazing performance. Another missed fountain Coke," he says, shaking his head disappointedly.

"I know! I know, I'm sorry," I say, stepping back so he can walk in. "But after this interview I'm free again. And I promise you we will give New York Coke a chance after our show tonight."

"I'm going to hold you to that, Bird Barrett," he says with a very serious expression on his face.

"Okay, y'all, let's go," Dylan says. "I read that you have to get in line early for the Empire State Building."

Stella claps her hands excitedly. "I can't wait!"

"Yay," I say halfheartedly. Then I plop down on the desk chair and pout.

"Aw, Bird," she says, walking over and massaging my shoulders. "Just answer every question yes or no and then send her packing. I promise to keep any fun we have to a bare minimum until you can meet us."

I grin up at her. "You're the best."

"I don't think the Empire State Building is that far from our hotel actually," Dylan says, looking at a map on his phone. "If the line is as long as they say, you might be able to find us and cut."

"Oh yeah, that'd be great for my image," I say, rolling my eyes.

"Listen, if you want my opinion," Adam says, leaning on the desk, "you've already been more than generous with your time. Tell that woman this is the last interview, and you have to be somewhere in an hour. You don't have to say where even."

I perk up. He's right.

"Just be the boss."

And then I cringe.

Because I'm tired of being the boss. I want to be more than the boss, especially with him and especially today.

My phone beeps and I read a text from Jase. "She's on her way up," I tell them. "I'll see y'all soon."

I hold open the door and watch my friends walk down the hall toward the elevator, giddy at the big day we have planned, and I decide Adam is right. I deserve a day off, and this interview doesn't have to take forever. Surely Jase has gotten all she needs and more by now.

I set my coat and purse by the front door so that Jase can see when she walks in that I've got somewhere else to be. I pull on my sneakers—tour guide Dylan warned us about the blisters rookie tourists get from wearing the wrong shoes—and I have them tied just as she knocks on the door.

"Hi!" I say, getting up and swinging it open.

"Hi," Adam says, surprising me. He takes a step inside and grabs a hotel room key card off the desk. "Forgot my key."

"Oh," is all I manage because he is standing close, really close, right in front of me, with a look on his face like he has more to say.

"Meet us in an hour, okay?" he says, more serious about seeing the Empire State Building than seems normal. "We'll grab food and just walk around until you can meet us there. You'll meet us soon, right?"

"Yeah," I say, nodding. "I'll make it quick."

"Well, well, well! Good morning to the two of you," Jase says suggestively, popping up in the doorway behind him. My mouth falls open as I realize what this must look like.

"Um, I was just leaving," Adam says quickly. He smiles at her as he squeezes by and slips the room key card into his back jeans pocket as he heads down the hall.

"Now *that* is not the worst a girl can do when she wakes up in the morning, am I right?" Jase asks with a mischievous smile.

"Oh, he just popped by," I explain worriedly.

"Sure," she says, breezing in and looking around my suite. She eyes the place admiringly. "You definitely travel in style, Bird. I'll give you that."

"It's nice to sleep in a stationary bed every once in a while," I say, closing the door.

"Hey!" she shouts, turning around to face me. "Incredible show last night. I think you saved the best for last."

I beam at her, relaxing some. "Thank you."

"Your energy is intoxicating," she goes on. "Seriously."

She takes a seat on the couch and pulls out her notebook. I sit in the chair next to her, happy that she seems as eager as me to wrap up this story.

"So, I feel like I know the Bird you want me to know," Jase begins, looking up at me intently, "but I don't feel like I know the *real* Bird."

"Really?" I say, surprised. "Jase, this is me. What you see is what you get. And trust me, I've let my guard down a lot more around you than I ever have with any other reporter."

144

"And I appreciate that," she says, "but I think it's time to ask some real questions, you know?"

"Real?" I ask. "Has all this other stuff been fake?"

"Not fake, just surface stuff," she says. "But now I want to get down to it. And speaking of fake," she says, glancing up at me, looking the teensiest bit apologetic. I brace myself. "A lot of people say that about you. So what do you say to those people who think you're too sugary sweet to be true?"

I'm surprised by such a direct and negative question right off the bat, and it takes me a second to answer. "Haters gonna hate," I say simply.

"Right, but there are *a lot* of haters," she continues.

"Well, I have *a lot* of fans, too," I say, a tad defensive. "Every celebrity has people trying to knock them down, and sometimes we do it to each other. That's the message behind 'Shine Our Light.' If we could just focus on being our best selves instead of trying to bring out the worst in somebody else, we'd all shine brighter."

Jase looks at me like, *Oh, please.*

"I just try to block out the negative stuff and focus on the positive."

"Okay," she says, pulling an iPad from her bag. She loads something and passes it to me. "Then how do you feel when you see sites like these?"

I look down at a Twitter account called NotBirdBarrett and am stunned by what I see. This person has uploaded a profile picture of me, but all the tweets are stuff I would never post or say or do:

Just biding my time until I can go Pop.

Hey birdies, go crap on somebody today. It's good luck.

Does this chastity belt make me look fat?

"This is terrible!" I say as I scroll down. I read one out loud that cuts especially deep. " 'Is it bad if your album makes your own ears bleed? Hashtag sorrynotsorry.' That's so mean," I whisper. "I worked really hard on those songs."

Jase doesn't reply, but she reaches over and swipes the screen to Instagram. "Check out the hashtag 'birdface,' " she says.

I gasp. I scroll down the page, attacked by images of person after person making wide-eyed expressions or over-exaggerated duck lips, a few pretending to hold a gun to their head. I feel tears spring to my eyes, and I set the iPad down on the coffee table in front of me.

"How does stuff like that make you feel?" Jase asks softly.

"Oh, like a million bucks," I say sarcastically. "Thanks so much for your concern."

"Come on, you have to have seen stuff like that before."

146

I dab under my eyelids. "I'm actually telling you the truth when I say I try to avoid it. Nobody around here mentions that stuff. We keep it positive. My *core group*, people who actually hate to see me upset, shield me from as much of this garbage as they can."

"Speaking of your 'core group,'" she goes on, in full attack mode, "what really happened with your dad? Why isn't he your manager anymore?" This is definitely not the Jase who's been on tour with me the past few days, and I'm not only fed up right now, but also a little hurt.

"Because it's a lot of work and he decided to put his family first," I answer hotly.

"'Family first'?" she repeats. "Then why isn't he here? Who's watching over his teenage daughter?"

"I'm eighteen years old, Jase," I say, frustrated. "You moved to freaking New York City when you weren't much older, remember? I'm an adult and Dylan's here—"

"To hook up with your best friend," she cuts in.

I pause and take a very deep breath. I remember dealing with Kayelee Ford last year at the New Year's Eve party, how I let her goad me, how I let her win. I do not want to lose my cool with this reporter.

I collect myself.

It is difficult.

"Dylan is here," I repeat slowly, "to play in the band and help me out if I need anything. Not to babysit, but so that

I'll have family if I need it. As for my father," I continue, "he *is* putting family first. His own father broke his hip, and as much as it killed him, he and my mom decided to stay in Tennessee and help Granddad get back on his feet. They meet me on the road all the time and will be joining me again at the next stop actually." Unable to bite my tongue, I give her a fake smile and add, "They would've come sooner, but it's been cramped quarters around here lately with our *Rolling Stone* VIP."

Ignoring me, she plows forward. "Do you ever wonder if your 'core group,' as you call them, might be using you? You know, for jobs, money, fame, whatever."

"What?" I ask. "No."

"Being in Bird Barrett's entourage is a pretty good gig," she says.

"They're my family."

"And you've always said that your family is very close," Jase continues.

"Yes."

"Do you think you'd be this close if your younger brother hadn't died?"

"Yes."

"Care to talk more about that?"

"No."

"Do you think he'd look up to you if he were still alive?"

"I like to think so."

"Even with all the catfights you've had with Kayelee Ford?" she presses. "You think he'd admire the fact that you dropped one of your best friends, Devyn Delaney, because she tried to befriend your nemesis?"

I look at her like she's crazy. "First of all, do not even dare to tie the death of my little brother to a stupid spat with a celebrity. That's base and it's vile, and I thought you were better than that," I snap. "And secondly, get your facts straight, *reporter*, because that's not at all what happened. The only reason I don't see Devyn anymore is because I've been really busy—maybe you've noticed that I'm head-lining a *national tour*—and when I am in LA, I don't have time for that party lifestyle. As far as Kayelee Ford is concerned, I have absolutely no ill will toward her. I have no idea how this weird feud got started, although I can tell you that it's been sustained by questions like these. Those girls party, I don't, otherwise we'd hang out. Maybe we will after this tour, but for now, I couldn't even go to any VMA after parties because I had to get back on the road."

"No time to party, huh?" Jase asks, amused. How can she look so unruffled when I feel like I could explode?

"I work a lot," I say through clenched teeth.

"And you're too good for that anyway, right?"

I take a deep breath. "It's not something I would make a priority."

"Interesting," she muses smugly as she pulls up the photo

album on her iPad. "That's not what Colton Holley had to say." I look at her quizzically. "I contacted him when I saw some photos of the two of you. At a casino? In Vegas? Admittedly, they were grainy, but he confirmed the two of you partied well into the night, although he sadly confessed that you did not make it to his penthouse."

I am fuming now.

"But he did send me a couple of these pictures." She swipes the iPad screen as images of Colton and me appear. I look pretty, but in one I am red-faced and sipping from a daiquiri, in another I am screaming as I cheer at the roulette table, and in the worst pic, I look like I'm in love as I snuggle against Colton for an ussie. "Obviously we won't use these because we're *Rolling Stone* and not *InTouch*. But after denying that you're a party girl and selling the world on your goody-goody image, now what would you say to the haters?"

"I'd tell them that maybe I'm not as sweet as everybody thinks I am," I snap. Then I stand up and point toward the door. "And off the record, Jase, I'd politely but firmly tell them to get the hell out."

16

*Anita's going to kill me. Anita's going to kill me. Anita's
going to kill me.*

For the past hour and a half, I have been lying on my
bed with my arms over my eyes, replaying the terrible, horrible, no good, very bad interview that just went down and
the mixed expression of surprise, satisfaction, and even
admiration from Jaded Jase as she scooped up her bag and
left my hotel room. "See you at the shoot tomorrow," she
called smugly as the door slammed closed behind her. She's
probably on her way to the *Rolling Stone* offices right now,
taking notes on how all the haters are right about me.

I look over at my own iPad on the bed next to me and
feel tears well up in my eyes. I made the mistake of Googling
"Bird Barrett Hate Sites," and there were so many that I got

upset all over again. People hate me. People literally hate me. They don't even know me, but they want me to die or drink their urine or get blown up in the next terrorist attack. *Who are these people? What did I ever do to them?*

Tears stream down the sides of my face before I can stop them.

And my music. I work so hard on my music.

"Bird?" Adam calls from the living room.

Quickly, I sit up and wipe my face with my shirtsleeve. "What are you doing here?" I call.

"I came back for a heavier coat," he says, walking toward the bedroom, "but I must've grabbed the wrong key card earlier. I somehow got yours."

"Oh."

"We called and texted, but finally Stella and Dylan just went ahead and got in line and I thought I'd come back and pull you away—" He stops short when he sees my face, and his own looks really worried as he sits down on the bed beside me. "Hey, what's wrong?"

I start crying full out and lean against his chest, his arms wrapping around me immediately. "I messed up, Adam," I sob. "I just messed up so bad and Anita's going to kill me and Dan's going to be so mad and my fans—" I stop, taking a deep breath, before just crying harder. "My fans are going to hate me!"

"Bird," he whispers. He shushes me, rocks me, and

runs his fingers through my hair as I cry against his chest. "When you can," he says quietly, "tell me what happened."

I sniff, lean back, and reach over for a box of tissues. I hate that I'm crying like this in front of Adam, but at the same time, I love that he's here. "Ugh, I feel so stupid," I say. "I let her get to me. It was just like when I lost my temper with Kayelee on New Year's, and I'm so mad at myself. I try so hard to be nice to everybody, but when somebody pushes me and pushes me and pushes me, I explode."

He nods.

"And this reporter," I spit out. I blow my nose and shake my head. "She acted so cool this whole time. I'm following her on Instagram and everything, and I thought, you know, we might even stay in touch. But it's like she was just reeling me in. Like, 'This isn't an interview, Bird, you idiot. This is just a bunch of friends hanging out on tour for a few days.' And then, bam! She sits me down a while ago and shows me all these hate sites about me and mean tweets and memes and—" I exhale loudly. I take a shaky breath and go on. "I know I shouldn't care what people think about me, but I do. It hurts. They don't know how hard I work and how much I care about my music or what it was like to lose my brother and then ask my family to give up the one thing that kept us together during the worst time of our lives. They don't know anything, but they spew all this venom and—I don't get it."

Adam nods, his eyes filled with real concern.

"Why?" I ask, my eyes filling with fresh tears. "Why do they hate me, Adam?"

He gives me a small grin and kisses my temple. "Nobody hates you, Lady Bird," he says sweetly. "You're un-hate-able."

I scoff. "Not according to the I Hate Bird Barrett Facebook page," I say bitterly.

"You can't read that stuff," he says when I reach for my iPad. He turns it facedown and grabs my hands. "You can't let pathetic trolls—cowards who hide behind their computer screens at night—do this to you. You just can't let them. There are people out there who are so miserable that they're not happy unless someone else is miserable. They are broken and bruised and scarred, and the only way they can cope with the depressing lives they are forced to live is to try to bring other people down with them."

He is staring at me so intently that I finally nod. "I know," I say softly.

"You can't let broken people break you."

I sniff and reach for another tissue, letting his words sink in. "I like that," I say. "You're right."

"Good," he says. "Now what's this reporter's home address? I need to go egg her house."

"Adam!"

"Come on," he says, throwing an arm around my shoulders. He is grinning from ear to ear. "Wouldn't that be fun?"

"It'd be awesome," I admit.

I smile over at him, his face right next to mine, his impossibly long lashes low as his face softens. "I really want to kiss you right now, Lady Bird."

I gulp. "You should," I say quietly.

And so Adam leans in, his hand tightening around my shoulder as he draws closer, and I shut my eyes. His lips are so soft and perfect against mine that when our mouths meet my whole body melts into his as he pulls me near. It's not our first kiss, but it's gentle, it's sweet, and it's been a long time coming. My heart isn't skipping; my pulse isn't racing. My whole body is relaxed, comfortable, and content, like this is the person I was born to kiss. He pulls away a little, rubs his nose against the side of mine, and lays his forehead against my own. "Bird, I've wanted to do that again since that first time in my truck and every single time I've seen you since that day."

I pull back some and look him right in the eyes. "I was hoping you'd give us another chance," I admit softly. "With the tour and my schedule being so crazy—my life hasn't gotten any *less* complicated—I wasn't sure you'd want to try again."

"Oh, I do want to try again," he says, kissing me. "And again," he says, kissing the tip of my nose. "And again." He kisses both cheeks.

I laugh. "I was talking about 'us,' but this works, too."

Then Adam scrunches up his face and pulls away. He licks his tongue on the sleeve of his shirt.

"Oh, there's every girl's dream come true," I say sarcastically.

"No." He laughs. "I love kissing you, Bird. It's just—your makeup's smudged all over your cheeks and that last kiss..."

I grab a tissue and stand up, horrified after I run to the bathroom mirror and see my reflection. "I look like a zombie!"

"A cute zombie," he calls.

I turn on the water and grab my face wash, chagrined that Adam finally kissed me on the day I have mascara streaming down my cheeks and a runny nose. This is what Hollywood always gets wrong. The major moments are never flawless.

When I turn the water off, I hear music as I grab for a towel. I dry my face and apply some moisturizer, smiling as Adam picks out a melody on my guitar that I've never heard before.

"That's pretty," I remark, walking back to the bed.

He nods and grins up at me. "I think there may be a

song in this room." He stops playing and passes me my iPad. The only app open now is Notes, where he's typed, "Broken People."

" 'You can't let broken people break you,' " I say, repeating what he told me earlier.

He starts to play again and I nod my head, feeling the notes wrap around me like a warm hug. I start typing quick phrases, images flooding my brain as he strums, and I feel power in responding to the hate that had me in its grip before Adam walked in. Adam: this boy who's like my mirror image in so many ways.

There *is* a song in this room, one beating against my rib cage, one that we're going to write together.

17

"FLYING COMMERCIAL, HUH?" Adam jokes over the phone the next night as I deplane in Nashville. "Like a peasant?"

"Ha-ha," I say dryly. "There was some kind of maintenance issue with the label's jet, and I really wanted to get home." After our second show at Madison Square Garden, the rest of the tour headed back to Nashville while I stayed behind for my *Rolling Stone* shoot.

"Is Anita with you?" he asks.

"Nah, she wanted to stay and visit her family on Long Island. Big Dave is here," I say, glancing over my shoulder. A string of passengers file out behind me, and I lower my ball cap again, always feeling weird in disguise. "But yeah, I'm so glad I called her. She wasn't thrilled about me losing my cool in that last interview, but she took half the blame for leaving me alone with a reporter for so many days in a row."

"That's cool."

"Yeah."

"Was Jase there this morning?" he asks.

"Yeah, she skirted around the perimeter," I say, still feeling so stupid and betrayed. "But all the other people at *Rolling Stone* were really welcoming—even the photographer was easy to work with—so I tried to block Jase out and stay focused on how big-time it is to have a feature in their magazine."

"Good."

"And while Jase is intimidating, she's no match for Anita."

"Nobody is."

"Got that right," I say with a grin. I follow the signs toward baggage claim and switch my phone to the other ear, hoisting my carry-on bag up higher onto my shoulder. "You happy to be back home?" I ask. "A few days off and then a couple shows at Bridgestone. Feels like a vacation."

"It does," he says. "And I have plans."

I can hear the smile in his voice, and my heart flutters. "Oh, really?"

"I thought *maybe* you could do me the honor of a redo."

"A redo?"

"Yeah." He pauses before going on. "The real reason I

came up to your hotel room yesterday is because Stella and Dylan had helped me plan this second-first-kiss thing at the top of the Empire State Building."

"Oh no!" I say, stunned.

"No, listen, no big deal," he rushes on. "I still got my kiss."

I can picture his lopsided grin on the other end of the phone. "Yes, you did."

"But having to leave you in New York killed me. So I want a redo," he says.

I laugh out loud and say, "You going to kiss me at the top of the AT&T Building?"

"Oh, I have big plans," Adam says. "I'm going to date you like a normal person."

"Hey, I am a normal person!"

He laughs. "No! I mean, let's go to the movies, let's crash the bluegrass jam at the Station Inn, or get fried chicken and biscuits at the Loveless."

"Yes!" I say with a hop. "Let's be normal!"

I feel like skipping, like running through the terminals with my arms wide or riding the conveyor belt at baggage claim singing something from *The Sound of Music*.

But then I stop short, the person behind me nearly running me over, when I see a kiosk to my right with shelves stocked high with Bird Barrett merchandise. "Oh my gosh," I whisper.

"What?"

"This shop," I say as my feet, almost as if of their own volition, carry me over to the tiny store. I am stunned by what I see. Obviously, "merch" is a big part of being a performer—I know my label and manager are licensing my image and "brand," as Troy calls it—but I mostly leave those decisions up to my parents. Of course I've seen the T-shirts, posters, and hats, and I've autographed thousands upon thousands of CDs for sale at my concerts. But as I walk around this shop, letting my fingers graze Bird Barrett souvenirs and tchotchkes—magnets and mugs and pillows and playing cards—I am positively stunned. It's unnerving.

"What is it, Bird?"

"It's just—" I start. "There's all this 'Bird' stuff. Like, my face and my signature are everywhere."

"Well, you have to expect that stuff in Nashville," he says.

"No, but Adam, it's so much more than—" I stop. It's like I'm in a house of mirrors at a carnival. "Okay, the Bird Barrett doll is kind of cool, if a little creepy, and the calendar and the book are okay. But what in the world would someone want with a Bird Barrett robe or my face crocheted on a blanket?"

"Oh."

"Yeah."

"So I should hide my Bird Barrett Kleenex dispenser when you come over?"

I chuckle. "Yes, please."

"It's pretty cool, actually. You pull the tissues right out of your nose. Could've really come in handy yesterday."

"Adam, you do *not* have a Bird Barrett tissue box."

He laughs. "No, but I wish I did."

Then my eyes fall on a square magnet of me playing my fiddle. It's the only image in this whole shop of Bird Barrett wonders that I recognize as the real me. I snatch it without thinking, remembering some advice I got last year from Bonnie: *It's just very important that through it all, you remember who you really are.*

I place the magnet on the counter and reach for my wallet. "Just this, please."

"You're buying your own stuff?" Adam asks loudly through the phone.

"Shh," I say, setting my phone down as I pay.

I glance up at the cashier, knowing she'll recognize me and probably want me to sign a bunch of stuff or snap a picture with her. But she just scans the magnet, takes my five bucks, puts the souvenir in a gift bag, and hands me my change and receipt. Then she says, "Have a good evening, sweetie."

"You too," I say, stunned as I pick up my phone and walk away. It's surreal. I am totally separate from the image of me that I'm selling. "Well, Mr. Dean, maybe the normal-person mini-break has already begun."

"She didn't recognize you?" he asks incredulously. "And she's surrounded by your face all day long?"

"I took a page from the Adam Dean Pro Disguises Handbook," I joke as I pass through the security checkpoint. "I'm in sweats and no makeup. Nobody suspects a thing."

"Well, I'd know you anywhere," he says, and suddenly I feel strong arms wrap around my back and his face appears next to mine.

"Adam!" I scream.

He spins me around to face him, and I don't even know what to say. I just stare at him, blinking, with my mouth in an O.

Adam is here.

I know he wants to kiss me as badly as I want to kiss him, but I can also see that he is aware of the people all around us. So he just takes my bag, and as if floating on a cloud, I follow him through the airport. Like a normal person. WELCOME TO NASHVILLE, a sign says near the baggage area, and with Adam at my side, there's nowhere else on earth I'd rather be.

"So this is our redo?" I ask as Adam parks his truck at Percy Warner Park.

"Consider this whole week in Nashville one giant series of redos," he says, getting out.

I step out of the truck as well, taking in the gorgeous October day and my handsome hiking partner. "This will be fun."

"Yeah, and Yelp said this place is romantic"—he stops and makes air quotes—" 'yet public enough in case you still don't know if your date is certifiably insane.' "

I laugh. "I know your brand of insanity isn't certifiable, so I'm not worried."

He grins. "Maybe I was worried about yours."

I swat his arm, and he grabs my hand, squeezing it as he leads me toward a hiking trail. We walk a little ways and are soon hidden from the world, under a dense overhanging of trees with leaves just starting to change colors. I hear the buzz of forest life, so peaceful and yet so alive with birds chirping and twigs snapping beneath our steps. "I do kind of love that you researched your redo date," I say now.

"Hey, when you go and botch something as epic as the Empire State Building, a guy has to dig."

I smile and we walk. I trail behind him when the path gets narrow, and he helps me up when things get steep. About twenty minutes in, I've definitely worked up a little sweat and it feels good to be outside and free, the very opposite of being cramped on a tour bus. "This is awesome," I say when we walk past a bunch of wildflowers. "Adam, look. They're so pretty."

"They really are."

"Wildflowers remind me of you now," I admit, linking my fingers through his. Ever since I told Adam I was named for Lady Bird Johnson, a First Lady of the United States from the sixties who was crazy about wildflowers, he's gone out of his way to get me flowers. Twice I've gotten hand-picked bouquets, and he even sent me wild poppies when I moved to California.

"You know," he says, "I used to hike around Lady Bird Lake in Austin all the time."

"Really?"

He nods. "It was so crazy because we had just, um, left things alone between us, and I'd moved to Texas to work on my music and, you know, free myself of any distractions. And then bam! There you were smack in the middle of the city I moved to."

I chew on my lip and start walking again, thinking back to that time and how heartbroken I was when he moved away. I liked Adam so much, thought about him constantly, dreamed of going out with him; then it finally happened and he dropped me faster than a hot potato.

"Anyway," he says after some silence. "Made me think of you every time I was downtown."

"I thought about you a lot after you left, too," I say, letting go of his hand.

"I wish I could say I shouldn't have left, but I think it

was good for me," he says. "Got my demo, met some cool people, signed with the label. All good things."

I nod, feeling my throat constrict, surprised by the sudden emotion rising up in my chest.

"You okay?" he asks as we walk over a wooden bridge.

I nod and step ahead of him.

"Bird, wait," he says, pulling me back. He stares at my face while I look beyond the bridge, watching as the water from a small creek flows over the smooth rocks below. "What's wrong?"

"Nothing," I say, swallowing hard. I do not want to get emotional right now. We're having a fantastic day on our first "normal" date, so the last thing I want to do is ruin it by hiking down a dark patch of memory lane. "Just tired. Might rest a sec."

I squat, sitting down on the bridge and letting my legs dangle over the edge, studying my sneakers as they swing back and forth over the water. The rushing sound is so soothing. I stare at a feather caught in a little whirlpool, wondering how long until it frees itself and carries on. Adam waits a bit and then sits down next to me, cautiously, as if feeling me out. *Ugh, I've already made things weird.*

"Hey," he says. "Talk to me."

I sigh, closing my eyes.

"What is it?" Adam asks softly. He squeezes my shoulder. "You know you can tell me anything."

I open my eyes and watch the ripples dance in the stream, deciding to be honest. Even if it's painful, I'll just be honest. If it goes badly, maybe I'll get a chart topper out of the deal.

"This might sound crazy, but when you brought up Austin and how you left..." I glance up at him and then back down at my hands. "It just—that was a hard time for me. I was really into you, I was crazy about you, and then it seemed like the minute things got hard, you left. Sayonara. Peace. The end."

He looks puzzled. "You had a lot going on. *A lot.* And I wasn't really sure you were all that into me, to be honest."

I stare at him. "Are you serious?"

"Bird, we only went out one time," he says. "And you squeezed me in at, like, six thirty in the morning."

"I had to finish my album!"

"Right, and you had to do publicity stuff all the time, like that date with Jason Samuels—"

"That was *not* a date," I interject.

"Okay, but it was just another major thing going on in your life that, I don't know, was more important than me," he says quietly.

"And then I missed your show," I say, groaning as I drop my head into my hands. "I'm sure that was another red flag on top of the Jason red flag that all added up to *she's not really into me*, when, Adam, I totally was." I look up at him, feeling so vulnerable as I search his eyes and my heart picks up pace. "I just feel like maybe we could've, I don't know, made it if it weren't for that whole debacle."

"Looking back on it all, I think it was timing," he says honestly. "But yeah, missing my show..." Now he looks away. "Truthfully, that one hurt. I was really into you, and I wanted you to hear my new stuff." Embarrassed, he glances over at me. "You're not the only one who's written a song about a crush, you know."

My heart cracks a little. He had written a song for me. And I missed it.

"And I saved you a seat—"

"Ugh, that sad glass of Coke at the bar!"

"It was supposed to be a romantic gesture," he says.

"It was so sweet." I pause. "It killed me."

"So anyway, I knew you couldn't make it to *my* performance because *you* were performing. I knew you didn't really have time for a boyfriend, or whatever, because you were in the studio all the time. And then I knew there'd be press and a tour and everybody would see how special and talented you are and..." He looks up at me and simply but softly says, "I guess I just wanted to end it before you accidentally broke my heart."

Tears completely blur my vision. "I'm sorry, Adam."

He smiles. "But it was timing, Bird. Don't you see? Maybe all of that had to happen so we could be right here right now."

He starts to move toward me, but a group of hikers appear out of nowhere and trod over the bridge behind us. The second they're gone, he grabs my face and pulls me toward him with urgency. We've laid it all out and we want to risk our hearts again...for each other. We sit on this wooden bridge in the middle of the gorgeous Tennessee landscape and we kiss and kiss and kiss, wrapped up in this new, old feeling.

18

"So he dropped you off last night, and you left it how?" Stella asks a few days later. We're hanging out at her mom's apartment in East Nashville, and I'm debriefing her on all the time I've spent with Adam lately, going to the movies, eating out, watching TV, just being together like a normal couple. It's been amazing.

"We left it at, I don't know," I say. "At good night."

"And you're boyfriend-girlfriend now?" she asks.

"Um, I wouldn't say that," I say, shifting in my seat.

"What do you mean? You're not official?"

"We haven't really talked about it."

"Bird!" she says impatiently. "You've been inseparable all week and you didn't DTR?"

"They've only been more than friends for a few days,"

Shannon says as she joins us on the couch with a big bowl of chips. "Give them a minute to figure it out."

"Mom," Stella says dramatically. "This is not their first take, okay? And this go 'round they have already taken it *so slow.*"

"Well, not everybody locks it down after one kiss," I say pointedly. "You and Dylan got together and it went from zero to sixty."

Stella glances at her mom and then shoots me a look, and I realize that as cool as Shannon is, Stella might not want me giving a tell-all interview here.

"I just mean that with Adam and me," I recover, turning the convo back around, "I think we're both a little gun-shy. It didn't work out the first time and now—"

"Now you're getting a second chance!" Stella interrupts. Then she bats her lashes and adds, "And it's *so* convenient for double-dating."

Shannon smiles. "Well, I'm happy for you both. But the guys should be here soon, and I have work to do. You going to watch the movie in here?"

"Is that okay?" Stella asks.

"Yeah, I'll close the door." Shannon gets up and heads to her work space, an amazing little in-home studio that was the inspiration for the one I had built in our new Nashville house.

"Adam was so sweet after the *Rolling Stone* thing," I

say when I'm alone with Stella again. "I'm still freaking out about what Jase will print."

"She's a snake," Stella says bitterly. "But forget her. The problem at hand is Adam plus Bird equals Adird. Ew. Or Birdam." I roll my eyes and she giggles. "Okay, well, your names don't go together but *y'all* do! I say you lock it down. You were meant for each other."

"Yeah," I say with a smile. "I guess there's really nothing keeping us from being exclusive—"

"Exactly!" she says. "Not like a psycho ex-girlfriend or something."

I look at her quizzically.

"Whitney's been tagging Dylan in some throwback Instagram pics lately, and it makes me want to murder somebody."

"Whitney Jehn?" I ask, shocked. "But she broke up with Dylan forever ago."

"Well, now his little sister's famous and he's on tour," she says, clearly annoyed. "And the worst part is that she's making problems in *our* relationship."

"How?"

Stella looks at me like I'm stupid. "Um, maybe because I've acted crazy jealous about it, like, twice now, which makes me even madder because that is so not me. But I don't like my boyfriend rekindling a friendship with his ex."

"I don't think you should worry about her," I say. "She was okay, but she's no Stella Crossley."

Stella rolls her eyes.

"And anyway," I go on, "he's obviously in love with you."

"Did he say that?" Stella asks, her eyes wide. "Bird, did Dylan tell you that? We haven't said it yet."

I wince, this being the exact kind of conversation I try to avoid. "I mean, it's pretty obvious, right?"

She frowns. "So he didn't say it?"

I exhale. "I don't know what to tell you..."

"You tell me the truth," she snaps. "God, Bird! Channing Tatum's ex-girlfriend is trying to worm her way back into his life, and your *best friend* is feeling a little crazy-girl about it and could use some reassurance."

"Okay, well, *Channing Tatum* also happens to be my brother, so it gets a little complicated sometimes," I fire back.

"Whatever," she says, rolling her eyes again.

"Yeah, whatever is right," I say with the same level of attitude. "I don't need this right now, okay? Neither of our boy problems is as stressful as what a national magazine might print about me after my blowup the other night, so I've sort of got some real problems to worry about."

Stella looks like I've slapped her in the face. "Oh, *real* problems? Okay, my bad. I'll take my fake problems and leave you alone." She grabs the remote and turns on the TV, fuming. I feel like I should apologize, but I also feel like *she* should apologize. I made it crystal clear when "Stylan" got together that I didn't want to be in the middle of it—*ever*— and this conversation is a perfect example of why.

"Stella—" I start.

But the doorbell rings and she stands up before we can smooth things over. "Whatever. They're here."

While she goes to answer the door, I get on Instagram, trying to do a little digging on this ex-girlfriend situation. I used to want to kill Whitney for breaking my brother's heart, but now I want to wring her neck for causing me unnecessary drama.

"If you'll recall," Stella announces as they all enter the living room, "we watched a shoot-'em-up movie last time, so Bird and I get to pick today. I think I want something serious, an indie maybe, something with *real problems*, you know?"

My jaw drops. *Did she really just take it there? In front of the guys?*

Dylan crashes on the big chair-and-a-half and Stella plops down next to him, her legs over his. "'Sup, Bird," he says, as she aims the remote at the flat screen. I shoot him an annoyed look and he looks surprised. "What's your problem?"

Stella whips her head around, giving me a *let it go* look that reminds me I'm not supposed to know about their fights. But that just irks me even more. *If I'm not supposed to know, don't tell me!*

"Just some big-star stuff," Stella says, waving me off. "You know, real problems."

"Hey, you," Adam says, sitting next to me.

I take a deep breath and shake off the Stylan drama. Instead, I focus on Adam's cute smile and force my happy back. "Hey to you."

Stella searches the guide, and for every romantic comedy she suggests, the guys groan or try to talk us into some alien or war movie they see on the list. Then finally, Stella's face lights up, and she clicks on Jason Samuels's last movie, the one with my song in it. "Winner! This is the best of both worlds. It's got war for you boys, it's got Bird's hottie ex-boyfriend Jason Samuels for her, and it's chock-full of national suffering, dying, and *real problems*. What do you think?"

She looks over at me with a huge fake smile on her face, and I feel my own flush.

"You know, I don't even think I'm up for a movie," I say. I stand and grab my bag.

"Bird, come on," Stella says, annoyed. "I was just joking."

"We see each other all the time," I say, trying to fake lightheartedness. "And I told my mom I'd help her in her garden today."

"Fine," Stella says. "See you at Bridgestone tomorrow."

"Super."

I walk toward the front door, my blood boiling, and I don't even know what just happened. What I do know is that my real life has been hard enough lately without dealing with Stylan drama or her ideas of where I should be in my own relationship.

"Bird," Adam calls in the hallway. I press the DOWN button on the elevator and wait for him. "Hey, are you okay?"

"Yeah, totally."

The doors open and I walk on, Adam right behind me.

"You're not okay," he says, standing near me. I press L and stand next to him, leaning into his side as he wraps an arm around me.

"Just something stupid with Stella," I say.

"Everything okay?"

"Yeah, I don't even really know what happened," I say with a shrug. "Just stuff about Dylan, and Jase . . . and you."

He nods, not prying. "Too much time together."

"Probably." The elevator doors open and as we step off, I catch a glimpse of us together in the mirror. "Not too much with you, though."

I already feel better now that I'm alone with Adam.

He throws his arm over my shoulder, and I wrap mine around his waist as we head outside. I lean against him as we walk, trying to shake off my sour mood. "Honestly, part of me doesn't even want to go back out on tour," I admit. "Which is ridiculous because this is my dream. But all week it's been like we're regular people, you know? No autographs or pictures or screaming fans."

"Yeah, it's definitely been more calm."

"I guess I've just felt like the old me this week. And I've loved it."

At my car, he takes my keys away and leans me up against the driver's door, placing a hand on the window at either side of my head. "Hey," he says intently, looking me straight in the eyes. "I don't know what you mean about feeling like the old you, but the fame and all that? You handle it more gracefully than I ever could."

I lean forward to peck him on the lips. "Thank you."

He rocks back and grabs my hips, shaking me from side to side playfully. "Really. I watch you all the time and think, 'Take notes, Adam.'"

"Oh, please," I say, rolling my eyes. "You're a natural."

"Not like you. Like with the way that reporter treated you and then facing her at the photo shoot the very next day, that took real courage." He looks at me with sincere admiration, and I feel myself blush. "I don't think I could've done it. And how generous you are with your fans, how you retweet them all the time and give one hundred percent at every single show. It's inspiring." He kisses my forehead. "And it's exactly like the Bird I knew way back when."

"Agh," I say, as unexpected tears spring to my eyes. I grab the hem of my T-shirt, dab at my eyes, and laugh as I say, "I think you may be blinded by love."

I stop cold. I can't believe I just used the *L* word.

Luckily, Adam laughs it off. He steps back, unlocks my car, and hands me my keys. "You really going to hang out with your mom?" he asks.

"Yeah, I told her I'd be by in a few hours, but I think I'll go on now," I say. "Which means you and I will have more time to hang out later."

"Cool," Adam says, looking past me. "Maybe I'll go see my mom, too."

"Oh," I say, surprised. I don't know all the particulars, but I know they're not close. He always crashes with friends when he's in Nashville instead of staying with her.

"I've texted her a few times today and haven't heard back. Just might check in."

"You know, I'd love to meet her," I say. "I could go with you."

Adam looks back at me, and I can't read his expression. He rarely opens up about his past, and I bite my lip, worried I crossed a line but also really hoping he says yes. He knows my family; I want to know his.

He twists his mouth, contemplating.

I lace my fingers into his and press on, "Let me drive you over there. If you want me to come inside, I will. If you just want me to drop you and go, I'll do that."

Adam scratches his head and kicks at a piece of asphalt at his feet. Finally he nods and says, "Okay."

He walks around to the passenger side, and we get into the car. I start the engine as he settles into the seat next to me, pulling on his seat belt, rolling down his window, and staring out into the sunny day. I turn the radio on, knowing not to push conversation right now. I wonder if he'll let me come inside. I wonder if I upset him by inviting myself. Clearly the topic of his mom is touchy, but I want to be part of his life, the good and the bad. I want to be there for him in every way.

Because I'm dating him, yeah, but also because...I think I might be in love with him.

Do I love Adam?

As I pull out of the parking lot, I think about how quickly a person can go from a first kiss to the real thing. But how do you know if it's really love? I thought I fell in love with Kai last summer, but now I barely think about him. And even though Adam and I aren't "official," I feel like there's so much more at stake.

I sneak a glance over at Adam, his shaggy hair blowing around, his unshaven jawline tense. If it doesn't work out with us this time, my heart may well break into a million pieces, and for the rest of my life, anyone I ever meet will immediately know I'm damaged goods.

⟡

"Okay, so I don't know how to prepare you for this," Adam says nervously. Truthfully, I think he's glad I'm here, but I can't imagine having this much anxiety about introducing anyone to either of my parents. His knuckles were tense and white on his knees the whole drive over, and his body is rigid, like he's turning to stone right in front of my eyes. As we get out of the car, he says, "Make sure you lock it."

The apartment building looks like an old motel. The place is clearly run-down, paint chipped on the doors and a few windows boarded up. "Is this where you grew up?" I ask Adam quietly as I follow him across the parking lot.

"No," he answers crisply.

And that's all I get.

We climb up some old metal stairs to the second floor, and he heads right for apartment number 6. Before pounding on the door, he takes a quick breath, and I watch him visibly steel himself. I wasn't worried when I asked to come along, but the guy standing in front of me is suddenly unfamiliar, and now I'm feeling pretty nervous, too.

"Mom!" he yells as he pounds on the door. "Angela, you in there?"

I hear movement, maybe a chair scraping against the floor or something, and I hear voices. Adam must, too, because he lowers his arm and takes a step back.

"It's not Roger," I hear someone say in a very loud whisper...someone who can't judge their current volume level. "Oh hell, it's my son." I know before she opens the door that Adam's mom has been drinking, and from the heartbreaking look of disappointment on his face, Adam knows it, too.

"Let's go," he says, nudging me back down the hall while we hear her fiddle with the locks.

"Adam?" a woman's voice calls from a few feet behind us. "Adam, where you going?"

He stops. Takes a breath. Turns back around. "Hey, Mom," he says, affecting a friendly demeanor that doesn't reach his eyes. "Just wanted to check on you. I thought you'd be at Aunt Lu's earlier, and I was worried when you didn't show up."

She smacks her forehead. "Was that today? Oh hell, I completely forgot all about that." Then she squints her eyes and takes a few shaky steps toward us. "Who's this pretty little thing you got with you?" she slurs.

But before either of us can answer, recognition registers on her face and she immediately stands up straighter. "Holy smokes, you're Bird Barrett."

She stares at me, astonishment all over her face, and I nod. "I am."

She hurriedly runs her hands through her hair and tucks in her wrinkled T-shirt. "It is such a pleasure to meet you. I'm a huge fan. Huge fan. You are just a superstar."

I let her shake my hand until I worry it may fall off, then I manage to remove it from her clutch and grab Adam's arm. "Your son's something else, too. He's been an absolute godsend for my tour."

"I didn't realize y'all were friends," his mom says, shooting him a mean look like he should've warned her. "I figured you just let him play a few songs at your shows."

"Oh no," I say. "Adam has been an important part of my life for a long time."

Her mouth opens in surprise. "A long time?"

"Yeah, way before I was famous, Adam was there."

"Well, I'll be," she says softly, glancing at her son accusatorially. I feel like I've said something wrong.

Adam's arm clenches in my hand, and he starts to back up. "Okay, Mom. Well, I'm glad everything's okay. Just wanted to check in."

"Don't run off, now you're here," she practically shouts, grabbing my arm and pulling me back toward her apartment. "I got to get you to sign something. And my friend Lacy loves your music, too. And Jeanne! Oh, Jeanne from down at number five has hair just like yours. From a bottle, but the color is close, I'm telling you, just like yours."

I look at Adam for help, but he is clearly just as surprised as I am. She yells, "Lacy! You'll never believe who's out here. It's Bird Barrett! The real Bird Barrett from that song. *Just rise! And fly!*" she sings at the top of her lungs. Her breath is so skunked I have to turn away.

"Oh, we're flying all right," a woman says, stepping out of unit 6 and cackling. She's holding a fifth of Jim Beam in one hand and a cigarette in the other. "Well, butter my butt and call me a biscuit, it really is her." But instead of introducing herself, she starts pounding on doors, shouting, "Bird Barrett is here! Y'all ain't gonna believe it!"

"Adam," I say in a low, worried voice. People from the courtyard below look up at the commotion, and I suddenly wish I'd thought to bring a bodyguard.

"Mom, let go of her arm," Adam says, stepping between us.

"Well, I just want her to come sign a few things for me," his mom snaps. "Don't want Miss Bird to go *fly* away now." She laughs hysterically at her own pun—wheezing, her voice rough like sandpaper—and waves us inside her dark apartment. We only step far enough inside the front door that I can get out of sight from her neighbors, but it's so dank and dirty that I can't believe someone actually lives here.

"Here's my CD from your first album," she says, frantically looking around for a marker. She runs out to the hall and shouts, "Lacy! Bring a marker!" Then back inside she says, "And maybe you could sign a T-shirt for me. This one I'm wearing is fine. And what else, what else . . . a coffee mug maybe or this Doritos bag . . . you could sign anything really."

The kitchen table is small and covered with packs of cigarettes, a couple of ashtrays, and at least five empty whiskey bottles. There are clothes strewn around the apartment, and the furniture looks like generic motel pieces, like the place was rented out this way. When she brings me a stack of completely random things to sign and a ballpoint pen, it hits me that she's going to sell it all—that she wants my signature to pay for the next round.

"Mom, we have to go," Adam says, taking the pen from her and putting it on the table. "Bird's not feeling well, and I need to get her home."

"Adam, something. Anything. She can sign just this piece of paper even, or maybe you can take a picture of us with your phone. Would that be all right?" she asks, throwing her arm around me.

Adam hesitates, but I want desperately to get out of here. "Sure," I say, leaning down and quickly scrawling my *BB* on her scrap piece of paper.

Then when Adam lifts his phone she wraps her arm around my waist, pinning my arms, and yells, "Cheese!" like a little kid. Once he takes a few quick shots, she calms down a little bit. "You print and get me that, okay? Print me a few."

"Okay, Mom," Adam says, leading me back out to the hallway, where a crowd has started to gather. "You take care. Call Aunt Lu if you need something."

"Can't I call you?" she asks, hanging back in the doorway. Then, in an awful attempt to whisper, she says, "You said you were going to help me out with rent this month."

"I did, Mom," he says. "You're covered for the next three months. I sent it to the office already 'cause I knew I'd be out of town."

"You gave *my* money to that crook downstairs?" she cries. "He'll steal it! He'll throw me out!"

"I have a receipt, Mom," Adam says. "You're good."

"I'm not good!" she shouts. "I need that money! I need it! And you gave it away?" At this point a few people in the now-crowded outdoor hallway have asked for a picture or an autograph, and I'm smiling like a ceramic doll as they snap away, still in shock that this is how my day is ending as I sign whatever they pass me.

"I took care of your rent, Mom," he fires back. "You're welcome."

"Oh, I'm supposed to thank you?" she spits. "If it weren't for me, you wouldn't be nothing."

"Yeah, you were my motivation all right," he growls.

"Adam?" I say through a tight smile as I pose for a picture with Lacy's boyfriend. What he lacks in teeth he more than makes up for in facial hair, and he is way too close for comfort.

Adam exhales loudly. "We have to go," he says as he backs away and throws one arm around my shoulders. He parts the crowd with the other. "I'm sorry, Mom."

"*You're* sorry?" I whisper, incredulous. "Sorry for paying her rent?"

"Not now, Bird," he scolds, pushing people to the side as we work our way to the stairs. By the time we're down to the parking lot, there is a little group of curious onlookers gathered near my car, too. The people upstairs wave from the balcony, and someone starts up an off-key, pub-style chorus of "Shine Our Light" that just makes me sad.

Once I'm behind the wheel, I lock my door and reach over to open Adam's. Out his window I see a toddler in a diaper standing in one of the first-floor doorways. It breaks my heart. It literally brings tears to my eyes.

"This is how you grew up?" I ask gently once we are safely out of the parking lot and back on the main road.

"It was a little better than that," he says. We are quiet for a few blocks, both of us lighter with each stop sign we put between his mom's place and ourselves. "But not much," he admits.

I look over at him, so clearly hurting but also so accustomed to a life that is unfathomable to me. I reach my right hand over and squeeze his knee, wanting to touch him and let him know that I am here—that I will take care of him—that I can be his family.

"You know, she went to college. She was a nurse. She helped a lot of people before my dad left," he says, almost like he's defending her. He looks out his window and goes on. "But after that I guess she drank 'cause she was sad. And then she drank when she went out on dates and stuff. And then she drank on her long stretches of days off."

"Do you ever see your dad?" I ask.

"Nah, when he left he left for good," Adam says. "I guess that's one thing about my mom; she didn't abandon me. She might've disappeared a lot, but she always came back."

I purse my lips together tightly, knowing what I want to say won't help: *seems like abandonment to me.*

"I'm sorry you had to see that," he says. "She's really not bad when she's sober."

I nod, not sure what to say.

He swallows. "She's just hardly ever sober."

Again, I'm not sure what to say. So I start to sing, softly. I want him to hear the tune of the song we just wrote together: "Broken People." I want him to hear the chorus in his head as we drive:

"He said they'll try to knock you down, they'll
    break your heart in two.
But you can't let broken people break you."

19

"ARE YOU TRYING to kill me?" I snap at Marco several days later when I run into the wings for my encore. Jordan passes me a hand towel and a bottle of water, but I feel like I could use a chair, too. The crowd is on their feet, begging for "Shine Our Light" as always, but ever since we left Nashville, the tour has been going nonstop and I'm exhausted.

"What do you mean?" he asks, eyes narrowed.

"Six shows this week?" I ask hoarsely. I guzzle some water and continue. "Six shows in seven days? That's insane."

He matches his attitude to my own when he replies, "You were at the scheduling meetings, Bird. Remember how you wanted to 'go hard'? *I* do." He does a very effeminate impression of me. "'More shows, Marco. I want to go hard.'"

I lean my head back and stare at the rigging overhead as a couple of people chuckle nearby. I do remember that. I also remember Marco telling me that by this point of the tour, most artists get into a funk and need a little downtime, although I don't really want to bring that up now. He knows he was right. The bags under my eyes ought to tell him as much.

"Okay," I say, looking back at him. "But a, that's a horrible impression of me. And b, next time, you need to use your veto."

He gives me a sassy grin. "I have one?"

"Bird, you ready to get back out there?" Jordan asks. The band is huddled around her podium, and when I nod, they walk back onstage to ecstatic fans.

I jump up and down in place, trying to reenergize myself. "Let's do this," I say, exchanging my water and towel for a microphone.

"Go hard, now!" Marco shouts behind me.

I don't even turn around. I just slap my butt and take the stage to the sound of his uproarious laughter.

"Knock, knock!" Marco calls from the front of my bus later before we head out. "I come bearing gifts!"

I dry my face and reach for my moisturizer, rubbing it

189

in as I go see what he's got. After the breakneck schedule we've been on, all I want to do is sleep for days.

"Yes! Thanks, buddy," Dylan says, taking the box of pizza from Marco's hands. "I'm starving."

"You're always starving," Stella and I say at the same time, but my voice comes out raspy. I hope I'm not getting sick. I *cannot* get sick right now.

"And a couple of things for just you, Bird," he says. "This packet from Anita. She FedExed it over today and said you should review it."

I roll my eyes. "Probably talking points for the radio interviews in Texas."

"*And* a little something from me," he says, holding out a small white envelope. I take it hesitantly and look at him with a skeptical expression. "What?" he asks. "Can't a guy do something nice for his favorite artist?"

I tear open the envelope and gasp when I pull out the printed piece of paper inside. "A full spa treatment at the hotel?"

"Three o'clock," he says. "I think your parents land in Fort Worth around noon, and your schedule is open the rest of the night, so relax. You've got another big week after this."

I groan. "Don't remind me."

He grins but also looks at me with real concern. "Listen, take it easy. Your schedule is brutal, so make time for rest. It's important."

"Thank you, Marco," I say.

He squeezes my arm. "You work hard. You deserve a break."

I must really be exhausted because all of a sudden I feel like I could cry. I clutch my T-shirt at my chest and say, "Thank you so much. Really."

"It's a spa package, not a Grammy," Dylan teases through a mouthful of pizza.

But it's so much more than just getting a massage. Marco exits the bus and I walk back to my room, staring at the certificate. In the "for" line it says:

GOING HARD. BECAUSE YOU ALWAYS DO.

And it's not that I feel like I deserve a medal or anything—I mean, it's my tour; I *should* be giving one hundred percent every day—but it's nice that someone noticed.

"Bird," my dad whispers, stirring me from my sleep.

After the tour pulled into Fort Worth, I spent the afternoon at the hotel spa getting the most heavenly facial, a luxurious pedicure, and then an absolute dream of a massage. Literally, I fell asleep and dreamed right through the massage. I don't think I've had that much alone time since the tour started, and it hit me that constantly being around people is almost as draining as performing for them. It was so blissful to be alone and just *be*.

After my afternoon of pampering, I went upstairs to shower and get ready for dinner but must have fallen asleep. "I hate to wake you," my dad says now, "but I'm assuming you'd want me to get you up in time for dinner, right?"

"Huh?" I ask, looking over at the hotel clock. I napped for forty-five minutes, but rather than feeling refreshed, I feel like the victim of a cruel joke. "When's the reservation?"

"Seven thirty," he says.

"Mmmmm." I stretch and consider if I can squeeze in fifteen more minutes.

"Anita called me," he goes on. "Said she thought she'd have heard from you by now."

"About what?" I ask groggily.

"She said she sent you the images from your *Rolling Stone* photo shoot and wanted to know what you thought."

"What?" I'm up in a flash, stumbling over to my bag for the manila envelope Marco gave me last night. "I thought these were notes for my radio interviews in the morning."

"Oh, she mentioned that, too, but I think she said she e-mailed those."

I sit back on the bed beside my dad and carefully peel open the top flap. When I pull out the thick, slick paper inside and see the contact sheet, I feel shaky. I knew this session was unlike any I'd done before, but I wasn't sure I'd be able to pull it off. As I peruse the thumbnails, scanning the different poses and outfits, I hardly recognize myself.

"May I?" my dad asks as I turn over the contact sheet and stare at an 8 x 10 with a Post-it from Anita.

"Yeah, sure," I say absentmindedly.

Congratulations, Bird. There isn't a more deserving musician for this honor.
xo Anita

"I made the cover," I whisper.

"What?"

I look up at my dad, my eyes wide. "This is a cover mock-up. I made the cover of *Rolling Stone* magazine."

"Oh, Bird, honey, that's fantastic!" he says, his joy mirroring my own.

We hear the hotel door slam and my dad shouts, "Aileen, that you?"

"We're back!" my mom shouts.

"You have to get in here and see this," he says, taking the contact sheet into the living room portion of the suite. "Bird just got her *Rolling Stone* pictures. She's going to be on the cover!"

"You are going to be on the cover of *Rolling Stone* magazine?" Stella screams, racing into our bedroom. She jumps on the bed and tackles me with a giant hug. "Oh my God, that's so freaking crazy awesome amazing, I can't!"

I'm laughing and also fighting back tears. The shock, the honor, it's just overwhelming. I've been on covers before, but to be on the front of *Rolling Stone*? I can hardly breathe.

"Let me see those pictures," my mom says, snatching the stack off the bed before I've even gotten a good look.

"I just texted Dylan," Stella says. "They're on their way over. This is so exciting!"

As my mom goes through the pictures, she passes them to my dad, who passes them to me. Stella is right over my shoulder, checking out each image with narrowed eyes. When the guys come in, she passes them on to Dylan and then Adam.

"Who is that?" Dylan asks. He's not being mean. If I hadn't been at the shoot myself, I wouldn't recognize me right away, either. I've never seen myself look so *editorial*. They used extremely dramatic makeup, dark intense eyes, and metallic glitter powder over my face. My normally flowing red waves were pulled back in a sleek ponytail, and the way the light caught my face, it's as if there are curves and contours I've never seen before. And I knew the wardrobe was edgy—I mean, I wore it after all—but somehow in the photographs I look fierce, sexy even, in a way that I couldn't see in the mirror.

Stella mumbles as she studies the images, already talking to herself about which is her favorite, which styling choices she likes—and which she doesn't—as well as what each picture says.

"I'll tell you what they say." My mom takes off her glasses and looks up at me, disappointment all over her face. "They say, 'I am a pretty girl who looks ten years older in these pictures than she ought to.'"

"Mom!"

"I mean it, Bird," she says. She picks up the cover image. "People are going to be walking through the grocery aisles and seeing this. You think they're going to buy it for their daughters?"

"I doubt *Rolling Stone* is sold in the express lane of the Piggly Wiggly, Mom," Dylan says. "What do you think, Adam?"

He shrugs. "She got the cover. I think it's cool."

"I didn't say it wasn't cool," my mom says, clearly flustered. "I just think they could've made her look a little more like herself. She's a beautiful girl. Why slather all this makeup on her?"

"And would it have killed them to put some clothes on you?" My dad finally speaks up, standing and unable to meet my gaze.

"Dad, it's a bandage dress," I say. "I'm wearing clothes."

"A black-and-gray dress, leather or something a biker would wear, and so tight it looks like you were sewn into it." He gestures around his chest, and while his dramatics are pretty embarrassing, even I have to admit I am surprised to see cleavage. "I knew better than to miss that shoot," he grumbles. "I knew it."

"Dad, the stylists had a specific vision," I say, defending the images. They don't look at all how I'd expected, either, but I do like them. I think I do really like them.

I pick one up, looking closely at my stare, at how defiant it feels. I see the Bird my mom can't, the one who's headlining a national tour and who's in charge of her own career at eighteen, the one who is tired of everyone else telling her who she is.

A small smile settles onto my lips. It's surreal to hold these images in my hands, pictures that represent an enormous accomplishment in any musician's career. I still don't know what Jase will write, and I'm a little uneasy about the kind of story that will accompany photos like these, but I made the cover of *Rolling Stone* magazine.

My dad shakes his head. "I need to play a stronger role here," he says to himself.

I roll my eyes at Dylan, who makes a face that lets me know he has my back.

"Congratulations on the cover, Bird. You deserve it," my mom finally says, walking around the bed. "I just don't like seeing my baby this grown-up." She kisses me on the forehead and says, "Judd? Take a walk?"

He nods. None of us say a word as we hear them grab

their stuff and leave, but the minute the door closes, I get real reactions.

Stella grabs her favorite and holds it up to my face. "Are you kidding me? You are a ten! Suh-mokin' hot! I hope they use this one as a spread."

"It's weird to say this about my sister, but this is kind of like looking at a model," Dylan says. "And it's strange to see you not smiling."

Adam has remained pretty quiet throughout the whole exchange, which makes me nervous. "What do you think?" I ask.

He sits on the bed and rubs his hand across his jaw, the stubble making a scratchy noise. "They're pretty," he says simply. "They look like a fantasy version of you, I guess. Like you're in a futuristic space movie or something, but then I still see the real you there, too. Like in this one." He points to a close-up of me playing Maybelle, my fiddle, a traditionally bluegrass instrument in such a stark juxtaposition to the crazy hair and makeup. "That's my favorite."

I beam at him. "I like that one, too."

"I feel like I can really hear you playing," he says. Then he looks up at me and says, "I miss that."

I frown. "I fiddle almost every night."

"For the show," he says. "But we never just jam out anymore, you know?" He looks up at Dylan. "We need to play for fun sometime."

"Definitely."

I stay quiet. When I dream of such a thing as free time, playing music is the last thing on my mind. Sleep, yes. Netflix, yes. Playing music after playing music nonstop? Not exactly at the top of the list.

"But the cover," Adam says, staring at the mock-up again. Then he looks up at me with his lopsided grin and says, "Now, that is something to celebrate."

20

"WE JUST WANT a ride!" the emcee of the Stockyards Championship Rodeo calls over the mic. "Just a ride. Come on, folks, let's cheer him on. Local boy, real Texan spitfire from right here in Fort Worth, and he's going to do it! He's going to do it! Come on!"

We are on a double date, Stella and Dylan, Adam and I, and on our feet. This kid seems like some sort of crowd favorite. He went the full eight seconds on quite an angry bull earlier, and now I'm watching him lay on a bareback, broncing horse, his head getting banged by the horse's rear on every jump.

"How is he not dead?" I ask Stella over the applause.

"He did it!" the announcer calls. "He did it, he did it again!"

Adam puts his fingers in his mouth and whistles, and then he turns to me with both hands up. I give him a double high five, loving the excitement on his face. "Now that's a real cowboy!" He leans over me and Stella to get Dylan's attention. "You see that, man? No helmet! Just his cowboy hat!"

"He's a warrior!" Dylan calls back.

I sit down and laugh, loving everything about this impromptu adventure. When Adam showed up at our hotel room this morning with his crazy idea to spend our day off at the rodeo, it took a little convincing. It's been a really busy month, and I'm dog tired. It's Halloween and I was hoping we'd spend the day snuggled up together watching scary movies and eating popcorn, but after his time in Austin, Adam is a big rodeo fan and he begged us to come out with him.

"Adam," I had protested, although his enthusiasm was catching, "what if we get recognized? People know I'm in town. We just did two shows, and it's been all over the radio and TV. We'll be mobbed."

"No!" he said, his eyes lighting up even more. "We can go as cowboys and cowgirls for Halloween! Nobody'll recognize you."

"Am I going as a rodeo clown?" I asked skeptically.

He laughed. "Come on. It'll be fun."

I still wasn't entirely on board. My Texas interviews and shows have been okay, but my throat is really sore and I've been blowing my nose a lot. My mom thinks it's from the change in climate, but I'm worried I might be getting sick.

But here we are, our fun-lovin' foursome, and surprisingly I am having more fun than I've had in a long time. I bought a big cowboy hat and kept my head low through the parking lot, worried I'd be mobbed right away, but so far so good. As the night goes on, I relax more and more to the point of asking my bodyguard to give me a little space. The events are super fun, and although not everybody here is in costume, even in my fringed suede vest and flouncy skirt, I still don't feel like I stand out in public like I normally do.

"Woo-hoo!" I holler as the fan favorite exits the arena.

"Guys, confession," Stella says as everybody sits. "This is my first rodeo. And it is more gloriously redneck than anything I could've ever imagined."

"Yeah, Adam," Dylan says, nodding. "Good call."

"Oh! The clowns are coming back out!" Stella shouts, standing up and clapping.

Dylan smiles, and it is evident from his face that watching her watch the rodeo is more fun than any of the events we've seen so far. I take off my cowboy hat and lean my head on Adam's shoulder. "Thank you."

"For what?" he asks.

"For giving me a night off," I answer truthfully. I look up at him, our faces close. "For giving me a chance to go on

201

a normal double date. For, you know, just being the greatest boyfriend a girl could ever ask for."

The rodeo clowns bring out a yellow car-slash-airplane contraption and try to ride it, failing hilariously. We laugh, the crowd cheers, and as Adam tilts my chin up to kiss me, it's like they're voicing the sound my heart makes every time his lips are on mine. I am the luckiest girl in the world.

"Folks, folks, folks, you aren't going to believe it," the announcer calls. "You just aren't going to believe it, I'm telling you." We stop kissing and stand up to see what the fuss is all about. "You'll see everything from rodeo queens to steer wrestling tonight, but I just got wind of something that's going to take the cake. Going to blow the whole night out of the water."

The crowd is attentive. The clowns dramatically gesture to one another, trying to figure out what all the fuss is about.

"I just heard that we've got a special guest in the audience tonight!" the announcer continues. He holds for applause, and as people start to look around, I feel my stomach drop. "A young lady that has fans all over the world, but especially here in cowboy country, is sitting out in the stands tonight, and I think we ought to give her a big warm Fort Worth welcome. Everybody, put your hands together for Miss Bird Barrett!"

I hear a couple of screams but mainly the din of voices

asking one another where to look. I shove my cowboy hat back on my head and duck down to grab my purse, pretending to look for something. "Oh, we see you, Miss Barrett," the announcer calls. "Let's say, we 'notice' you!"

The audience is buzzing now, and I feel like a trapped animal, frantic as I consider what to do. I don't want this. I want a night off. I want to enjoy the rodeo like everybody else in this stadium. I want to have fun for once!

I see a couple of people down in front of us turn around to snap pictures. Adam raises his other arm and waves, playing along, but I don't want to. I love my fans—I really do—but aren't I entitled to one freaking night off? Ever?

"Bird, they see you," Adam says, his voice low. "You probably ought to wave or something."

I take a breath and look up. Right when I do, a teenager a couple of rows down from us leans over and screams, "OMG, they *are* dating!"

"I saw that in *Us Weekly*," her friend says.

"But it wasn't confirmed. This is incredible." And the minute she holds up her phone, I realize that this is not how Anita wants to "control the narrative."

I turn around to Big Dave and say, "Let's go." My bodyguard immediately jumps down to my row and makes a path as he leads me from the crowd. I force a smile and wave as I squeeze past Stella. "Y'all ready? I want to get out of here."

"Bird, are you okay?" Dylan asks. He lets Dave get by him. It seems like every single person we pass has a phone in my face.

"Where you going, Miss Barrett?" the announcer calls. "Don't run off just yet. Come on down here and give us a song. What do you say?"

As we make our way down the stands, I wave and smile but shake my head. Fans call to me as we descend, a couple reaching out to touch me, and I'm in a near-panic. I don't feel like singing. My throat hurts and I'm playing huge shows all week, so the last thing I want to do is sing.

"Bird," Adam says, pushing his way down the stairs to grab my arm. "Hey, stop."

"Adam, please. I really want to get out of here. Can we just go?"

"Come on, Fort Worth, let her hear you," the emcee persists. Now the rodeo clowns are into it, one running toward me as our group gets near the ring. I suddenly feel closed in—caught—as he climbs up on the rail and holds a mic out to me, the fringe of his sleeve waving back and forth as he gestures for me to join him in the ring.

"I really don't want to sing tonight," I say with a smile.

"Hey crowd, let's 'Shine Our Light,'" the announcer continues, really riling them up now.

"'Shine Our Light,'" the crowd repeats, chanting. "'Shine Our Light'! 'Shine Our Light'!"

"This is crazy," Stella says, grabbing my hand. "Are you sure you don't want to just go sing real quick?"

"No," I say firmly. "What I *wanted* was to have fun with my friends without it turning into a publicity stunt for once."

"Bird," Adam says, close and low. "It's not a big deal."

"It *is* a big deal," I say, a little frustrated now. "People just take from me all the time, and I'm tired."

"They're your fans," he says. "They love you."

"I love them, too," I say. "I love them so much I'm hauling my butt all over the country to sing to them. Don't I deserve a night off?"

"Just give them a song," he persists, standing close. "Any song. I know Anita would tell you to do it, and I'm sure my publicist will kill me if we just bail. Come on. I'll sing with you if you want."

"God, Adam!" I say, pulling away. The crowd is still chanting, and I feel my throat tighten as hot tears prick at the corners of my eyes. "If you want to sing so bad, go sing. Here," I say, grabbing the mic out of the clown's hand and shoving it in Adam's chest. "Sing your heart out."

Then I turn around and clutch Dave's elbow, incensed as he leads me to the exit. I'm crazy about Adam, but I wish he'd care about his girlfriend a little more than his image. As I stomp off, I feel the anger build. I'm mad at the crowd for being so selfish and at myself for thinking I could have a piece of that old anonymity back. That week in Nashville was a terrible tease.

Then I hear booing. I stop in my tracks and look back to see people throwing trash over the rails. "Are they for real?" I say, shocked. "What if that stuff actually hit me?"

All because I didn't give them what they wanted. All because I wanted one freaking night of me time.

I wipe tears from under my sunglasses and follow Dave to the parking lot. Part of me thinks it would be easier to just go back, to give them what they want, but isn't there any merit in being true to myself?

I glance over as Stella and Dylan catch up to me, looking completely dumbfounded by the whole turn of events, but I don't see Adam. I don't see him, but then the crowd roars and I *hear* him. "Hey there, Fort Worth," his voice booms through the speakers. "Everybody having as good a time as I am tonight?"

The audience cheers, and now I am in shock, stopping still as a statue. *Is he serious? Did he really just show me up like that?*

"My name is Adam Dean, and I'm on the Bird Barrett Shine Our Light Tour right now—" He is interrupted by booing, and I feel my chest constrict. "Come on now, Fort Worth. Come on. She just gave y'all two amazing shows over at the American Airlines Center in Dallas, and she's feeling a little under the weather tonight or she would've been over those rails in a heartbeat. She lives for her fans."

"That's nice," Stella says quietly. The crowd boos again. "Yeah, real nice."

I march off, my vision blurry as I weave through the parking lot.

"Over here, Ms. Barrett," Big Dave calls, leading me to the car.

In the distance, I hear Adam telling the crowd that he'd love to sing a song for them, "if they'll have him," and of course they go ballistic. *Prince Charming, saving the day. What a guy.*

I assume he's going to sing "Make Her Mine," and all I can think as I climb into the car, angry and hurt and now crying so hard that the sobs are embarrassing, is how I may not be his much longer.

21

"BIRD, WHAT HAPPENED at the rodeo?" Anita says over FaceTime the next day. She looks like she could strangle me. Troy and I are on my tour bus, and the minute he told me she wanted a conference call, I knew there was trouble.

"Nothing," I say hoarsely as I grab another tissue. All that crying last night did nothing to help ward off the cold I knew was on the way. I feel like I'm in a tunnel, her words sound far away, and it's painful to look at the bright screen. "Somebody spotted me and they wanted me to sing, but I didn't feel like it. I wanted a night off."

"Why did Adam sing instead?"

I feel my jaw tighten. "We haven't really spoken much since last night," I say, thinking about the awkward and very tense ride back to the hotel after his performance. "He said he was 'trying to help,'" I say, making exaggerated air quotes.

"Adam's a good guy, Bird," Dylan says, exasperated as he walks back to the bathroom.

"Yeah, he's a great guy, Dylan," I call. "But I doubt he's in trouble with his publicist today."

My brother slams the door, and I roll my eyes. Just another example of someone who has no idea what it's like to answer to a million people.

Anita purses her lips. "Well, I won't sugarcoat it. Your decision to have a night out on the town did a few things. One, there are now rumors about you and Adam turning the Shine Our Light Tour into a hook-up tour."

"What?"

"Two, he's getting amazing press," Anita says pointedly.

"Okay, okay," I say, my head pounding. "Is that all?"

"I wish," she says, her fingers at her temples now. "The worst thing is that the local news interviewed some kids and their parents after the event last night, and frankly, it doesn't look good."

I blow my nose and sniffle. "What do you mean?"

"I'll show her the links, Anita," Troy says. "We'll talk it over after she sees the local segment—"

"Local?" Anita asks loudly. "We should be so lucky. Troy, this thing has gone national. I just saw Kathie Lee yapping about it on the *Today Show*. You two talk, then call me back. We need to get a grip on this thing."

"Got it."

"Bird, take a NyQuil and a nap," she says. "You look terrible."

"Thanks, Anita," I say, rolling my eyes again.

"And make sure you're perfection for the Houston crowd tonight," she says.

"Perfection. Got it."

"We'll talk soon. Ciao."

Anita hangs up and I stare at my iPad, amazed that one innocent night out could turn into this much drama. "Show me," I tell Troy quietly.

My hands tremble as he pulls up a video from the Fort Worth local news last night. The reporter asks a group of kids if they were excited to be at the rodeo with me. "We were," one kid answers, "but not after she didn't want to be there with us." Then they ask a mother about it, and she says she was shocked by my actions and would never buy another one of my albums. "I'm not even going to listen to her on the radio," she goes on. "I'll change the station before I support Bird Barrett again. Look, my little girl is still crying."

"Oh no," I whisper as they zoom in on the girl's swollen face.

The reporter continues, "Barrett was attending the rodeo tonight with her brother, her best friend, and her tour partner, Adam Dean, when she was spotted in the stands and asked to give an impromptu performance. The general thought around here is that Barrett most definitely did not want to 'Sing Anyway.' Back to you."

The clip stops, and I drop my head into my hands.

"Bird, she's right," Troy says delicately as he searches the Internet. "It's gone national."

I take my iPad from him and pull up my Twitter account. For once, it does not feel good to be trending. "Hashtag rodeo-runner?" I ask hotly. "Seriously, that's the best they could do?"

Troy's phone rings. "Bird, don't go too deep down the rabbit hole," he warns as he stands up and walks toward the door. "The mob is angry, but we're making a plan."

While he's on the phone, I check all my social media sites, and the more I read, the worse I feel:

Bird Barrett won't be roped into singing for free.

Bird performs for ticket holders, not rodeo clowns.

No time for the little people. Bird Barrett is full of bull.

But the worst thing I read is an article already picked up by *The Huffington Post*, by a blogger who talks about how desperately her daughter wants to see my show—how she's a young fiddler like I once was and how it's her life's mission to meet me—but how that dream will never come true because my concerts all sell out in two minutes, are too expensive, and single-income families should just be lucky they get to catch clips on YouTube. The entire premise of the post is that wealthy entertainers are willing to entertain only their fellow wealthy Americans, and if they do ever pander to their poor fans, they want to make sure there's a camera there to promote it.

"That's not true," I whisper to the screen.

And there is a lot about Adam and me:

Is Bird Barrett shacking up with Adam Dean?

Adam Dean > Bird Barrett. #forthefans

Is Bird Barrett sporting a baby bump?

"What?" I shout when I read the last one. "I hate this! I *hate* this!"

And before I can stop myself, I fling my iPad across the room, knowing before it even hits the back wall of the bus that the screen will shatter. I start crying again, just like I did all night long, pulling tissues out of the box and shaking.

But when Troy boards the bus immediately after hearing me scream, the only thing I give him by way of explanation is, "I'm going to need a new iPad. And more tissues."

Then I run back to my room, desperate for some alone

time and a power nap before the show...which, of course, must go on.

"Fantastic performance," Troy says a couple of nights later as I breeze into my Tulsa dressing room. I always feel this insane mixture of alive and dead tired after a show, my body completely at odds with itself. Makes me think about that traveling Pilates studio Jolene Taylor had on tour and how maybe that wasn't such a diva move after all.

"Thanks, Troy," I say, crashing on the little couch. Usually I head right for the chair at my vanity mirror and start taking off my jewelry, but tonight I'm just too tired. "Did I sound nasally?" I ask with my arm thrown over my eyes. I was hoping to beat this cold by now, but I was sweating like a beast through the entire performance, and even Sam commented on how pale I was when he did my makeup earlier. I really hope it's not the flu.

"I think you sounded great," he says.

"Mmmm. The fans were all in. I'm hoping some other celebrity scandal will overshadow the stupid rodeo thing, but at least my real fans are out there every night holding up sweet signs and singing along." I yawn, so sleepy. "It makes me forget the haters for just a little while, you know?"

He clears his throat. "Yes, that's...wonderful. Truly."

I pause. "What's going on, Troy?" I ask, looking up at him.

His face falls. "Oh, Bird, Anita always tells me to give it to you straight, but I have a hard time seeing you upset."

With great effort, I pull myself to a seated position. "Why would I be upset?"

"Well," he says, pulling at his shirt collar, "with all the brouhaha surrounding this rodeo fiasco, *Rolling Stone* rushed their cover story." He holds up an open envelope, and I know before looking that it's bad. "They FedExed our copies. It'll be on stands everywhere tomorrow."

"She provoked me," I say softly, knowing Jase used our final interview in her article. He reluctantly hands me a copy, and I sit back against the couch cushions, staring at the cover in my lap as my pulse starts to pound in my ears.

The picture is provocative. My parents were right. I see it now. Especially since the headline reads:

BIRD BARRETT: AMERICA'S TOO-SWEET HEART?

Inside, it's not any better. Jase paints me as a judgmental and hypocritical Goody Two-shoes who plays the part of the wholesome all-American girl but parties behind the scenes. And even though Adam and I barely even saw each other while she was with the tour, she must've climbed aboard the rodeo romance bandwagon, because she strongly insinuates that the real me—the one she "got to know" on tour—might secretly be dating my opener, who spends long hours on my bus and in my hotel room.

"She can't say that," I say to Troy. I am so angry that I'm shaking, but my voice comes out strained.

"Bird—" Troy starts.

"No, she can't do this," I say, so over all the crying but fighting tears yet again. "Call Dan. I want to talk to Dan."

Troy never pushes me, never tries to talk me down, always guides me by letting me express what I need. In this case, I need to talk to the president of my label. In this case, I need to know how screwed I am. He immediately makes the call.

"Dan, it's me," I choke out. The tears are flowing freely. My stage makeup is streaming down my cheeks.

"It's bad," he says. "I know."

"My first *Rolling Stone* cover," I say in gasps, "is this load of bs?"

"Bird," he says after a mighty exhale. "I'm sorry. I know it's hard to read. It certainly took me off guard. Anita is spitting nails. We never should have let her on your bus. One of us should have been there."

"No," I say. "Don't take any blame. This is all from the twisted soul of that jaded, miserable reporter who had a crappy life and is only happy if the rest of us do, too." He doesn't say anything. Troy brings me a box of tissues from the vanity and squeezes my shoulder. We sit there in silence for almost a full minute as I get myself together, blowing my nose and dabbing at my eyes. "Dan," I finally say, my throat raw. "What can I do? How can I make this right?"

"Well, if songs like the one you just wrote with Adam come out of these tough times, then I'd say it can't all be bad, right?"

"You liked 'Broken People'?"

"We loved it. Makes me very optimistic about your third album, Bird."

"Oh, but it was his song," I say.

"So why did you send it to me?"

"I don't know," I say with a sniffle. "Just thought you'd want to hear it. I guess I should check and see if Adam's going to use it."

"*Oh*-kay," Dan replies, sounding annoyed.

"But don't we have more important things to worry about than credit for a song?" I ask as I hold up the magazine, clutching it tightly in my fist. "What about this stupid article? And the rodeo thing?"

Dan sighs heavily on his end. "Well, Bird, it's tricky. Anita is trying to manage the *Rolling Stone* press, and I really wish you'd just sung at that rodeo—"

"I know!" I say, closing my eyes and leaning back against the couch. "You and everybody else in the world."

"But what's done is done." Dan sounds defeated, which doesn't give me a lot of confidence. Actually, his condescending attitude makes me mad. I think back to that night a couple of years ago when I gave a free, impromptu performance at Stella's high school fund-raiser. I thought he and Anita were going to murder me. Yet now I'm supposed to sing whenever someone asks me to, like a doll with a pull string.

I sneeze, lean forward, and wipe my nose for the millionth time today. "Maybe I should take a little break," I suggest. "I'm not feeling well at all. What if we reschedule the next few shows and give the media a chance to feed off someone else's mistakes? Let it all die down a little, you know?"

"Reschedule?" Dan practically shouts through the phone. I hold it away from my ear, shocked. "You must be out of your mind. If anything, I'll be speaking to Marco about extending the tour, adding more cities, maybe going abroad."

I blink fast a few times, stunned by his reaction. "More dates?" I say quietly.

"Bird, you can't afford to take a single wrong step right now," he goes on, all brass tacks. "Don't you see that? It's *you* they're feeding off of, *you* they're still talking about, so it's *you* that has to hold your chin high and prove everybody wrong. You think your fans are angry now? What do you think will happen if you go canceling the concert they've been looking forward to for months?"

My head pounds. I hear what he's saying, but I honestly don't know how much longer I can keep this up.

"Fansfirst," Dan says, quoting a hashtag I use a lot on social media.

I steel myself for another rough patch and weakly reply, "Fansfirst."

22

By the time we reach Tupelo, Mississippi, the next day, whatever crazy virus I've been fighting has finally taken hold of me. I slept the whole way in a NyQuil-induced haze, and now I'm halfway through the show, running on fumes, but determined to be perfect. I can't give the media or these Southern fans even a moment of negativity to latch on to. Dan was right: After the rodeo and *Rolling Stone* fiascos, I cannot afford a misstep.

"Hey, are you feeling all right?" Stella asks during the quick change for "Before Music." Dylan and I bring the whole show down for this special number, lights low and everything. We perform on stools at the very end of the T, almost in the center of the floor seats. It's intimate and sweet, but I only have a short video promo to hold the crowd over for my quick change, so I always stress this part.

"Yeah," I say as I dive into the dress she's holding out for me. "But I flubbed a word in the second verse of the third song, and it's been on my mind ever since."

"Nobody noticed," she says as she pulls the dress down and fluffs the skirt.

"I noticed," I say, my throat on fire. "Jordan, can I have a drink?"

My stage manager hands me a bottle of water, and Stella stands back and looks at me, smiling. I return her gaze, wondering what the heck she's doing. "You always look so pretty in this dress," she says.

"Thanks," I say, reaching a hand around my back. "Are you going to zip it up, or is it just as pretty hanging open?"

"Oh my God!" she says, running around me. "I totally flaked."

"And the belt?" I ask as I hear the video wind down. I'm glad that I can stay in the same cowboy boots at least.

"Yes, it's right here," she says. But when she bends down to grab it off the floor, we both realize that it's already connected. "Oh no," she says, fumbling with the buckle as the lights start to lower.

"Bird," Jordan says, taking the water from me. "You need to get out there."

"I know my cues," I snap. "I wish my wardrobe assistant did."

I jerk the belt from Stella's hands, looking away from

219

her big hurt eyes to wrap it around my own waist, tucking it in as I walk forward, since there's no time to buckle it. I hear Dylan start to play the opening melody and freak out. "I need my mic! Come on, come on!"

"Bird, I'm sorry about the belt," Stella says as I grab the microphone from Jordan.

"Either hit your cues, or I'll request Amanda from now on," I reply angrily before heading toward the stage. I hear the harshness of my words the minute I say them, but there's no time for apologies. The truth is that these days on this tour Bird Barrett has to be perfect.

The tension is thick in my dressing room after the show. Stella and Amanda work quietly as they take inventory of my wardrobe and pack it away for tomorrow's show. I crank up the P!nk playlist on my iPhone and slam my jewelry on the vanity, still fuming about the flow of the show and how it was basically the worst one of the tour so far. "I feel like I ought to give those fans their money back," I grumble.

"Adam had to take a call with his manager, so he went on out," Dylan says as he lets himself into my dressing room. *Oh no, Dylan. Please, whatever you do, don't knock.*

"Thanks," I say. It's not like I was going to get a Coke with him anyway. Ever since Fort Worth, I've headed right for the bus after my shows, pushing myself through these performances and running on empty. He's apologized a thousand times about the rodeo thing, and he was supportive about the *Rolling Stone* article (although he used the dumb cliché that "all publicity is good publicity," which really irked me), and for the past week, things between us have been super tense. He may have meant well, but the way he's reacted to the chaos surrounding my life just magnifies the fact that he has no idea how different things are in the big leagues.

"Hey, what's wrong?" Dylan asks.

Surprised and a little moved at my brother's concern, I turn to face him. "Everything," I say honestly. "I think this virus that I've been fighting has finally turned into a full-on flu, I'm under tremendous pressure, and I feel like I'm losing my mi—"

But I quickly realize that my brother isn't talking to me. He has made his way around the clothing rack, where my best friend is now crying in his arms, her shoulders shaking as he rubs her back. I feel a pang of guilt—I know I shouldn't have snapped at her during the show—and suddenly I feel the kind of exhaustion that literally weighs me down, my chest constricting as if I were pinned under a boulder.

I spin back around in my seat and chug an entire bottle of water. Then I throw my things in my big purse and turn off my music before making my way to the door. I need to think of a way to apologize to Stella, I guess, but I really don't have it in me right now.

"Who died and made you queen?" Dylan demands, cutting me off before I exit the room.

"Excuse me?"

"People make mistakes, Bird," he says. "And that girl over there? The one you *supposedly* think of as your best friend? She's completely torn up because you spoke to her like a piece of dirt during the show."

Fire flames in my gut. I want to kill somebody. "Hey, I'm just taking the tour seriously like my big brother asked me to back in Vegas. Remember that? Remember when you went off on me in front of the whole band and crew during rehearsal? How all these people are counting on me for their jobs? *I* do. I remember it like it was yesterday."

"That doesn't mean you have to go diva on everybody," he says. "You can still show a little respect."

"Respect?" I laugh bitterly. "Yeah, you're right. Stella, I'm sorry I didn't respect you enough when you messed up your cue and interrupted the flow of the show. Dylan, I'm sorry I don't respect you enough when I let y'all shack up on my bus every night and pretend not to hear you making out."

"You're acting like a jerk," Dylan says, his blue eyes steely.

I'm sure mine are the same as I step toward him. "You

have no idea what it's like to be me right now," I say. "This is a big old fun adventure for everybody else on tour, but when one thing goes wrong—anything—it's *my* name that gets dragged through the mud. Okay? It's *me* that everybody hates. So you two hate me now, too? Fine. Join the club."

I storm past him and speed walk through the passageways toward my bus. I don't want to run into anybody, talk to anybody, or be around anybody. I want to fall into my bed and shut out the world and turn off my brain and cry myself to sleep...again.

When I swing open my bus door, I race up the stairs and run smack-dab into Adam. "What are you doing in here?" I ask.

"Bathroom on my bus is broken," he replies.

"Still?" I ask, squeezing past him. "God!"

"Hey, what's wrong?"

"Nothing. It's just—you can't just come over here anytime you want."

"Why not?" he asks from behind me. "I'm your boyfriend."

I spin around. "And I'm your boss!" I exclaim.

Adam looks like he's been slapped in the face. Immediately, I put my head in my hands and feel it pounding. This has been the worst night. "Adam," I say, calmer. But before I can make it right, he turns on his heels and leaves me standing in the aisle alone, wondering how I got here.

"Bonnie?" I say later when she answers the phone.

"Honey, what's the matter?" she asks, immediately hearing the sadness in my voice.

A quick sob escapes. "Everything."

"Oh, Bird, I've been there, sweet pea," she says, her voice soothing through the phone. It hits me how badly I miss her, how I miss life off the road, how I miss... myself.

"I know what's been eating you," she finally says when I sit quiet on the phone, afraid to talk too loudly because I don't want Stella or Dylan to overhear. "There's not exactly a Bird Barrett lovefest going on in the media these days, is there?"

"No," I manage. I put down the phone and blow my nose before talking again. "And I don't know what to do about it. I don't know how to make it right."

"Listen, you can't please all the people all the time," she says.

"I know, but now—" I try to catch my breath. "Now it's like I'm becoming the person they say I am. I've been so sick and I don't know if that's why, but I was really rude to my best friend tonight, I had a fight with my brother, and for some reason, I just completely treated my boyfriend like the hired help. *Who am I?*"

I sob again, crying hard into my pillow to keep the noise down, my chest heaving.

"Come find out," Bonnie gently suggests. "Take off a few days and come stay with me at the farm. Let me nurse you back to feeling better, and I don't mean just getting over that cold. You need to walk barefoot in the grass or jump in a pile of leaves. We can ride horses, and I'll make you sweet tea, and we'll write a song. Just come home a little while, Bird."

"I can't leave the tour right now," I lament. "We've got two more shows this week, and my fans already hate me. Imagine if I cancel on them."

"Everybody needs a day off, Bird," she says. "Exhaustion is a real thing. What will your fans think if you collapse on the stage? Or if your crew leaks it that you've become a prima donna?"

I chew my lip.

"Maybe before Thanksgiving," I say.

"You going to make it that long?"

"It's just a couple more weeks, and then we've got a break."

Bonnie sighs. "Well, you take care of yourself until then, girl," she says. "And remember, the door's always open."

Fresh tears fill my eyes. It seems like such a small thing, but it feels good to be worried about. "Thanks, Bonnie. I'll see you soon."

We hang up the phone, and I close my eyes, lying back on my bed still fully clothed as I let the recent events of my life replay in my head. I have to get ahold of what's happening to me and around me. I have to be better.

My phone beeps, and I look down at a text from Adam:

Dear Boss, thought you might want to know about this.

Attached is a link to a story about Kayelee Ford setting up a special concert at the next Fort Worth rodeo, the theme of the article being about how she's giving the fans what I couldn't.

"No!" I shout.

Ignoring Adam, I text Bonnie a second later:

Prepare the guest bed. I'll be there tomorrow.

23

"WELCOME TO BELLE Holler Farm," Bonnie says as her truck bounces along the gravel driveway. I've spent lots of time at her condo in LA, but this is the first time I'm visiting her Tennessee oasis.

"That's a pretty name," I murmur.

Her husband, Darryl, glances back at me in the rearview mirror and grins. "Named her that because my Bonnie has the prettiest holler I've ever heard." Then he puts his finger in his ear and gives it a shake. "And let me tell you, I've heard it... a lot."

"Oh, hush," Bonnie says, waving him off. "This is what I've had to put up with for twenty-five years, Bird."

"The best years of your life," he teases.

She nods. "Probably right there."

Bonnie and Darryl picked me up at the airport, swooping in like they were rescuing a damsel in distress. Darryl wouldn't let me carry any of my own bags, and Bonnie handed me a pack of throat lozenges and a thermos of tea as soon as she saw me. Now I'm squeezed in the back of the extended cab, my luggage thrown in the truck bed, with the wind from Darryl's open window blowing across my face and whipping my hair around. I've heard a lot about their farm, but I've never seen pictures and I am certainly impressed by what I see. There is so much land. We aren't that far from Nashville, but I feel like I'm worlds away.

"Down that path are the horses," Bonnie says, pointing. "We can ride a little later if you're up for it. Or tomorrow."

I shrug.

"And over that way is the barn for the milk cows and chickens."

"Fresh eggs in the morning, Bird," Darryl says. Then he leans over his steering wheel and slams on the brakes before yelling out his window, "Hah! Get on, Wilbur! Hah! Hah!" I've been like a zombie this whole ride, my forehead pressed against my window as I zone out, but now I lean forward and see a cute pink pig mosey out of the driveway and into the yard. "And if that dad-blamed pig keeps getting under my wheels, we'll have fresh bacon, too."

"Looks like 'Some Pig,'" I remark, quoting *Charlotte's Web*.

Bonnie laughs out loud, and even Darryl allows a small smile. "Yeah, he's some pig all right."

When we pull up to the house, it's exactly what I expected, if a little larger. It is a white two-story farmhouse with a gorgeous wraparound front porch and the quintessential swing. There are no fancy columns or anything, but it's grand in that it's nestled between giant trees that must be ten times as old as me. It's picturesque, classically beautiful, and the perfect place to hide from the world.

"Home at last," Bonnie says, hefting herself out of the truck. "Here, Bird, grab my hand and don't miss this step."

I climb out of the F-150 and stretch. Arms in the air, chest to the sky, I feel my hair fall down my back as I twist and breathe deep. Then I start coughing, and my head explodes in pain. Bonnie leads me to the front door. I feel like a weak, fragile old woman, but as the sun beats down on me, on the autumn-speckled leaves of the trees all around us, and on the small pond I see way on past the house, I think I'd much rather be miserable here than anywhere else.

"Bird?" Bonnie says softly.

I open my eyes and see her perched on the side of my bed, sunlight streaming in through the lace curtains. She passes me a cup of water, and I gulp it down. "What time is it?" I croak.

"About ten," she says. "You've been sleeping for a while now."

I push myself up to a sitting position and pile a bunch of pillows behind me. "Did you feed me chicken noodle soup in the middle of the night?" I ask, wondering if that was a dream.

"I did," she said. "You hadn't had lunch and you slept through dinner, so I wanted to make sure you had something in your belly."

"Wow," I say, pushing stringy, wet hair off my head. "I think my fever broke. I feel better."

"You look better," she says. "You've been here less than twenty-four hours, but you've slept for about nineteen."

I grin at her. "You know my mom would've called nine-one-one by now."

"Well, mommas are supposed to be a little crazy when it comes to their babies," she says. "You feel like taking a shower?"

"I do," I say, astounded. "Yesterday I felt like fresh roadkill, but today I feel like eighty bucks."

"Only eighty?" Bonnie says with a grin.

"Still got a sore throat and a little congestion, but no more body aches. And oh! My head. This is the first day I haven't had a headache since—" I feel my face fall, remembering the rodeo incident...and then the *Rolling Stone* article...and the fights with Stylan and Adam...and how angry Dan was when I left the tour, forcing him to cancel a week of shows—

"Let's tackle those other headaches one at a time," Bonnie says. She stands up, turns off the humidifier, and brings me a couple of towels. "In the meantime, take a hot shower, and I'll go make you some breakfast. If I don't have you feeling like a hundred bucks by the time you go back to Nashville, then I haven't done my job."

"I can't believe this is your first time riding a horse," Bonnie says as we ride a pair of her Tennessee Walkers away from the stables and across her land. It's been a relaxing couple of days around the house, not doing much besides watching TV and exchanging short, tense texts with Adam, but my caregiver demanded that I have fresh air and talked me into coming along on a riding tour of her farm. Tomorrow I leave for a couple of days at my Nashville home, so it's now or never.

"You're a natural, Bird!" Bonnie says encouragingly, although anyone with two eyes can see that I'm not.

"I don't think I'm actually riding him," I say, gripping the reins firmly, my legs squeezed tight over the bulging tummy of my horse. "I'm pretty sure he's in charge."

Bonnie chuckles. "Chico's a gentle giant. He's too fat and lazy to run off with you, so he's a good starter horse.

It's Blackjack I have to keep my eyes on." She leans forward and pats his neck, her horse's impressive muscles as defined as an Olympic athlete's. "He's the high-spirited one."

"Why are they called Tennessee Walkers?" I ask.

"Let me show you," she says mischievously.

We were going at an okay pace, a nice slow walk, but all it takes is Bonnie tsking twice for our horses to crank things up a notch, which completely throws me off guard.

"Whoa!" I cry, instinctively clutching the reins tightly to my belly. Chico stops dead in his tracks, and I nearly dive over his head. Then I scream.

Bonnie looks over her shoulder and laughs, bringing her horse quickly around to where Chico and I have stopped still. "Can't go saying things like 'whoa,' unless you really mean it," she says, as if she's telling me a secret she doesn't want our animals to hear. "Good boy," she coos to Chico, leaning over and running her hands through his brown mane. "Good boy."

"Oh yeah, really good boy," I say sarcastically. "You almost killed me, so fantastic."

Bonnie arches an eyebrow and says, "Bird, you're in charge here. You gave him a command and he listened. If you didn't mean what you said, you shouldn't have said it. You understand?"

I nod, feeling properly scolded. Her words strike a chord. She might be talking about my horse, but all I can think about right now is the tour and Adam, Stella, and Dylan.

"All right now," she says, turning her horse around. "We're going to let them pace, then work them into a flat walk, and then a run-walk. The run-walk is what makes these guys special. A Tennessee Walker has the prettiest gait. They can pick up some good speed without making you feel like you're going too fast."

I take a big breath and double-check that I'm in the saddle the way Bonnie showed me at the barn: feet in the stirrups, hands on the reins. "I felt like we were going pretty fast."

"Maybe eight or ten miles an hour."

"On. A. Beast," I remind her with a grin.

She chuckles. "Here we go," she says, and tsks again.

Later that night, using the flashlight on my iPhone, I make my way gingerly down the gorgeous wooden staircase toward the kitchen. I never thought I'd say this, but I think my body has actually gotten *too much* sleep. When I first got here, I was so flu ridden and exhausted that I shut my brain off and just gave in to its need for rest. But now that I'm feeling better, all I can think about is how royally I've screwed up lately and how impossible it seems to fix. I've tossed and turned ever since we all said good night, and at this point, I'm tired of fighting it. Plus, I've got my appetite back.

I go straight for the fridge, knowing Bonnie put the left-over cobbler in there somewhere.

"Well, I figured it was a raccoon or a prowler, but I'm glad it's just you."

I scream as the lights are flipped on. "Bonnie!"

"Sorry!" she says, laughing. "Sorry, sorry, sorry. Didn't mean to scare you. I was out on the porch swing and wanted to make myself known so I wouldn't scare whoever was in here."

"Too late," I say, fanning myself dramatically.

She laughs harder, a sweet melodic laugh that's almost like song. "Well, I reckon so. Here, take a seat. I was just about to heat up a piece of cobbler."

"Really?" I say, stepping aside. "I just happen to be in the market for a piece myself."

"Is that so?" She pats the bar top, indicating I sit, as she gets out the cobbler, a tub of ice cream, and two bowls. "What are you doing up anyway, missy? This is supposed to be your hideaway, R-and-R stay before you get back on tour."

"Couldn't sleep."

"Any particular reason for that?"

I sigh. "It's been so nice today, riding over the farm, skipping rocks on the pond, and just being away from it all. Even listening to Darryl's take on how ESPN has no respect for the SEC was mind-numbing enough to be relaxing," I say with a wry smile. Bonnie laughs. "But I don't know. I never would've dreamed my life would be filled with this much drama."

"Is it that Kayelee girl again?" she asks.

"Well, she's not helping," I say, rolling my eyes. "But it's typical Kayelee Ford. She retweeted all the *Rolling Stone* stuff. She posted a pic of Adam playing in *her* band a couple of years ago at her debut release party, with the hashtags belikeme and shineourlighttour. And now she's doing this big free concert at the same rodeo where I got that bad press. And I know it shouldn't, but it eats at me a little."

"Hmmm," Bonnie murmurs.

I look over at my reflection in the French doors and realize my hair is wild, frizzy and sticking out every which way. I try to smooth it down and finally just take the pony-tail holder from my wrist and pull it up in a loose bun on top of my head. It makes me think that's kind of how my life is, like I think I look one way but the world sees me in another. I think about how easy today was and how differ-ent my life would be if I'd never been discovered in the first place. Nobody cared about anything I did a few years ago. Now it's like every step I take is in the wrong direction.

"At the end of the day," I admit as I swallow a lump in my throat, "I guess I just feel like I'm letting everyone down."

Bonnie grabs two spoons and brings over our midnight snack.

"In what way do you feel like you're letting everyone down exactly?" she asks.

I shrug. "I guess it's like, I don't know, maybe I'm living

a lie." I glance over at her, and she raises one eyebrow but doesn't say anything. I take a bite and think about what I want to say as I chew. "Like my fans and my family and my friends—well, everybody—they all think I'm this charming, easygoing, sweet, perfect role model when in reality, sometimes I just want to cuss or spit my gum on the ground or flip off the paparazzi. Sometimes I want to scream at reporters and tell everybody to mind their own business and get a life instead of constantly commenting on the way I live mine."

Bonnie nods as she eats.

"And yes, the clothes are amazing, but I don't love being constantly dolled up and paraded around. My shows are exhausting, so on my days off, I want to wear sweats and go a day without showering and watch a marathon of *The Voice*, which I can't say in interviews because then the *American Idol* people would get mad. It's all so bananas!"

I start to take another bite, but my mind is racing now. "But no, I can't say anything off script because my team is carefully curating my aura, my ever-important image, and God forbid I stray from the perfect Bird Barrett that my fans—no, my fans' *parents*—want me to be."

I glance over at Bonnie, whose blue eyes are bright and crow's-feet are deep. "Feel better?" she asks.

I take a big bite of peach cobbler and grin. "Actually, I do."

"Oh, Bird, they all know you're not perfect," she says. "You're human. You can't be charming or sweet every minute of the day, because you're a human being. Sometimes people forget that about celebrities, but we're real people. They think we're real when we're putting on a show, and they think we're fake when we do something real."

"Yes!"

"No one, in reality, is the person they project, even and especially celebrities. But take the average Joe, too," she says. "Everybody's on Facebook writing things like, 'Little Johnny ate all his organic vegetables!' so they rack up all those likes and comments and such, but they aren't posting, 'Little Johnny still sleeps in my bed. And he's nine!'"

"True," I say with a laugh.

"Nobody's putting it all out there, Bird."

"Yeah, but it's one thing for my fans to not know the real me, but now I'm not even getting along with my family or closest friends. I have to be so many different versions of myself: boss, friend, sister, girlfriend. And when those things conflict, it all blows up in my face. Or rather, I seem to blow up, and it's not pretty."

"You're tired, honey," Bonnie says. "And I'll tell you another thing—you're jealous."

I scrunch up my face. "Jealous?"

"I'm telling you," she says. "People would think I'm crazy to say that the rich, famous girl is the one that's jealous, but your family gets to go eat wherever they want whenever they want. And your friends can date and make new friends without ever wondering if the people they meet have ulterior motives."

I take another bite and chew on that. She's right: My friends and family have a certain freedom that I don't have, but it's not fair of me to hold it against them.

"And they all get to make mistakes, little ones or—" She pauses, sets her spoon down with great concentration, and I can tell she's going back in time. She swallows hard before she continues. "Or big, fat, humongous ones—but they all get to make their 'just human' mistakes behind closed doors."

Gently I ask, "Are you, maybe, talking from experience?"

She sighs and nods. "Bird, honey, I ran with a wild crowd when I was younger, and I was the wildest of them all. I had more money than I had sense, and there was always a party or an after party or some way to 'relax' after a show." She shakes her head.

"So you quit singing when you sobered up?" I ask.

"No."

She looks out the window for a few seconds and finally says, "Bird, I quit singing when my boyfriend and I went joyriding, three sheets to the wind, and ended up with our car wrapped around a tree." I feel my jaw go slack. Bonnie answers me before I can ask. "He didn't make it."

"Oh, Bonnie," I say, reaching over for her hand. "I'm so sorry."

She pulls away and pats my own hand before picking

her spoon back up. "So I got sober, I eventually got married, and I quit the business."

"I can't believe I didn't know all that," is all I can say.

"There wasn't a soul on earth who *didn't* know about it at the time," she says. "You want to talk about image and judgment and all that? I was every water cooler or dinner party conversation topic for months. Thank God they didn't have the Twitter yet."

"I can't imagine."

"But then somebody else's scandal came along. I was out of the spotlight. And since I had stopped singing, I was able to start over."

"But didn't you miss it?" I ask. "I don't know how I would've gotten through something like that without music."

"Oh, I've written enough songs about that time to fill five albums," she says. "No, I can't live without my music, but I can certainly live without the fame."

I take a bite and ponder that.

"But you, young lady, should absolutely not quit," she says, turning toward me. "Do not let that be the takeaway from my sad story. Instead, you remember this: The greatest lesson I ever learned is that life is short, every moment spent with the people you love is precious, and every moment spent *doing* what you love is a gift."

" 'Every moment,' " I repeat.

"Don't let your last be one you'd regret."

24

"KNOCK, KNOCK," I say when Darryl and Bonnie drop me off at my house in Nashville the next day.

"We're in the kitchen!" my mom calls.

I drop my bags and take off my jean jacket, both excited and anxious to join everybody. My dad gets up from the counter and gives me a big hug, and when he goes to pull away, I squeeze tighter. I thought I'd want all this freedom on tour, but in reality, I've missed having him around. My mom is making dinner, so her hands are too messy to give me a hug, but she leans back and plants a loud smooch on my cheek when I walk around the counter to greet her.

"You have a good time, sweetie?"

"Oh, Mom, I needed that," I say truthfully. "I really needed that."

"Dylan, your sister's home!" she calls into the living room.

My brother is sprawled on the couch watching something on his computer. He looks up and gives me a nod but doesn't remove his headphones, and his eyes soon refocus on the screen.

I walk back to the front door and dig inside one of my bags for the Tupperware I borrowed from Bonnie. Dylan's not one to hold grudges, but I know him well enough to know that a thoughtful gesture goes a long way. So I grab a couple of forks from the kitchen drawer, walk over to the couch, and sit down at his feet, placing the plastic container between us and removing the lid.

He pulls his headphones down around his neck. "What's this?"

"Humble pie," I say with a small smile. "I baked it last night at Bonnie's."

He leans forward. "Looks a lot like pecan pie."

I nod. "Yeah, I think the recipes are close, but to make this kind of pie you have to stir in a lot of self-reflection, a cup of remorse, and a dash of shame. The final touch is an apology—and I owe you a big one."

He picks up the Tupperware and fork and takes a bite.

"Dylan, I'm sorry," I say. "I shouldn't have gone off on you the other day. I've probably been pretty crappy to be around lately." I gulp and look down at my hands. "I feel so terrible about the way I treated you and Stella and Adam. I was a jerk to a few crew guys, too. It sounds like such an excuse, but I really let the...well, all the stuff people have been saying about me..." I suddenly feel a lump in my throat, and I choke it down before going on. "I guess I've been letting it get in my head. But I shouldn't have taken it out on you guys, and I am sorry."

"What?" he says, pretending he didn't hear that last part.

I look up and blow air through my hair. "I said I'm sorry."

He chews thoughtfully and then says, "You're right. Humble pie is much better than pecan pie."

I squint my eyes at him. "Hardy har-har."

He smiles and then he says, "You know, Bird, you were right about one thing: I have no idea what it's like to be you. While you were gone, Stella and I Googled you. You haven't been acting like yourself, and we try to avoid the tabloids and Internet trolls and stuff, right? But I had no idea what was really happening—how badly people were giving it to you. There were some things that got me so mad *I* wanted to punch a hole through the wall."

"Yeah," I say, looking down at my hands. "That stuff hurts."

"Well, for what it's worth, they're all pathetic," he says. "Don't let scumbags like that get to you." I nod, my eyes filling up with tears. He turns back to the pie and changes gears. "Hey, just six more shows before Thanksgiving break."

"Yeah, I probably should've tried to push through, but honestly, I felt like I was losing it," I admit, dabbing under my eyes.

"Eh, you do what you got to do," he says with a shrug. Then he lowers his voice and says, "Jacob got a tattoo."

I inhale sharply and glance over at my mom, who doesn't seem to be listening. "He'd better hide it when he comes home," I say.

"He'll have to hide it for 'Infinity,'" Dylan jokes.

I gasp. "No!"

He grins smugly and finishes off his pie.

One apology down, two to go.

"Stella's coming over," Dylan says as he passes my bedroom later that night.

I look up from my guitar. "When?"

"In a few minutes. We'll probably just binge watch something on Netflix. It's cool if you want to hang."

"Is Adam coming, too?" I ask quietly.

"Haven't heard from him."

Sighing, I strum absentmindedly. "I owe both of them an apology, but Adam was short on the phone earlier and

Stella's been freezing me out on text. I don't think she wants to see me."

He leans against my door frame and crosses his arms. I can tell he's weighing his words. "She's pretty hurt, Bird. She feels like you've been acting differently toward her ever since we started going out."

"I try to stay neutral," I say, defending myself. "I just don't always know how to be there for her when the stuff's about you."

He nods. "I get that. It'd be weird if Adam tried to talk about your relationship with me. But he doesn't. 'Cause we're dudes."

"Lucky."

"But she's also miserable, Bird," he confesses. "So I think you should come down. Make her listen. She's like Dolce without Gabbana."

I look at him skeptically. "Do you even know who they are?"

He shrugs. "No, but I've heard her talk about them, and I know they go together. Just like you nerds."

The doorbell rings and he takes off, hopping down the stairs like he hasn't seen her in months when they're actually together all the freaking time. I doubt *my* boyfriend wants to see me that bad. After the minimal texts we've sent since I left the tour, I wonder if he still wants to be my boyfriend at all.

"Hey, Stella, can I talk to you alone a minute?" I ask my best friend after the first episode of *Sherlock*. I joined them once the show got started and waved when she looked up, but she barely even acknowledged me before turning back to the screen.

She shrugs. "I'm pretty comfy."

Dylan pulls his arm from around her shoulders and stands up, flopping her back against the couch abruptly. "Hey!" she protests.

"I'm hungry," he says by way of explanation. "Be right back."

I look at Dylan gratefully as he walks past, and then it's just the two of us.

Stella rolls her eyes. "I *was* comfy."

I had put my guitar and songwriting journal by the door when I came downstairs, and I grab them now. Then I sit on the opposite end of the couch, giving her space, but facing her. "So," I begin, my voice shaky, "you know how you always tell me that I'm better at saying stuff in a song?"

"Yeah?" Stella answers hesitantly.

"Well, there's something I need to say to you." I open my songwriting journal to the last used page, where I wrote a song inspired by my talk with Bonnie. "I am so sorry, Stella."

"Okay," she says simply. She hates confrontation, so I know that while she says it's okay, that's only because she wants to get this over with. To really get things back to the way they used to be, it's going to take more.

"I am truly, deeply sorry for exploding at you the other night," I go on. "First of all, it was totally unprofessional of me, but more important, I can't believe I treated you like that. I'm really embarrassed."

"It's fine," she says, waving me off, but I need to say more.

"Obviously, I wasn't myself—I haven't been myself for a long time actually—but hurting you at the Tupelo show hurt me, too. I'm mortified every time I think about it, and trust me, I've been thinking about it nonstop."

"You weren't feeling good," she says. "You'd had some bad days."

"Don't make excuses for me," I say. "You deserve an apology. And I'm sorry."

She finally faces me full-on, looking almost relieved. "Thanks."

"I went to Bonnie's and was able to relax and unwind and *sleep* and, I don't know, refocus on the things that are important to me. And you're one of those things, Stel. You're my best friend. My sister from another mister, right?"

She smiles.

I start to strum. "Bonnie and I were talking about how I'd lost my footing, not just with my career, but also with the people closest to me. And I realized that maybe I've been stumbling in my relationships for a while, which led to the recent . . . blowups. She told me to treasure every moment in life, and it got me thinking about how you've been there for me through really rough times—breakups and bad publicity—but how you're also there for me *always*— like just to help me pick out an outfit for an interview or something—and those moments mean a lot, too. So I wrote this song. It's for you."

I look down at my guitar and focus on the chords, on the new song, on the apology and the heart behind it. And I sing from that place:

"Every moment I'm awake, the show goes on.
On stage for each mistake, I can't be me, I'm just
    a pawn.
The press says I shouldn't sing like that,
They say that dress makes me look fat,
So I'm here.
But I'm gone."

I glance up at Stella, who is nodding along, not just to the beat but also to the message behind it, and I belt the chorus.

"I'd fly—if you weren't waiting on the ground.
I'd say good-bye—if I thought you wouldn't be
    around.
I'd cry—if you weren't here to hold my hand.
And I'd die—if you weren't here each time I land."

She sniffs, and I glance up, see tears in her eyes, and look back down. I hope those are happy tears. I hope they're forgiving tears.

"Steady, strong, and true," I sing, emotion choking my own voice a little, *"every moment with you, gets me through."*

There's more to the song, another verse, chorus, bridge, the whole shebang, but Stella is crying pretty hard now, and my eyes have blurred over so completely that I can't see the lyrics scrawled in my journal anyway. I stop and lean forward, and Stella meets me in the middle. We hug, there on our knees in the middle of my enormous sectional, and I feel a weight lift off my shoulders.

When we finally pull away, Stella passes me a few tissues from the box on the coffee table and we both wipe our faces and blow our noses. "You'd think we were watching a Nicholas Sparks movie in here," she finally says.

"We *should* be watching one," I say. Then I get an idea. "Let's queue up *Dear John* so when Dylan comes back in and thinks he's getting *Sherlock*, bam! Chick flick."

Stella's eyes shine bright, and she gives me a high five. "Oh, buddy. It's good to have you back."

"Come in!" Adam calls when I knock on the studio door.

Sheepishly, I enter. "Hey," I say, testing the water.

"Hey, Bird," he says, looking surprised to see me. I can't exactly say he looks pleasantly surprised, but he's not unpleasantly surprised, either. Perhaps neutrally surprised. I've got a long row to hoe.

"Um, I was hoping you'd stop by for dinner last night, but you never showed."

"I sent you a text," he says, somewhat defensively.

"No, I know," I say, not wanting to sound accusatory or anything. "I just—we missed you, that's all."

He runs his hands through his hair, and the engineer looks up at us, not sure if he should stay or go. "Yeah, I went over to my mom's actually."

"Wow," I say, stepping toward him. "That must've been—"

"Take five?" the guy at the soundboard cuts in. He stands up and awkwardly makes his way past us to the door. "I need a coffee anyway, so, let's take five. Or ten. Or whatever."

He opens the door and bolts.

Adam spins around in his chair and looks through the large glass window facing the recording area. Finally he says, "Sometimes I like to sit in the calm of these places before I lay anything down. I try to think about all the magic that's been made before I come in. It's overwhelming."

I nod, looking at the microphone, pop filter, headphones, and music stand. "It's humbling."

He takes a breath, coming out of whatever head space he was in before I got here, and asks, "What's up? How was your time away?" as if we're old friends and everything is just peachy between us.

"It was good," I say, inching closer. I want to crawl into his lap and hug his neck tightly and stop talking like robots and acting like strangers. "Adam, I'm so sorry about the other day," I rush in. "Or days actually. Or weeks. I don't know."

He simply nods so I go on.

"And that boss stuff." I cringe. "I'm mortified, and I'm so, so, so sorry."

Adam looks away. "It's partly my fault. You said you didn't feel well, and I dragged you to the rodeo. Then you said you didn't want to sing that day, and I made you look bad when I sang—which was totally not my intention."

"I know."

"And then there was all this distance between us," he says, looking hurt. "You stopped wanting to get Cokes after shows, and the few times I rode on your bus after that, you basically stayed back in your room like a hermit."

I swallow a serious lump in my throat as I see him do the same. This sucks.

"Do you want to break up?" he asks quietly.

"No!" I say, sitting in the chair next to him and grabbing his hand. "No, Adam, I do not want to break up. You're the best thing in my life right now. I am so sorry, seriously. Okay?"

He finally looks at me, searching my eyes as if he can see the truth there.

"Adam, I promise you, that distance had nothing to do with us. I really did have the flu. Then all that bad press kept piling on, and it's like everybody had all these different expectations from me. I was drowning trying to meet them all. It was unhealthy. I let too many people get in my head, and I'm sorry," I say, on the verge of tears. My voice comes out high-pitched and weak. "I'm sorry, okay?"

"Aw, Lady Bird, I could never stay mad at you," Adam says with a sad grin. He turns his chair toward me and leans forward, looking straight into my eyes. "But listen, I want you to know that if this is all going too fast or if it's weird that our relationship is also a business one and not just a—"

"No!" I cut in.

"I mean, if you need a little space, I understand. We can slow things down. It's no problem," he says. He squeezes my hand. "On tour it's like I'm right there in your face all the time and—"

"Adam, the *last* thing on earth I want is space," I say adamantly.

"But I want to get it right this time," he says. "I want us to work."

Tears spill from my eyes and splash onto our hands. "Me too," I squeak.

I use my other arm to wipe at my face with my shirtsleeve, and Adam pulls me into his lap. He stares at me, wiping my cheek with his thumb, and then pulls my chin toward him and kisses me slowly and deeply. I am relieved. In Adam's arms, I am home.

After a few seconds, I pull away and grab his face with both of my hands. "Listen, space is never what I wanted. Space is what kept us apart for too long." I fall into the depths of his gorgeous hazel eyes and say, "Adam, I—"

But then I stop myself. I'm about to say *I love you*—and it hits me that I do, that I love him with every part of my being, that maybe I have for a long time.

"You what?" he asks softly.

I watch his eyes searching mine . . . but I don't know if he feels the same, especially if he's suggesting space, especially after the way I've treated him lately.

"I—I—" I stammer, letting my hands fall. "I'm sorry. I just wanted to say I'm really, truly sorry. I want to be me, the real me, but sometimes it's like I lose sight of who that even is anymore."

Adam gives me a small smile and brushes my hair off my shoulders. "Cut yourself some slack, Bird. Apology accepted, but don't turn a few bad days into a full reevaluation of your character." His hand is at the back of my neck, the other rubbing my thigh. "You are the full package and I told you before: I'm all in."

He leans forward and kisses me again, passionately. My hands are instantly in his shaggy hair, and my heart pounds a hallelujah beat in my chest. *We're okay.* I kiss Adam and he kisses me back hard, running his hands up my back to pull me nearer. I melt into him, snuggling closer.

"Um, I can come back," the sound engineer says when he slams the door open against the back wall and scares the living daylights out of me.

"No," Adam says, laughing at how loud I screamed. "No, I want to get this song down." We stand and I know it's my cue to leave, but now that we're okay, I don't want to go. "We're making a rough cut of 'Broken People,'" he explains as he opens the door and we walk into the recording space.

"Oh, are you going to use it for your album?" I ask.

He grins. "I'd like to," he says, "but your people want it awfully bad."

"Oh my gosh, no," I say, putting my hands on his chest.

"That was your idea. I told Dan! No. No way. That song is yours."

Adam wraps his arms around my waist and pulls me toward the center of the room with him. "It's *ours*, actually," he says. "And I was hoping if we worked things out you might want to sing it with me. It *is* a duet after all."

I feel a flutter in my chest. *Record a song with Adam? It's so perfect.*

"Wait, is your label cool with that?" I ask.

"Cool with a multiplatinum country artist singing a duet on my debut album?" he asks. "No, but I forced them into submission."

He flexes his biceps, and I laugh out loud.

Then I kiss him again, just because I can, just because I'm *still* his girlfriend, and say, "Get me a pair of headphones, stud."

25

"How are we going to fit on the bottom bunk?" Adam asks as he flips me over on the bed in the back bedroom of my bus and runs his hand over my belly.

"You'd think the headliner would have a little more sway," I agree, pulling his face back to mine.

When I rejoined the tour, we played the remaining pre-Thanksgiving shows with ease. Everyone was well rested, and it was nice knowing we were headed right back home. I actually found myself having fun again!

Now, after the holiday, everybody is supposed to meet in Nashville for the next leg of the tour. Adam picked me up early so I could "clean out the back bedroom for my mom and dad" since they'll be joining us through Christmas. My granddad is up and moving finally, and he practically shooed my folks out of Tennessee, saying they belong on the road with their kiddos. I don't think it took much since it's my personal opinion that they miss touring. And while I'm looking forward to having them around, it means I'm stuck with the bottom bunk now.

Well, not *right* now. Right now, I'm on the master bed with my hands under my boyfriend's T-shirt. I'm scratching his back as he leans over me, peppering my face with kisses. His lips trail my jawline and start to move down my neck, causing me to shiver. I kiss his forehead and he moves to my clavicle, kissing across that delicate bone and scooting my bra strap and shirt down over my shoulder. I keep my eye on the clock and my ears open for my folks, but it's difficult to concentrate.

"Welcome back," Troy calls as he climbs the stairs of my tour bus.

I push Adam off me with both hands and jump off the bed, adjusting my T-shirt and knowing just from the look on Troy's face that he'll definitely knock from now on.

"Hey, Troy," I say as nonchalantly as possible as I walk out of the back bedroom, past the bunks, and up to the little kitchenette. Besides the fact that my cheeks are burning from the stubble on Adam's face, which would be a dead giveaway, my manager definitely saw us clawing at each other. His cheeks are just as rosy, although clearly from embarrassment in his case. "What's up?"

"Um, well, I—do you want to step outside for a minute?" he asks awkwardly.

"No, no, y'all stay here," Adam says, walking up behind me. "I need to get going anyway."

He purposefully brushes his hand against my butt when he squeezes past, grinning from ear to ear, and I think again how hard it's been for us to find any good quality alone time.

"Later, Troy," Adam says, as he takes the stairs in a hurry.

"Adam," is all Troy says in response.

I sit at the table, where Troy and I always do business, and prepare for him to debrief me on the next leg of the tour. First stop: Lexington, Kentucky, followed by Charlottesville, Virginia, followed by every-other-city-in-America, USA.

"Bird, over the break I worked with Dan and Anita on an idea for the tour that we think you're going to like," he begins.

I can still feel Adam's kisses on my skin and am fiending for the next make-out sesh, preferably one where we don't get interrupted. I text Adam under the table:

We need a secret make-out place stat.

I look out the window, see him get the text and nod as he replies:

Top priority mission. #classified

"Bird?" Troy says. "Bird, did you hear me?"

I look up at him across the table. "Oh, sorry. What was that?"

He exhales dramatically. Feeling thoroughly admonished by that one breath, I put my phone facedown on the table and fold my hands, giving my manager my full attention.

"I said that Dan and I have been working on a way to help manage your image as well as give you a chance to really connect with your fans," he repeats. "We know how much you love that special up-close-and-personal moment during your encore, and we were thinking that maybe more intimate meet-and-greets *after* your shows would interest you. Your fans would get to spend some real time with you, ask questions, and talk about their favorite songs or whatever they want to know. They'd actually get to know the real you a little bit."

"I love that idea," I say, beaming at him. "It's so great. I love it!"

"Good," Troy says, nodding his head. "We went ahead and had an IT guy build the webpage, but we didn't want to go live with it until we got your approval. So it's a go?"

"It's a major go!"

I immediately pick up my phone and text Adam about the idea, along with at least twenty smiley-face emojis. Then I run and grab my iPad from my bed and come back to the table, where Troy is already putting the wheels into motion on his phone, texting Dan and Anita and who knows whom else.

"How soon are we doing these things?" I ask as I type *birdbarret.com* into the search bar.

"I think the first one will be tomorrow night in Rupp Arena. Is that okay? All the preliminary plans were arranged during your, um, time away," he says delicately.

"I needed a break, Troy," I admit quietly. "I appreciate the way you and Anita handled that, by the way."

"We didn't lie. You were sick."

"Yeah."

Sure, I had the flu, but moreover, I was exhausted. My tank was totally empty. Physically and emotionally, I was a wreck, and nobody wanted to admit it, including myself. But now I'm healthy, I'm refreshed, and I'm determined to be my best self and take advantage of this amazing opportunity to continue headlining a tour, to write my own music, to be a positive pop culture role model, and to shake off those pesky haters. Bird Barrett on fresh batteries.

Troy and I sit in silence for a minute as we each get lost in our screens. I see where Anita has tweeted about the meet-and-greets from Open Highway's account, so I retweet that post and everything else I see about this idea. Troy mutters under his breath as he types on his phone, and then he stares at it as if it were his mortal enemy.

"You want to use my iPad?" I ask, looking up.

"May I?" he says, turning it toward him to refresh the site. "The page won't load on my phone, and I want to see how it looks."

My phone buzzes on the table next to me, and I giggle when I see a text from Adam:

How do you win one of those intimate meet ups?

I send my thumbs flying over the screen as I reply:

You'd have to buy me a Coke first, sir. Need I remind you? I am a Lady.

He sends me back a line of big smiley-face emojis crying tears, and I laugh out loud. Troy looks up and grins, which reminds me that my iPhone and iPad are synched on the cloud. I blush and look away, but I know Troy's relieved to see me so happy. Things are okay. Everything is okay. I just need to focus on my core group, my inner circle, and stay off the Internet.

"Damned Internet," Troy grumbles now. Shocked, I look over at the mind reader across from me, and he turns my iPad so I can see the screen. "We set these things up as a lottery through your website. Anita used social media to promote it as soon as I texted her that you gave the okay. That was only a couple of minutes ago, and the damned site's already crashed from too much traffic."

I laugh and grab my manager's wrist, shaking his arm. "These are good problems to have, Troy! Finally we have some good problems around here."

"I couldn't believe it when I got the e-mail that said I won," a fourteen-year-old girl named Sasha says to me backstage during my first meet-and-greet. "I was like, 'Agh!' and my best friend was like, 'OMG!' and then I was like, 'Mom!'"

"A riveting tale," the girl's mother says, her eyes dancing as she holds up her camera to take our picture.

"They said the meet-and-greets filled up pretty fast tonight, so I'm glad y'all could make it to one," I say as we smile together. "I think we're going to post them last-minute like this at every stop. It adds to the excitement."

"How many people got picked?" Sasha asks, wide-eyed.

"I think fifteen or twenty," I answer.

"That's so cool!"

It is cool. After my show, I headed straight for my dressing room and changed into regular clothes. Then I met my mom backstage and got my first glimpse of the "private lounge" she created, really just a small room decorated with wildflowers and candles. While Dylan isn't psyched about our folks being on the bus with us for the next month straight, I've liked being all together again and this job is perfect for her.

"Bird, may I interrupt?" Troy asks, smiling at Sasha and her mother. He gestures to a woman standing next to him with a daughter whose arms are cradling a fiddle and says, "I'd love to introduce you to Ibiza. She is the young fiddler I was telling you about a couple of months ago, whose mother wrote an article that was picked up by *The Huffington Post*—"

"Which is so embarrassing," Ibiza cuts in, stepping out from the arm her mother has across her shoulders. "I didn't talk to my mom for, like, a month after that went viral."

I glance up at her mother, who crosses her arms and smirks. "True story."

"What songs do you know?" I ask as I nod my head toward her instrument.

She blushes. "All of yours, obvi. And I learned that very first song you wrote when you were my age."

" 'Will She Ever Call?' " I ask surprised.

The girl nods. "And tonight when you covered that one section of Tim McGraw's song 'Where the Green Grass Grows' and changed it to 'Where the Bluegrass Grows,' I was screaming my head off with everybody else like, 'Um, I really love you now.' "

I laugh and offer her a fist bump. "I love you now, too, Ibiza."

"My friends call me Biza."

"All right, then, Biza. Want to get a picture? Did y'all grab some food?"

262

We join the other fans behind us on the couches and comfy chairs that will now become a standard part of our traveling production. The assembled group talks a little about which of my songs resonate with them and why, but mainly—and this is what I think I'll love about every meet up—they talk about their lives: what they deal with at school, what kind of heartbreak they've been through, whatever story is hot in the media right now, and even their viewpoints on politics and fashion. They ask me which other stars I know and who I'm actually friends with. And tonight, the big question is if Adam Dean and I are really dating.

"You can't believe everything you read in the magazines," I say. "But I will say that Adam is an old family friend, and he's one of the most talented singer-songwriters I've ever met. Hey, would y'all like to meet him, too?"

The *OMGs* and screams and fervent nods prompt me to pull out my cell phone, take an ussie with the group, and text it to him with the caption:

COME MEET MY FRIENDS!

I stare at the screen, and it's funny that the lounge has gone pretty quiet. "He may not be able to," I say, tempering their hopes a little.

But Biza reads over my shoulder and squeals, "He's

263

writing back. There's the dot dot dot. He's writing back!" which actually makes me as giddy as she is:

Be right there.

Biza and Sasha grab hands and scream. They met for the first time ten minutes ago, and now they're fangirling like besties. It's so great.

The mood in the room grows a little apprehensive as we talk about the Shine Our Light Tour, with everybody glancing at the door every few minutes. And now, as my adorably handsome show opener strides into the room in dark jeans, old boots, and a green plaid button-down, I get the same butterflies as all the girls currently gripping hands and trying to play it cool. We are all Adam Dean fangirls at this moment.

"I heard there's a party going on back here," Adam says as he makes his way over to the couch where I'm sitting and nudges me to scoot over. All the girls' faces are different shades of crimson, but Biza is the one to break the ice:

"Is the 'Make Her Mine' girl your girlfriend now?" Biza asks.

"Is that song about Bird?" Sasha asks on her heels.

Adam looks at me as if he doesn't know how to answer, and I guess, truthfully, he doesn't. We had the DTR between ourselves, but we haven't talked about whether we

264

should come out publicly as a couple. I'm sure our publicists will want some say in the matter, and after the rough patch we just went through, I'm not sure I can trust the media with the most special part of my life.

"I hate to be the party crasher," Troy says, coming over to save the day, "but our time is up. Thank you so much for spending a little extra time with us backstage, and we hope you've had an evening you'll never forget."

"Why don't y'all let Adam sign some autographs and take some pictures before we head back out on the road," I say, turning to the fans. The meet up really went by fast, and I hate the look of disappointment on their faces, but they are gracious as they pass us CDs, T-shirts, and posters. Biza is smart enough to linger in the back so that she's the last fan in the room, a strategic move I always admire in my most enthusiastic fans.

"Will you please sign my fiddle?" she asks, suddenly timid.

"I'd love to," I say, scrawling my name across the side with a black Sharpie.

"And can we take one more picture?"

"Of course," I say.

Biza's mom holds the camera up dutifully, but her daughter stops her.

"Mom, let Adam take it," she demands. "Yours are always blurry."

I try not to laugh as her mother shakes her head and passes the camera to a very amused Adam. I put my arm around the girl and smile, but then she points at her mom again and says, "And don't post it before me. It goes on my Instagram at least twenty-four hours before you can blog about it, deal?" Her mother nods, both exasperated and a little embarrassed to be put on blast like that.

But as Adam lines up the shot and Biza and I lean our heads together, smiling into the lens, it hits me that while my fans got to meet Bird Barrett in person tonight, the guy behind the camera knows the real me.

And hopefully loves me anyway.

26

"BIRD, I AM so sorry I can't be with you right now in New York," my publicist says a few days later over FaceTime.

"Don't sweat it," I say. "What's up?"

Troy, my mom, and I have just landed in the city and have a full day of promotion to do, post-Grammy nomination, before flying back to meet the tour in Duluth. We all know this will be a strenuous couple of months, balancing the tour with Grammy press and appearances, but I was nominated in *four* categories, so I've got some extra motivation. Troy is my lifesaver. He asked me to shoot him straight about what I really think I can handle. As opportunities arise, we're going to honestly weigh what their payoff will be versus the risk I take of pushing myself too hard again.

Anita picks up a bunch of large envelopes and holds them to the screen. "These are your invitations to the Clive Davis pre-Grammy party as well as numerous after parties. You and Troy need to start thinking about which of these you'll accept, if you want to perform at any, and how you envision your performance at the awards show itself. I want you to start brainstorming over the next few weeks so that when you're here during Christmas break, the entire Open Highway team can come together and create something extraordinary." She looks so smug as she says, "I want to show the world why Bird Barrett deserves Album of the Year."

"Every time I think about it, I get goose bumps," I say.

"And you need to think about your date," she goes on. Before I even reply she holds up a hand and says, "I know, I know. The Grammys aren't until February, but the paparazzi have snagged some good pot-stirring shots of you and Adam, and I think it's something you need to consider. Do you want to come out publicly as a couple? Are you ready for that?"

I look over at my mom, who raises her shoulders and shakes her head. Clearly this is a personal decision, and I don't get to make many of those, so I ask Anita if I can think about it.

"Please do," she says. "And ask Adam what he thinks. I'm sure his publicist will have some thoughts as well, but if it were me running this show, I think attending the Gram-mys together on Valentine's weekend would be the perfect way to let the world know that you're walking the red carpet with your special someone."

"Oh my gosh," I breathe.

I look at my mom, and she smiles. "It does seem kind of perfect, like your Cinderella moment."

"You'd think I'd have reached my life's quota on those," I say.

Mom reaches over and squeezes my hand. "It also gives you a couple more months to keep things to yourselves, which I know has been important to you."

I consider it as our plane taxis to the gate, picturing the whole thing. It really does seem perfect, and it would be amazing to take Adam to his first Grammys. I can just see his expression as he sits in an arena full of music icons and legends. And if I win one, he would be the first person I'd want to share it with anyway.

"I like it," I tell Anita as Troy unbuckles his seat belt and stands up. "We've got to go, but I'll talk to Adam and let you know."

I can't imagine that he would turn down the chance to go to the Grammys, but I don't know how he feels about taking our relationship public. After this conversation with my team, I really do feel like a fairy-tale princess on her way to a ball. Now to snag my prince...

"How is this happening right now?" Adam asks as he takes another shot from the free-throw line at the Smoothie King Center in New Orleans.

I rebound for him, bouncing the ball back his way. I'm just relieved to see him in a good mood. When we landed in Duluth, I was all set to tell Adam about Anita's plan. I figured he wouldn't need much convincing, but I had my whole spiel ready about how important he is to me and how I'm ready to take things to the next level, aka let the public know about us. I ran right over to his bus when we got back, but when his drummer opened the door for me, I immediately felt the tension. His band was fighting. One guy was threatening to quit the tour, and Adam looked completely helpless. Probably not the best time to talk about "us."

"I'll come back," I told him.

But it seems like our schedules haven't been lining up at all lately, with me flying off for press appearances about the Grammy nominations and him ducking out for local interviews or to record here and there. His label really wants to take advantage of the momentum he's gaining by being on my tour, so they've booked him in studios at a few stops so he can record on his days off or in his early-morning free time. It doesn't seem like the best idea to me, but Adam's still in that hungry stage. He wants so desperately to be successful.

270

I want that for him, too.

But still, I miss him.

We play here tomorrow night, and since we're both off today I asked Marco to pull some strings to get us court access. Adam and I have floor seats tonight for the Pelicans game, and we get to meet the team afterward, but right now, we're shooting hoops on the regulation floor. We only have about twenty minutes, but it's been enough to send him over the moon...and to put me at the top of the list of greatest girlfriends of all time.

"I just sank an NBA three-pointer on an actual NBA court!" he calls, his hands in the air. "Somebody pinch me."

"I think it's safe to say that this is what heaven looks like for guys," I remark.

"I think you're right," he replies with a silly grin. He grabs the ball and runs toward the basket, laying it in effortlessly. "Want to play around the world?"

I rebound and put the ball on my hip. "Sounds like the perfect game for a couple on tour," I say. "How do you play?"

He takes the ball from me and banks in a shot from the hash mark under the goal. "Usually you play around the three-point line, but we can play around the paint so it's a little easier, okay? We'll shoot from each of these little lines."

I look up at the basket. "Okay."

He steps to the line next to me and sinks that shot, too. I rebound, bounce passing the ball to him, and he moves to the next spot. "You're good," I say when I watch him make yet another basket.

"You sound surprised," he says, mock hurt.

"No, I just—I'm not a very good athlete."

He finally misses and chases down his own rebound.

"Yeah, but you're tall," he says. "Look how close your first shot is."

I stand on the white box to the right of the basket, and when I miss, he gives me another chance. When I miss that one, he walks around and helps me with my form. When I miss that one, he laughs and gives up, dribbling the ball back to his spot. Soon we fall into a fun groove: him making shots and moving easily around the world and me staying put at the first position while he laughs harder at my every attempt.

"Bank it, Bird," he finally says, grinning as he shows me how to bounce it off the box on the glass.

I throw another miserable attempt, and he nearly cries from laughing so hard. "You may break a world record soon," he chokes out. "Good thing you don't play for the Pelicans."

I laugh, too, and even if the jokes are on me, it's nice having Adam to myself again. He is now on his way back to the start, getting closer to where I've stayed put, when he looks at me with wonder and says, "You know, it's crazy enough playing this arena the way we do, but can you imagine what it's like for these guys? At least we're up on a stage. They're right in the belly of the beast, in a fishbowl, living and dying with each free throw." As he says that, he misses his. "And the opposing team cheers."

"Hooray!" I tease as I grab the ball. "Okay," I say, focusing on the rim. "This is my moment."

He stands right in front of me. "Take your shot, Bird."

"You're standing too close," I complain. "I'm afraid I'm going to hit you."

Adam moves behind me, and whispers in my ear, "Is this better?"

"No!" I squeal, pushing him back. I take my shot and miss, then rush him. "Cheater!"

"Oh yeah, like you would've made it if it weren't for me." He laughs and when I catch up to him, he throws both arms around me. "You know, it's been too long since I kissed you."

He does, briefly, and I notice that we both glance around to see if anyone is watching. *I know what he means about those guys in a fishbowl.*

"Adam?" I ask, attempting nonchalance as he loosens his hold on me. "Have you given any thought to all the tabloid speculation and stuff about us?"

He shrugs. "Not really. They ask me about you in

interviews and stuff, but I tell them you're an important person in my life and personal stuff is off-limits. I just say I'd rather talk about music."

I nod, following him as he goes for the ball. "Yeah, that's kind of what I've been doing, too."

He makes another shot and asks, "Is everything okay? Did I do something wrong?"

"No!" I say quickly. "No, no, no. Nothing like that."

"But something's on your mind," he says. An employee approaches us and lets us know that our time on the court is up. We give the ball back and thank him profusely, then leisurely walk toward the exit, neither of us saying anything.

Finally, I start up again. "It's just that I was thinking about the Grammys."

"Oh!" he says, looking over at me with fake surprise. "Are you going to that?"

I laugh and swat his arm.

"Bird, I know all that stuff is pretty carefully orchestrated. You don't have to worry about me. My feelings won't be hurt if I'm not your date."

"What?"

"Who's the lucky guy?" he asks. "Your brothers said they had a great time last year, but I know you've been missing your dad a lot, too."

"Well," I say, stopping in the tunnel, "Anita thinks I should take you."

He looks stunned. "Really?"

I nod.

He cocks his head, looking at me like there's a catch. "So Anita wants me to go, or you want me to go?"

"I'd love it if you went with me," I reply honestly. "I just want you to know that it'd be more than a regular date." I gulp. "The show's on Valentine's weekend this year. We'd be coming out, like, publicly. As a couple."

"Wait a minute," Adam says, a huge smile across his face. "So somebody's going to pay for me go on a romantic Valentine's Day date in Los Angeles, where I'll get to meet all my music heroes and cheer on my smoking-hot girlfriend?"

I grin and nod.

He walks toward me and kisses me, leading us backward until I'm leaning against the wall of the tunnel with his hands on either side of my head. When he pulls away, his eyes are twinkling. "Yeah, I think I'm in."

I beam at him.

"But full disclosure?" he says, trailing little kisses around my ear. "I'm irresistible in a tuxedo."

I clutch his shirt, bringing his mouth to mine again.

I don't doubt it.

27

"HEY," I SAY a week later, opening the front door of my Nashville house for my clearly exhausted boyfriend. "It's almost midnight. I was worried."

"Sorry," Adam says as he comes inside. He kicks his boots off and gives me a peck on the cheek before walking to the living room and crashing on the couch.

I can't read his mood, but I remember how hard I worked when we recorded *Wildflower*. Every phrase, every instrument, every lyric and the accompanying tone had to be perfect. It was torture, but then when a song was finished, it all felt worth it. I hope he's happy with what he's recording, but he hasn't wanted to talk about work after work. I sit down on the tiny bit of couch his body isn't occupying; he's sprawled out on his belly like a dead man. I run my fingers over his forehead and around his neck, gently, knowing how tired he must be. He puts his hands around my hips and pulls himself onto my lap, his eyes still closed as I play with his hair.

"We missed you at the movies tonight," I say softly. "I was a total third wheel with Stylan. Not even Zac Efron shirtless could make up for your absence."

"The *High School Musical* kid?" Adam asks, opening one eye.

"He's, like, almost thirty now," I say, flicking him in the head.

"Should I be jealous?" he asks with a lazy grin.

"Of his poster maybe," I say. "If you keep up these crazy hours, I'm going to need a stand-in."

He closes his eyes again and squeezes my waist. "They wanted to finish 'Let Her Preach' since we're off tomorrow and Friday for Christmas," he mumbles.

"Are you still coming over for the Second Annual Barrett Family Christmas Bash tomorrow night?"

He yawns so big and loud that it's almost laughable. "Definitely," he finally says.

I don't pester him anymore, knowing how important it is that he rests. Instead I play with his hair and watch the lights on the Christmas tree twinkle red, green, blue, and white. I left my phone on the kitchen counter, so I slip his out of his back pocket to put on some music. He doesn't even move, already knocked out on my lap, and when I slide my thumb across the screen to unlock his phone, I accidentally pull up a text message he hasn't checked. It's from his mom:

> I didn't realize a hundred bucks for a Christmas tree was asking so much. You're rich and famous now but can't help out your own mother?

Instantly I know I wasn't supposed to see this. I know I should push the HOME button and pull up his Music app like I had originally planned, but it already shows that it's a read message, so that's not what I do. Instead, I read more. Even though it's a pretty big violation of his privacy, I tell myself that Adam and I don't have secrets, or at least I don't. I glance down at his peaceful face to make sure he's still sleeping and then slowly scroll through their text thread, sickened by the things I read. Some messages are full of typos and mean rants where she's clearly intoxicated, some are little updates about him paying her phone bill or rent, but others are just pitiful, begging him to come home more often or call her once in a while. I feel like I'm in the head of a crazy person. His replies are always short and noncommittal, but I don't know how he stays so grounded while being pulled in so many different directions without any support at home. I suddenly feel protective of Adam, suddenly knowing with all my heart exactly how I feel about him.

"I love you, Adam Dean," I whisper. I bend over and kiss the top of his head, tears filling my eyes. "I love you now, and I always will."

"So you told him you love him?" Stella asks the day after Christmas. She came over on Christmas Eve, but so did half my extended family, including our boyfriends, so we didn't have time for intense girl talk. I texted her today that I wanted to hang out, just the two of us, and she suggested we go shopping. Why we thought the mall the day after Christmas was a good idea is beyond me, but I'm in disguise and I have security with me, so I'm hoping all goes well.

"Yeah, but he was asleep," I say.

"And you didn't tell him again?" Stella asks, confused. "Like, you know, when he was conscious?"

I shake my head. "I think I'm going to wait." I don't want to break his confidence by going too deep into the details about his home life, but I try to explain to my best friend how I'm feeling anyway. "It's like with Adam, he has this wall up. He didn't have the greatest childhood, and he protects himself by being this easygoing, fun-loving guy that everyone likes to be around. I feel like he probably doesn't want to get hurt, so he doesn't invest in many real relationships. Even you've said how our relationship has moved at a snail's pace—"

"So slow," she cuts in. "I don't see how you do it."

I ignore her tone, sidestep a distracted shopper, and go on. "And now that he's opening up to me, I don't want to scare him off."

"I see that, I guess," she says, looking at a cute phone case at a mall kiosk. "But maybe he's scared to say it first because you're a bigger star than he is and he doesn't want to look like an opportunist."

"Stella," I say. "Come on."

"What?" she asks, walking with me again. "Men can be intimidated by powerful women. I think he's just trying to show you that he's in it for you, not for your connections."

"Well, I already know that!"

"Yeah, but guys are dumb," she says, shaking her head and pinching her mouth up. "So dumb. So, so, so, so, so, so very dumb."

Clearly we aren't talking about Adam anymore.

"What'd he do?" I ask reluctantly. Then I add, "Broad strokes."

She rolls her eyes. "I know, I know. Boundaries."

I sigh. "Stella, I want to be there for you, but it's hard when the dumb guy is my brother."

"Look at this," she says, pulling me over to a bench.

"This is what Dylan got me for Christmas. *This.*" She pulls a gray hoodie out of the shopping bag she's holding. It says, *Don't follow me, I'm lost.*

I smile. "That's so you."

Stella's mouth falls open. "Are you serious right now?"

Immediately I realize I've reacted in the wrong way. I try to backtrack. "No, not like '*That's* so you,' because I know you don't really wear that type of clothing—"

"Bird," she interrupts. "It's a lace-up hooded tunic made out of sweatshirt material."

I think it looks comfy, but I know it's not her style. I screw my face up and hope it's the reaction she wants.

She blows air through her bangs and shakes her head. "I'm bummed because I spent a lot of time thinking about what to get him. I found a local artist to turn a selfie from the night of our first kiss into this gorgeous oil painting," she explains. "It was really special and thoughtful, and then he gets me this sweatshop piece of crap that he probably waited until a couple of days ago to get because he forgot."

I nod along, trying to stay neutral, but I know Dylan, and in his mind stores like Aeropostale, Abercrombie & Fitch, and Hollister are high-end. "Right, so you don't wear a lot of sweats—"

"Any."

"—and I can see where the lace-up sides are a little much—"

"A corset on a sweatshirt? That should be illegal!"

"—but I can also see how, for Dylan, it was a sweet gesture." I can't help but defend my brother a little.

Stella looks at me like I've personally betrayed her. "Never mind. Let's get a pretzel."

She stands up and starts walking away so that I have to chase after her. "Stella, seriously," I say. "Dylan loves that store, and I know he didn't wait until the last minute because I saw my mom wrapping it for him over Thanksgiving break. And it actually *is* thoughtful, because on tour it's like, Stella, seriously, you know you never know where we are. And you are a terrible navigator. Remember when we drove around Seattle trying to get to the Space Needle, which was so big that we were all like, 'It's right there!' but Google Maps kept telling you to circle the block and we wasted, like, twenty minutes driving around it?" She breaks a little, softening. "See? It brought back that good memory for me, so I can see where he's coming from. It's funny. I know it's not romantic or sentimental, but to be honest, you're not exactly dating a romantic or sentimental guy."

She sighs and looks down at the offending gift, her lip curled up on one side.

"I told him it was the wrong size," she says.

"So return it," I say. "His feelings won't be hurt."

She looks around the mall, at the throngs of people hurrying to capitalize on sales and exchange unwanted Christmas gifts, and shrugs. "I'll come back another day. Besides, even in that baseball cap and sweats, you're starting to get some stares."

"'Stars—they're just like *us*!'" I say. "'They return Christmas presents with their besties!'"

Stella laughs and links her elbow through mine. "Let's go, superstar. I want to get my nails done."

"Look at these sketches," Stella coos once we're back on tour after New Year's. My styling team handles the pieces of card stock as if they are ancient scrolls that could crumble at our touch. Tonight is Miami, our first show back from break, and Anita sent over a FedEx today with some Grammy dress options. Even though "Music's Biggest Night" is a little over a month away, planning for the big event has been in high gear over the past couple of weeks, and I've got a huge binder full of ideas and designs.

"The pleats here are perfection," Amanda whispers. My head stylist, who is impressed by very little that life has to offer, looks like she might faint. "Oh, and this one with the intricate print."

"Right?" Stella agrees. "And I just can't with these swatches. Feel this fabric, Bird."

"I like that one best," I say, pointing to a coral, form-fitting, floor-length gown with a high neck.

"That's my favorite for you, too," Stella says immediately. "Your body shape is perfect for this."

"I absolutely agree," Amanda says. "And I adore the way the fabric falls around the back, almost like a cape but also giving the illusion of fuller sleeves. It's genius."

"How do you think they'll want your hair?" Tammy asks as she puts the finishing touches on mine.

"I think we should go bold with the makeup for your actual performance," Sam chimes in. "But if that's the dress you go for on the red carpet, we should keep it sweet and natural with maybe a statement lip."

I stare at myself in the mirror and zone out as they buzz around me: Tammy fussing with a stubborn curl in my hair, Sam preparing his pouch for touch-ups throughout the show, Amanda steaming my opening dress, and Stella finally putting my sketches away as if it pains her to do so. They get back to dressing me, their doll. I think about the other celebrities who will be at the Grammys, the same ones at so many of my events, all of us contemplating how we will look and all of us parading down the red carpet, exactly like a string of paper dolls.

And inspiration strikes.

I lean down and grab my bag, ignoring Tammy's complaints. When I have a pen and my songwriting journal in my hands, I allow her to get back to work, but a song has taken hold and I've learned that nothing is more important than seizing the moment. This time the Grammys feel bigger than the other events, and it's not because I'm nominated for four this year or because I've been requested at so many other events that weekend. It's because Adam will be on my arm, and he never seems to care how I look.

I hear the melody in my head and chase it across the page with a pen:

> *Some see a paper doll.*
> *Strung out for all to admire,*
> *Who would curl and crumble in the fire,*
> *Two-dimensional.*
> *But there's more to me.*
> *I'm a different person than they see.*
> *I'm not a paper doll.*
> *Not their paper doll.*
> *At all.*

28

"Bird, there's Dave Grohl!" Adam whispers in my ear as we wait our turn to walk the red carpet together for the first time ever. I am giddy with anticipation.

"Be prepared for your mind to be blown over and over and over again," I tell him, both of us stupendously elated to be at the Grammy Awards after weeks and weeks of preparation. "You thought the Clive Davis pre-party was something? This is that times ten."

"Then my mind will explode tonight because I had a ten-minute conversation with Keith Urban at that party, and I don't think my brain has fully accepted it. I'm still in shock. I don't even know my own name right now."

I laugh out loud. "When my brothers and I were here

last year, we felt like we were in a Madame Tussauds museum. Like, are these people real?"

"Bird, Adam, are we ready?" Anita asks briskly, adjusting her diamond bracelet. She chose a deep-midnight Gucci dress that fits her like a glove; she's a complete pro at looking glamorous while blending into the background. "It's showtime."

"You're going to lead us down the carpet, right?" Adam asks, plainly nervous.

"I'll be a few steps ahead," she says. "And remember, you're not alone. Your date is an expert."

I smile over at him, and it hits me that it wasn't that long ago that I was as clueless and slightly terrified as Adam is now. But tonight, I'm not nervous at all, just excited to claim my man in front of the world.

The minute we are in view of the press line, I hear my name. I do as I've been trained, plastering on a smile and posing as they shout. Camera bulbs *pop* and flash as I pay homage to the gorgeous creation Zac Posen tailor-made for me. I fell in love with the coral color and luxurious fabric the moment I saw the first sketch and swatch, and tonight I hope to make the designer proud as I stand tall in his form-fitting gown, throwing my shoulders back to accentuate the fabric billowing freely to my midback. Sam kept my makeup light and natural, and Tammy styled my normally loose waves back from my face in a twist of delicate braids.

"You are radiant," Adam says, after giving me the initial moment in the spotlight as Anita instructed. But now that he's next to me, I feel even more beautiful. He wraps his arm lightly around my waist and rests his hand on my hip as we smile to our left, then slowly move our heads to the right so we aren't looking in opposite directions in all the photos. He had scoffed at the red carpet tip sheet Anita sent him, but now that he's here in the madness, I bet he's glad we went over it. I know he's nervous, but he looks totally cool and absolutely edible in his crisp black Calvin Klein tux.

When we're a quarter of the way down the carpet, Anita gives me the signal that it's time to be cuddly. I can show the world that Adam Dean is not just my tour opener or my date tonight, but also my boyfriend. I smile at him, not used to seeing his face free of stubble, and kiss him on the cheek, giggling when I see that I've left a lipstick mark. I hear a swell in the crowd's chatter and know that we are the center of attention. I beam at my date. "I guess we're official now."

"I don't know," he says, putting his forehead against my own. "I think it could be official-er."

The moment is perfect, it's magical, it's the stuff of my dreams from four years ago as his lips brush mine. I hear a little *pop* of excitement, see flashbulbs on the back of my eyelids, and know we made the press happy with our PDA.

Anita gestures for me to walk forward to an *Entertainment Tonight* reporter, and we give them the first "official couple" interview. Then we continue to pose our way down the red carpet, stopping occasionally to talk to reporters behind the press line as well as other celebrities we bump into. I introduce Adam to Bridget and Bria, reality show twins I ran around with when I first got a place in LA. He also gets to meet the members of Caitlyn's Cradle, a band I really like that was in the Best New Artist category with me at the last Grammys.

"Wow, are your cheeks hurting?" Adam asks me after half an hour.

I grin, totally able to relate on most occasions, but tonight I don't have to fake it. My cheeks don't get tired from smiling, my lips don't go dry, and I don't have to worry about my eyes bugging out. I feel so at home with Adam on my arm that when we finally enter the Staples Center, I know we're in for a night that neither of us will ever forget.

"You were incredible!" Adam says when I get back to my seat after my performance of "Shine Our Light." I've never seen him so pumped up in my life. The calm demeanor is gone now; he's losing it, shaking his head as he holds one hand to his forehead and the other tightly around my Grammy for Best Country Song. "That was phenomenal! People out here were going nuts, Bird. It was crazy!"

"Adam!" I laugh. "You are too much right now."

"Listen, I've seen you perform live for months, but *nothing* has come close to that. That was at another level completely, and that's not just lip service."

I grin. "Well, I sure could use a little of that."

He laughs, shaking his head at my corniness, and gives me a quick kiss on the lips. A few other Open Highway people reach over to compliment my performance, and we all take our seats as the host starts introducing the next presenter.

"Thanks for babysitting this bad boy while I was up there," I whisper, reaching for my golden Gramophone. I totally freaked out when they called my name—*I won my first Grammy!*—but somehow, I managed to read my thank-you speech without going over the time limit.

"You know," Adam says as he passes the Grammy toward me, clutching it tighter when I try to take it. "I can hold on to it a little longer if you want. Even stash it on my bus for safekeeping."

"Ha-ha," I say, jerking it out of his hands. Then I cradle the prize and whisper, "You're safe now, baby. Shh. Momma's here."

"Bird," Anita says, leaning over Adam to get my attention as the next presenters take the stage. "This is the moment. I sincerely believe in *The Road to You*, but no matter what happens, remember that the cameras will be right there." She points to a guy setting up in the aisle beside me.

"And you need to be gracious in your reaction either way. It sounds cliché, but it really is an honor to be nominated."

"Hey, I agree a hundred percent," I say, nodding.

A shiver runs up my spine as music goddess Beyoncé Knowles walks across the stage in a shimmery silver dress, escorted by her copresenter Adam Levine. As they approach the microphone to uproarious applause, everyone in the audience knows what's next.

"'Music's Biggest Night' celebrates music from all genres, represents people from all parts of the world, and celebrates cultural differences right here in our own country," Beyoncé says. "So do this year's nominees for Album of the Year."

My competition is stiff. As Adam Levine reads from the teleprompter, a snippet of each nominee's biggest hit plays over the speakers.

"*Catch Me Crazy*. Mz. Communication," he announces. "*Drifting*. Evangeline Grey," he continues as we clap. The same progression for Delightful Chaos, me, and Kingdom-Luxe. Then I see all our faces projected together on a humongous screen as we wait with nervous anticipation. There is a camera right at my feet, right there to capture my reaction, win or lose, and I can feel the eyes of the world watching. I grab Adam's hand and squeeze.

Beyoncé takes the mic again. "And the Grammy goes to . . ."

Adam's knee is bobbing up and down involuntarily, and a trickle of sweat drips down my side even though it's freezing in here. I can feel the nerves from the entire Open Highway team in the seats around me. It's one of those moments when you wish you could fast-forward a few seconds, or pause for a minute, because experiencing it in real time is absolute torture.

"If I can get this open," Beyoncé says. Except for a few random shouts, the Staples Center is eerily quiet as she prepares to announce the winner for the biggest award of the night. "Oh, I loved this album. *The Road to You.* Miss Bird Barrett."

My mouth falls open. My hand is at my heart. I know people are cheering, are squeezing my shoulders and slapping me on the back, but it's like I am watching it all from outside my body. Somehow I rise to my feet and then Adam has me in a bear hug, sweeping me into the aisle as Dan, Anita, and a bunch of other Open Highway people file out of our row. I give my first Grammy back to Adam and follow my Nashville producer, Jack Horn, to the stage, walking in a trance toward Adam Levine and Queen B.

When I get to the stage, I am fighting tears. "I can't believe I just hugged Beyoncé," I say into the mic, my voice quivering as I look down at the award in my hands. The crowd laughs, and it brings me to the present with clarity. "Oh man, this is unbelievable. Thank you, first and foremost, to my fans.

292

You did this," I say. I hold the Grammy up and repeat myself. "You did this, Birdies!" The upper decks go nuts, and it's the greatest feeling in the world. "I want to thank my family, my boyfriend, my publicist, my manager, and especially this man, Dan Silver, the president of my label, who believed in me from day one. *The Road to You* started off bumpy, and I'm so grateful that I can call Open Highway Records my home, that I get to write honestly and that I get to share what's in my head and in my heart. Thank you to all the producers up here who know me well enough that when I think I've given my best, they push me harder." I pause and see Bruno Mars nodding along and Adele smiling in the front row. I continue to scan the elite section: Mumford & Sons, Pharrell, Rihanna, and Taylor Swift all staring at me, all smiling as if to say, *Cherish this moment.*

"And to the other nominees, your albums were brilliant. To every musician sitting in the seats tonight, in every genre, you continue to raise the bar, you continue to create amazing beats and hooks and lyrics, you continue to touch lives with music from your soul, and you should see my iTunes playlist. I may be a country artist, but you inspire me. I want to be bold like Mz. Communication, vulnerable like Evangeline Grey, rock hard like Delightful Chaos, and be able to fuse sounds like Kingdom-Luxe consistently does so well. As I look out at this diverse crowd of musical geniuses, allow me to say: *I am a fan.*" Pockets of people start to clap, and I finish up over the applause. "I learn from you. Music is meant to be shared, and so I share this award with you all."

Much to my surprise, Wiz Kahlifa stands up and shouts, "Hell yeah!" Then Drake is on his feet. Jay Z, Justin, Katy Perry, the Black Keys, every person in the Staples Center stands up and applauds passionately. It is a beautiful chorus, a beautiful moment of unity. "Thank you, everybody!"

As the orchestra music swells, I follow my team across the stage a changed person, never again to be Bird the fiddler in her family's band or Bird Barrett an act to watch, but for now and forever more as Album of the Year Grammy–award winner Bird Barrett. I clutch my gold statue tight, just so I have something to keep me in the moment, just so I know that it's real.

29

"THIS PLACE IS packed," Adam shouts over the music at an after party later.

"Right?" I say. "But packed with megastars. It's like a weird dance club where everybody you pass is a little more famous than the last person you saw."

"Exactly!"

Every time Adam and I end up in a conversation with a huge celeb, we are downright starstruck. We completely gush over their music, but the cool thing is that it's not long before we and the celebrity find common ground and are just talking shop, like we've been friends forever. This event is like a fantastic otherworld, where every person here is in awe of some other person here. Rather than any one of us being the star of the room, we're all regular people having a good time. My brothers and I didn't hit up any after parties last year, so it's been fun to experience something completely new with Adam.

But it's been a long night. "How long do these things last?" he asks, trying to suppress a yawn.

I shrug. "Is it lame to leave?"

"Lame to call it a night at two in the morning?" he asks. "Not at all. And now we have His and Hers Grammys to snuggle."

I elbow him in the rib cage. "Lay off, Dean. You'll win your own soon enough."

"Hello, stranger," a low voice says behind me.

"Jason!" I say when I turn around. We do the standard Hollywood double-cheek air kisses, and even though nothing even close to romantic ever happened between us, I am a little nervous when I turn to introduce him to Adam. "You have got to meet my boyfriend, Adam Dean."

Adam doesn't look tired anymore. In fact, he looks quite alert as he reaches out a hand and shakes with the guy who inadvertently caused us trouble during our first go 'round.

"Hey, from 'Make Her Mine,' right?" Jason asks enthusiastically. "That song is terrific. I always blast it in the car. It's country but rock, and it's got a lot of heart, man. Jason Samuels is a big fan."

Adam's eyebrows nearly hit his hairline he's so shocked.

"Thank you. I had a pretty tempting muse," he says, nudging me with his shoulder.

"Bird, did you see Devyn? I'm sure she'd love to catch up," Jason asks, the most innocently clueless man on earth. "Or Kayelee? They're running around here somewhere."

"I haven't seen them," I say, trying to be sweet. "I've been on tour and haven't spent much time at our LA place lately. I did see Bria and Bridget on the—"

"Adam!"

I spin around, knowing that voice anywhere, and am dumbstruck when the devil herself comes running up to him with her cleavage about to spill out of her very low-cut dress.

"Hey, Kayelee," he says as she throws her arms around his neck and rubs her boobs all over his chest. He clumsily pats her back and tries to pull away, glancing at me like a kid in trouble with his mom.

"How are you?" Kayelee squeals as she finally pulls away from *my boyfriend* and completely ignores both Jason and me.

"Good, good," Adam says awkwardly.

"Are you loving this after party?" she shouts, sliding one hand over his chest and tipping back a mixed drink with the other. The music is loud, but she's clearly not aware of how much louder she is . . . or of the average personal space bubble.

"Yeah." He nods, looking around. "It's a lot of fun."

"So, Bird, what've you been up to since I saw you last?" Jason asks, realizing as I do that we are being completely iced out of their conversation.

"Still on tour," I say, turning my back to Kayelee. "My label added more dates, so it looks like I'll be playing in Europe in May."

"That's spectacular," he says. "You have to text me for suggestions. Jason Samuels knows Europe."

"Not as well as Colton Holley knows Europe," Colton Holley himself says, slinging an arm around Jason's shoulders. I look around, wondering how and why all these people just keep popping up out of nowhere. It's like I'm in some kind of weird horror movie. "Bird Barrett, you vixen. It's always a pleasure to see you," Colton says, his eyes shining as he grabs my hand and brings it to his lips. "You are as ravishing as ever."

"Hello, Colton," I say politely. I glance over my shoulder at Adam, who looks miserable as Kayelee blabs on and on about the direction of her next album, repeating herself a lot and having trouble keeping her balance. I don't even think she realizes that she's backed into me twice, because knowing Kayelee, she would revel in it much more if it were on purpose.

"Bird and I once had a very romantic evening in Las Vegas," Colton tells Jason now, his voice suggestive and his eyes full of mischief.

Jason looks over at me, astonished. "Really?"

"Unfortunately," Colton continues with a pout, "with Vegas being the cruel wench that she is, I did not get lucky."

"Oh, 'unfortunately'?" Kayelee repeats, spinning around and staring daggers into Colton's face as she stumbles between us. "Well, 'unfortunately,' I just spilled my drink." And taking everyone off guard, she slings her cocktail right into his face, splashing some on Jason and causing everyone nearby to gasp and stare.

"Bird, that's our cue," Adam says softly, tugging at my elbow. I don't even say good-bye to Jason. Instead, I let Adam lead me right out of that drama and we don't look back.

"That was insane!" I say once we've put some good distance between us.

"She's completely blitzed," Adam says, shaking his head. "She's got so much talent, but she's such a mess."

"You still ready to go?" I ask, changing the subject.

"Definitely."

We weave a path through the crowd toward the front entrance, where people are bottlenecking at the doors. I'd rather wait out the crowd than push my way through, so we hang back to the side in a quiet hallway and sit on a little ledge. "Was tonight what you expected?" I ask Adam as I lay my head on his shoulder.

"It was better," he says, kissing my head. "You won *two* Grammys, Bird. How sick is that? How amazing is that?"

I smile. "I'm not the same girl you met a few years ago, that's for sure."

"All that's changed is the wrapping," Adam says. "Your hair is redder, you wear nicer clothes, you go to Cinderella balls with a studly Prince Charming…"

I laugh.

"But none of that has anything to do with who you are," he says. He takes my hand in one of his and rubs circles on the back with his thumb. I feel him tilt his face down, and then his lips are at my hairline. "You're still the girl I fell in love with at the Station Inn," he murmurs. "And again at the Pancake Pantry. And again last Christmas Eve. And yet again during the food fight in Chicago."

I blink, feeling like the wind has been knocked out of me as I look up at him.

"You are still the most amazing person I've ever known. Money or fame or press or bad days? None of that is going to change the way I feel about you."

He stares at me, vulnerable, those eyes with brown-and-green-and-yellow flecks and lashes that go on for days searching mine. He stares at me and it's like I feel him looking at my bare soul, as if he knows my heart and already feels the sensation that courses through my veins, bringing my love for him to every fiber of my being.

"I love you, too, Adam." I say it with strength, with power, so he'll know it's not just a return-the-volley reply, but a truth that is as much a part of Bird Barrett as my blue eyes and beating heart.

When he kisses me, I feel my body go to jelly. Movie stars and rock stars buzz around us, but we are swept up in another realm, a different moment in time where I didn't win two Grammys and he isn't about to release his first album. We aren't two celebrities, we're just two people in love.

Adam pulls away and looks at me with a full smile. "You know I'm going to write a song about this," he says.

I feel my own smile rival his. "Not if I write one first."

"Hey, lovebirds," Kayelee sneers behind us. Reluctantly, I turn around. Her makeup is smeared, it looks like she's been crying, and she has ripped her couture gown. "Get a room. And not this room. Like a real—"

Kayelee pauses, looking like she might vomit.

"Are you all right?" I ask. "You look like you might be sick."

"*You* make me sick!" she shouts.

A few people in the hallway turn around, and the last thing I want is an awards show after party video of us going viral, so I stand up and softly suggest, "Hey, Kayelee, let's go into the bathroom. There's one down this way with no lines. Maybe splash some cool water on your face?"

"How 'bout instead you go straight to—"

And then she slaps her hand over her mouth. She heaves but doesn't puke.

"Come on," I say, getting behind her and pushing her toward the bathroom. Adam grabs one of her arms and, amazingly, she doesn't fight us. "Okay, in here," I say as she dives into the door at the end of the hall. It's not long before we hear her losing it and a partygoer flees the restroom with a look of disgust on her face. "Now this is a party!" I joke with Adam. "To think we almost left."

"Whoa," he says, looking a little pale. He has to step away when he hears Kayelee gagging again.

"Are you okay?"

"Yeah, just—weak stomach."

I look down the corridor and see a few people snickering, the gossip mill turning already, but nobody comes to Kayelee's aid. "Where are her people?" I ask. Adam shrugs.

I start to pace, not knowing what to do. I don't owe Kayelee Ford anything, but I don't think it's right to leave her in there by herself, either.

"Are *you* okay?" Adam asks, seeing the inner turmoil all over my face.

I pick at an already chipped nail and think it through. "I *am* okay because I have you. And Stella and my family and Dan, Troy, and Anita—and thank God for Bonnie. I have a lot of people, Adam. But Kayelee? I don't think she has anybody. Not really."

"Yeah."

I walk to the end of the hallway and scan the crowd,

hoping to catch sight of Randall or Colton or Devyn or *somebody.* "Who'd she even come with?" I ask Adam as I walk back toward the bathrooms.

He shrugs again.

I sigh mightily, knowing what I have to do. "I'm going to check on her."

Adam's eyebrows nearly jump off his face. "Really?"

I nod and walk toward the bathroom, but before I can open the door Adam is at my side. "See? Different on the outside, but the same sweet Bird on the inside."

I smile. "All right, Romeo. Just go find somebody that'll take her home."

"Kayelee?"

I push open the handicapped stall and see my arch nemesis, Kayelee Ford, passed out in her own puke on a public restroom floor. I'm pretty sure I need to establish she's breathing and wake her up, but I'm also pretty sure I don't want her to ruin my cocktail dress. It's Valentino, and it's Valentine's weekend, and of the three gowns I've worn tonight, it's the only one I don't have to give back. This is not how I imagined my night at the Grammys.

"Ugh," she groans.

Good. She's alive.

I step into the stall with her, and the stench is so disgusting that I worry I might get sick, too. I hold my breath and flush the vomit down, then I wipe the seat with toilet paper and flush that as well. I walk over to the sink to get some paper towels and catch my reflection in the mirror. I pause for a moment.

"Okay, Bird," I say, giving myself a pep talk. "This is your moment. You've made some big mistakes yourself, right? You wanted people to forgive you, right? So practice what you preach. Do it. Now or never. Let's go."

I grab a bunch of paper towels and run water over them, then head back to the situation at hand. "Kayelee?" I say softly, wiping her cheek and chin. I formulate a plan as I clean her up. "Okay, you know what? First, let's take off these Jimmy Choos. I couldn't even walk in these sober. And we have to clean off your dress, okay? It's disgusting. Kayelee? Can you hear me?"

She groans again but lets me pull her up to a sitting position and then starts mumbling some crazy stuff about dancing with dinosaur-sized unicorns. I remove a rubber band from one of my little braids and oh-so-carefully pull back Kayelee's hair to get it off her face and neck. I ask her to tell me more about the giant unicorns, partly to keep her awake and partly so she won't realize it's me helping her. I have a feeling that the minute she sobers up a little, I'm the last person she'll want seeing her like this.

Once she's clean, I wash my hands with the meticulous devotion of a neurosurgeon.

I grab a few more wet paper towels and hold them to her forehead as she dozes, dabbing her hairline and wiping away some of the makeup smeared all over her cheeks and around her eyes. I don't know what else to do.

Suddenly, her eyes flutter open, and I am face-to-face with a confused and very pathetic-looking Kayelee Ford. I flinch, worried she might go off on me. Instead, she slowly asks a simple question: "Why are you helping me?"

I don't answer. I don't *have* an answer. So I lead her to the sink and help her wash her hands. "Why don't you come over and sit down?" I gently suggest as I lead her to a bench below an open window. She plops down like a puppet without a master, her limbs splayed out at ungraceful angles, her head heavy and hanging forward. "Here, lean against me," I say, sitting next to her. She roughly tips her head onto my shoulder.

"Thank you," she says after a minute, turning her face up to mine. "I don't know why you're being so nice to me, but thank you."

I nod, not knowing what to say.

And then Kayelee starts sobbing. Not sniffling or fighting back tears, but full-on sobbing. "Kayelee," I say, alarmed. Tears stream down her face, and her body shakes violently. I wrap my arms around her shoulders and try to hold her still, but she's heaving and gasping for breath, a complete emotional release of anything she's ever held inside. I'm a little freaked out, but I think about what my mom would do if she were here and I affect a soothing voice. "Kayelee," I purr, trying to soothe her while keeping her upright as she bawls. "Kayelee, come on now. You're okay. Adam went to get help, and you're going to be okay. It's all going to be okay."

She wipes her face with her bare arm and gasps for breath, trying to get control of herself. Finally, when she stops shaking, she looks at me, her eyes tortured, and says, "No, it won't. I haven't been okay in a long time."

30

"THIS IS THE right thing," Bonnie says as she parks her car at Cumberland Heights Alcohol and Drug Rehab outside Nashville.

I called her the day after the Grammys and told her all about the Kayelee drama. Later that day, *TMZ* leaked a terrible headline, FORD PULLS INTO REHAB, and that's all everybody's been talking about since. When I wanted another scandal to overshadow my own, this wasn't what I had in mind. Taking care of Kayelee that night was scary. I wouldn't wish her demons on my worst enemy.

The first thing Bonnie suggested I do was reach out to Kayelee, the same way Jolene Taylor did for her years ago. But I had to get back on tour, my schedule was slammed, and it wasn't like I had Kayelee's phone number. So a few weeks went by and I moved on, went to Europe, stopped thinking about it. Kayelee was getting help, rehab is a good thing, and none of it had anything to do with me.

But leave it to Bonnie to start blowing up my phone the minute I was back in Nashville for a special concert at the Ryman. Text after text of sage counsel like:

I thought Jolene Taylor was my worst enemy, but when I hit rock bottom, it turned out she was the only friend I had.

All she can do is tell you to go to hell, but I guarantee she thinks she's already there.

You're always talking about burying the hatchet and making things right. Well, there's no Internet or press or spotlights in rehab. If there ever was a place and time, it's here and now.

Adam-the-Saint thought it was a good idea, too, especially since Kayelee and I had "bonded" at the after party, but I quickly reminded him that she had been so drunk, she probably didn't even remember it. Stella thought it made total sense that I didn't want to go, but the fact that I was on the fence about it meant that I'd have regrets if I didn't. And my folks, well, they just said they knew I'd do what was right.

So, reluctantly, I agreed to visit Kayelee in rehab if Bonnie would come with me. It took us about twenty-five minutes to get out here. It was a quiet, thoughtful ride. I'm sure Bonnie was reliving some rough memories, and I was going over in my head all the terrible outcomes that were likely to happen once Kayelee Ford saw my face.

"Don't you think rehab is hard enough?" I ask nervously now as we walk toward the facility's front door. "I mean, it was probably really hard to come here in the first place, and she has to know that everybody's talking about it: the media, her fans, industry people. Then I come strolling in, and she thinks I'm all smug, and we already know she hates me, and—"

"Bird," Bonnie interrupts as she opens the door. "All this visit does is show that we care. That at least two people on earth care."

"I'm sure her family cares," I say quietly as we enter.

"You never know," she answers with a shake of the head. I think of Adam and his mother. "And remember, I had to have this visit approved with her therapist. If she didn't want to see you, all she had to do was say no."

"I can't believe you're here right now," Kayelee says as we walk down the wide, tree-lined drive a few minutes later.

"Me neither, honestly," I reply.

We keep our eyes focused ahead, one foot in front of the other, my hands in my coat pockets and hers in her jeans pockets. We haven't made eye contact since she first came out to the lobby and asked me to go for a walk. Bonnie made herself comfortable in the waiting room with a magazine, and I was on my own.

"It's really pretty out here," I finally comment.

Kayelee looks up and breathes deeply. "Yeah. We moved to Tennessee when I was fifteen, but I feel like this is the first time I'm really seeing it. We don't have cell phones or Internet or anything here, so all we can really do is, like, be present. Every day I take long walks on this big trail they've got, and I'm like, 'When's the last time I heard the wind blow through the trees? When's the last time I noticed a little plant sprout through the dirt?'"

"It's almost spring," I say, thinking about the metaphor and how it could apply to her situation.

"Don't *even* say it's the perfect time of year for rebirth," she warns.

I scoff, giving her my best *as if* expression while I secretly worry she's telepathic.

Kayelee exhales and looks back down at her feet. "Sorry. I didn't mean to snap at you. They're really driving that home in group therapy," she explains.

I rack my brain for something appropriate to say. Nothing comes to mind. We walk.

"I feel like I've been going so hard the past few years that I've missed real life," she admits.

"I actually know what you mean there," I say.

I see her nod in my peripheral vision. We keep walking slowly. The sun shines down brightly on the expansive acreage, and I can see why someone would come here for a break during a breakdown. It reminds me of my time at Bonnie's.

"I really can't believe that you're here," Kayelee says again, shaking her head.

I glance over at her, but then look away quickly.

"We're in group sessions and individual therapy a lot during the day, and in the, um, twelve steps we have to acknowledge our wrongdoings and make amends with the people we've wronged. If it's possible." She takes a breath. We keep walking. "I knew I'd need to get to you. I don't know if you've noticed, but I had my mom deactivate my Twitter account. I'm sorry for . . . well, a lot."

"Oh. Okay."

Kayelee takes a deep breath, and then words start tumbling out of her mouth like water from a busted dam. "It was so weird when we were coming up together and everybody kept telling me that we looked alike and sounded alike, and I knew that Dan had poached you from

Randall and I—" She kicks a rock from the path into the grass. "This is going to sound so stupid—" She stops walking. "I just wanted to prove to Randall and everybody that GAM didn't get me as some kind of consolation prize. That I could be as good as you."

I feel her staring at me, so I look over at her. "Oh."

She starts walking again, and I match her pace. "My dad actually invested in GAM to encourage them to offer me a development deal," she admits, embarrassed. "He's always reminding me how much he's sacrificed. And I don't know if you know this, but my mom was Miss Florida, like, *way* back in the day, so she's constantly on me to be her perfect, pretty girl and—" She shakes her head. "I know this is all so dumb. When I hear it, I feel so dumb. But it got to the point that I was always 'on.' All these people were constantly around me telling me to do this event or that, to sing this type of song when I wanted to do something different, or they were in my ear about where *you* were on the charts."

"They pitted us against each other from the start," I say.

She nods, chewing her lip and thinking. Then, very quietly, she says, "It's like I'm always surrounded but somehow . . . I just feel totally alone."

I don't know what to say. I'm shocked that Kayelee Ford, my supposed rival, is opening up like this.

"So anyway, with you and these 'amends,' I figured one

day I'd have my publicist reach out to yours, or I'd try to contact you somehow to apologize for letting it all get out of control, but then my therapist said you'd reached out and—" Kayelee finally stops walking and looks up at me. "I don't know why you're here, Bird. I've been so mean."

I stop, too. I look at Kayelee, her face in a genuine expression of wonder. This is the first time I've seen her without intensely made-up eyes, without her violet-blue contact lenses, in jeans that don't look painted on. She looks like an average girl. She looks like me.

And I hug her.

I don't know why, but I reach out both arms and hug this girl. Because I know the pressure she's talking about— the pressure to make sure your parents didn't sacrifice everything for nothing, the pressure to make it to the top, the pressure to hone a public image, and then the pressure to maintain it. I know this hurting girl who wants a break sometimes, and I hate that she found it in alcohol. I hate that she doesn't have an Adam or a Stella or a Bonnie or a Barrett Family Band. And I am so grateful that I do.

I pull away and see that she's crying. I feel pricks at the corners of my own eyes. She passes me a tissue from the little pack in her pocket and smiles. "My therapist thought we might need these," she explains with a sniff. She rolls her eyes. "God, they act like they know everything."

I laugh out loud. "Now there's the Kayelee Ford I know."

"Hey, I'm here to stop drinking, not to stop telling it like it is," she says with a wry grin.

We start walking again and things feel, surprisingly, easy and normal. She asks about Adam and tells me she thinks we're a really good fit. "He's a great guy." And she tells me about a recent falling-out she had with Devyn Delaney, commenting, "She's such a user." She asks what people are saying about her online, and I try to soften the blow, telling her that all anybody wants is for her to get well. I tell her about my time at Bonnie's farm and how songwriting is always an outlet for me when I need one.

"You're lucky," she says. "I don't play an instrument and I'm not exactly poetic. I kind of have to go with whatever the label picks. Whenever I suggest something it's like, 'No, we know what's best for you.'" She sighs. "I feel like such a puppet sometimes."

Immediately, "Paper Doll" comes into my head, and I start to sing:

"Some see a paper doll.
Strung out for all to admire,
Who would curl and crumble in the fire,
Two-dimensional.
But there's more to me.
I'm a different person than they see.
I'm not a paper doll.

Not their paper doll.
At all."

Kayelee stops walking and grabs my upper arm. "Yes," she says. She squeezes tighter, and tears well up in her eyes again. "Yes, Bird."

"You're not, you know."

She nods sharply, pursing her lips. "Sing it again?"

I start the chorus again, and by the time we're at the end of the drive, she has joined me. We turn back toward the facility, and I harmonize as Kayelee carries the melody. It shocks me how well our voices blend together, what a pretty sound we make when we're not screeching at each other. When we finish the chorus, we walk the rest of the way back in comfortable silence, breathing in the fresh, cool air.

I know that while we may never be best friends, we will always have a respectful understanding of each other from this day forward.

And I'm so glad I came.

31

"I DON'T THINK she's coming," Adam says softly. Along with several other artists, I've been invited to play Opry Country Classics at the legendary Ryman Auditorium, the "Mother Church of Country Music." Adam and I are backstage, watching the show as we wait for my turn to go on.

He was so excited for me when I first booked this gig. Playing at the Ryman is a huge deal, something both of us have always dreamed of, but now, as I look at his desperately disappointed face, I can't see a trace of that enthusiasm. His mother bailed.

"All I hear about is how I've up and left her, how I don't care about my momma, how she's struggling in the poorhouse and I can't even toss her a few table scraps. And then you get her front row seats to the Grand Ole Opry, and she doesn't even show up?"

He sounds bitter, so much older than his age, and it breaks my heart. I rub his back as he closes his eyes and leans his head against the wall. I peer out into the crowd. There in the front row are Stella, Shannon, Bonnie, and Darryl, but the seat I reserved for Adam's mom is empty.

"I'm sorry, Bird," he says. "This is your big moment, and I'm a total downer, whining about my family drama."

"Hey," I say, pulling him around. I take his face in my hands, feel the stubble against my fingers, and look him right in the eye. "Adam, listen. *I'm* your family now." I nod toward the rest of the Barretts, also watching the show from a few feet behind us. "We're your family."

He nods, and although I know he appreciates us, I also realize that it's not the same. But he kisses me sweetly, like he's done a thousand times, and it's clear that right now he's putting on a brave face and concealing an aching heart. His mother sees him as a paycheck, not as a son, and every time he thinks they've made headway, she does something like this. I think I hate her.

When Terri Clark finishes her third song, the crowd showers her with praise. She's going to be a tough act to follow. I clutch Maybelle tight in one hand and say a quick silent prayer, gripping my lucky rock pendant in the other.

"You'll be great," Adam whispers in my ear.

"I can't believe that after all the arenas and stadiums I've played, I still get a little stage fright," I admit softly.

"This is the 'Mother Church,' " he says with a grin. "I'd be nervous, too."

I roll my eyes. "Thanks, babe."

"The next artist in the lineup tonight is cute as a button," the night's host, Trisha Yearwood, says into the microphone. "She wrote a song called 'Shine Our Light,' and, folks, I can't think of a better message." The crowd applauds in agreement.

I grip Maybelle tighter and shake out the jitters.

"Go shine, Bird," Adam says, squeezing my shoulders. "I love you."

I look over my shoulder and peck him on the cheek.

"Without further ado, ladies and gentlemen, it is my honor to welcome Miss Bird Barrett to the stage."

I walk to the circle of light at center stage and stand behind the iconic WSM microphone stand. I smile out at the crowd, take in the hardwood pews and gorgeous stained glass windows above the balcony. This may not be a sold-out arena, but it's better. I turn toward my band.

"One, two, three," I call, off mic. The guys come right in with the intro to "Shine Our Light," and I raise Maybelle to my shoulder, leading with an improvisational melody, a slight twist on the chorus that's both slow and soulful. As

I've come to do almost any time I play a show now, I get right into the music. I've learned that I've got to beat my nerves before they beat me, and the best way to do that is to play. Now as I wrap up the quick eleven bars, almost like a warm-up of sorts, I lower my fiddle and start the first verse, loving the intimacy of this hallowed music hall.

"You look at me like it's a natural rivalry," I sing. *"Like there's just room for one to succeed."* As I sing, I think about my time with Kayelee yesterday. I always think about her when I perform this song, but tonight it's different. Tonight I realize that what our relationship needed was time *away* from the spotlight. It was so refreshing to talk to her like a normal person, to go deeper than the spray tan and accessories. I sing with more joy now that I've actually *seen* Kayelee's light, now that I know it's there and that she's finally getting the help she needs to let it shine.

By the time I come to the final chorus, the crowd is singing along. As we cut the song, they erupt in applause. Stella even shouts out, "I love you, Bird!" like a crazed fan. It's a moment I'll never forget.

I take a bow and tuck Maybelle under my arm before leading into the next number, something classic that fits with the night's theme. "Y'all may not know this," I say into the microphone as the audience settles, "but tonight is sort of like a throwback for me. You see, I got my start in music with a fantastic little bluegrass group known as the Barrett Family

Band, and we only covered the classics." As I talk, Dylan steps forward from where he was playing with my band, and the rest of my family trickles onstage: Mom to my right on the mandolin, Jacob a little behind me with his upright bass, and my dad at the mic next to mine with his banjo. "We played everything from Bill Monroe to Ricky Skaggs, Emmylou Harris to June Carter, and to think that so many of those greats played this very stage is awe-inspiring."

"Sweetheart, one day somebody will be standing right where you are saying the same thing about you," my dad says into his mic. "Mark my words."

I smile wide as the crowd cheers, and I strum the taut strings on my fiddle. "Now we'd like to play a number that is deeply special to every member of our band," I go on. "This is the song they played at my little brother's funeral twelve years ago. Music is what pulled our family through the greatest grief we've ever known, and I don't know where I'd be without it . . . or without these people standing around me."

I nod to Jacob, who counts us into "I'll Fly Away," and just like the old days, we're off. I sing lead, my mom and dad harmonizing with me, and it starts as a sweet gospel; but by the time we're through the second verse, my dad starts nodding a little harder, stomping a little louder, picking a little faster. We follow. I see Dylan smiling, and I'm glad we decided to take this song to a fun place. We'll remember

Caleb's spirit on this night in an epic Barrett Family kind of way. Soon everybody gets a chance at the mic, Dylan tilting up his dobro for his solo, my dad crushing it on the banjo, Jacob slapping with all he's got on the bass, and even my mom smiling contentedly as she picks out a solo on her mandolin. I go last and give the crowd everything I've got, the pace so blistering that I'm starting to sweat as I work my fiddle over.

By the time we cut the song, the pews are empty and everybody in the "Mother Church" is on their feet. It's exhilarating. It's a feeling unlike any other. I glance over to the wings and see Adam with a thumb and finger up to his mouth, whistling his support the same way he did the night I was first discovered at the Station Inn.

And I know what I want to do. It wasn't planned, certainly wasn't approved or rehearsed this afternoon, but I've gone rogue before, so why not now? I'm slotted for one more song, and it feels like a member of our family is missing.

"Thank you, everybody!" I call. "Now we've got one more song to go before I pass the baton to the beautiful and incomparable Pam Tillis. It's a song I wrote with my family on the way down to Jackson for Christmas the first year we left the road so I could pursue a solo career. It's called 'Yellow Lines.'"

The crowd cheers, a lot of them knowing the song, but I'm not quite ready to play.

"Those yellow lines took us all over the country for seven years, but they also led us to a talented musician who happens to hold my heart," I say. I stretch my arm to him and see the surprised look on Adam's face. "Mr. Adam Dean, would you come out here and sing with us, please?" I look out at the crowd again and ask for their help. "He didn't know about this, so can y'all help me give him a little nudge?"

The audience applauds, and my family urges him on, too, so Adam walks toward center stage, running a hand through his shaggy brown hair as if there's any way he could actually tame that mop. Dylan stays on dobro and hands Adam his guitar.

"You've always got something up your sleeve, don't you, Lady Bird?" Adam asks, his voice deep in my dad's microphone.

"Get over here, buddy," I say, waving him around. "You're dating me, not my dad."

The crowd laughs, and my father hoots into the mic. Adam actually blushes as he steps over next to me, but as always, he has a great sense of humor and goes with the flow, leaning in close, cheek to cheek with me at my mic. "There, darling," he coos. "That better?"

"Well, hold on!" my mom calls, scooting over quick to share my dad's microphone. "There, darling," she says, pressing her cheek against his with both their eyes bulging. "That better?"

"Before and after," Adam quips, triggering a ripple of laughter through the crowd.

I laugh, too, and turn around, nodding for Jacob to count us in before this turns into the Minnie Pearl wannabes show.

The band starts up, lively and fun, and we bring an old Barrett Family Band number back to life, stripping away the contemporary sound and studio qualities the song has on my album *Wildflower* and performing it the way we originally wrote it back on the RV. The crowd loves it; their foot-stomping on the old wooden floors pounds through the auditorium. By the second chorus, they're singing along:

"We won't forget the journey,
Each mile makes us who we are.
We go when we feel ready,
But together it's not far.
Another school, another town,
Another round of good-byes.
Adventures wait and life unfolds along these
*   yellow lines."*

When the song ends, we wave good-bye, to a standing ovation. Then we all line up at the front of the stage, hold hands, and take our bows as a family who hasn't skipped a beat since our days in America's honky-tonks. I think about the song I wrote with Adam on tour called "Broken People" and how grateful I am that I have this glue to keep me together—how I'll never take it for granted again.

Backstage Dan and Troy give me hugs, but it's Anita who puts it perfectly when she says, "Now *that's* how you control the narrative."

I squeeze Adam's hand, and he kisses my forehead. It does feel nice to be the one telling my own story for a change.

ACKNOWLEDGMENTS

Thank you first to my early readers, Becky Bennett and Bobbie Jo Whitaker, for reading every single draft, chapter by chapter, one e-mail at a time, and for letting me know exactly where you stand. With skillfully crafted editorial notes like, "I hate that girl," "I need more Adam," and "I'm crying in public," and somewhat dramatic responses like, "Whoa, 50 Shades of Whitaker," I was motivated to keep the pages coming.

A heartfelt word of thanks to my actual editors, the pros, if you will: Pam Gruber, when you took over this project I knew I was in good hands from the start. I have felt that way ever since. Kathryn Williams and Dan Tucker, thank you for the conceptual notes and for all the little extras you do to make the trilogy something of which I think we can all be proud.

Alyssa Reuben, my agent, you are the best. I feel so lucky just to know you, let alone have you represent me. Thank you for always championing my ideas to hand-sell these books, to make appearances, and to get my work in front of the target audience. You go above and beyond. (And, Katelyn, holla!)

To Kristina Aven, my publicist for this Wildflower series journey, thanks for the support on promotion and for tips about the new neighborhood. To Wendy Dopkin and Chandra Wohleber, my killer copy editors, thank you for the attention to detail you always bring. Of course, you know my mamaw, Loretta Fryman, will still proof these pages, reading the whole thing aloud to my papaw, Joe Fryman, to make sure I haven't used the word *freaking* too much. Thanks to my awesome grandparents!

Megan Girvalo, I am so fortunate to have you in charge of my website. Ellen Hagan, I love bouncing ideas off you and being inspired by your need to create. Thanks also to Alisa Siwacharan, Joanna Pecak, Kim Pace, Micol Ostow, Cindy Johnson, and Whitney Grannis.

I adore my social media friends and followers and the help you give me when I'm stuck. So I thank Katherine Newman for recommending the word "dorks"; Bethanyelle_ on Instagram for the "Mz. Communication" and "Evangeline Grey" suggestions; Andrea Baker for "The Hicks from 36"; Judy King for "D-Lux," which got changed to Kingdom-Luxe still in your honor; Emily Case Curtsinger for the cool name "Jase"; and Sarah Lyons for "Delightful Chaos."

Many of my fans wouldn't get to read my books if it weren't for their school librarians and media specialists. Thank you for those who support my books and especially those who have invited me into your schools to meet your students in person. The fan mail I get proves how important meeting an author and holding a personalized copy of a book in their hands really is to them. LeeAnn Gamm of Maurice Bowling Middle School, I am so appreciative of the school visit video you and your students edited for me and allow me to use on my website. Renee Hale of Henry Moss Middle School, you are a goddess for creating my teacher's guide and making the Wildflower series curriculum connections.

Enormous gratitude goes to the Kentucky Bluegrass Awards committee for putting *Wildflower* on the 2016 Master List. Many

BEATS OF MY HEART
A PLAYLIST BY BIRD BARRETT

"Boys from the South," **Pistol Annies**

"I'll Fly Away," **Alison Krauss**

"Everything Has Changed," **Taylor Swift ft. Ed Sheeran**

"Just a Kiss," **Lady Antebellum**

"I Will Wait," **Mumford & Sons**

"We Were Us," **Keith Urban ft. Miranda Lambert**

"Can't Take My Eyes off of You," **Lauryn Hill**

"The Way You Make Me Feel," **Michael Jackson**

"Girls Chase Boys," **Ingrid Michaelson**

"Crazy," **Patsy Cline**

"You Could Be Happy," **Snow Patrol**

"Song for You," **Alexi Murdoch**

"I Won't Give Up," **Jason Mraz**

"Ring of Fire," **Johnny Cash**

"I Choose You," **Sara Bareilles**

"Love on Top," **Beyoncé**

"At Last," **Etta James**

schools have chosen the Wildflower series for their book clubs because of that, and I am happy to supply questions and discussion guides for those interested. And thank you to Chuck Coldiron for the opportunity to speak to eight thousand Kentucky students last fall with former first lady Jane Beshear at your annual Feed the Mind literacy event. It was an incredible experience. I was also thrilled to be the recipient of the Evelyn B. Thurman Young Readers Award from Western Kentucky University Libraries. I am humbled by the fact that although I have lived in New York for eleven years now, Kentucky literacy schools and programs always show me the "Way Back Home."

Thank you forever and always to my dad and mom, Glen and Vicki Whitaker, for being my biggest fans. I am able to model great families in my books because I was privileged enough to grow up in yours.

Jerrod, thank you for reading all my books and pressuring all your friends to read them, too. And to Knox, Rhett, and Wyatt Mae, I look forward to the day when you can do the same.

Proverbs 22:6